PINKERTON'S
SECRET

PINKERTON'S
SECRET

· A NOVEL ·

ERIC LERNER

A JOHN MACRAE BOOK
Henry Holt and Company
NEW YORK

Henry Holt and Company, LLC
Publishers since 1866
175 Fifth Avenue
New York, New York 10010
www.henryholt.com

Henry Holt® and ⊞® are registered trademarks
of Henry Holt and Company, LLC.

Distributed in Canada by H. B. Fenn and Company Ltd.

Library of Congress Cataloging-in-Publication Data

Lerner, Eric.
  Pinkerton's secret: a novel / Eric Lerner.—1st ed.
      p.   cm.
  ISBN-13: 978-0-8050-8278-4
  ISBN-10: 0-8050-8278-6
  1. Pinkerton, Allan, 1819–1884—Fiction.   2. Warne, Kate, d. 1868—
Fiction.   3. Private investigators—United States—Fiction.   4. Spies—
United States—Fiction.   5. Pinkerton's National Detective Agency—Fiction.
6. United States—History—1849–1877—Fiction.   7. United States—
History—Civil War, 1861–1865—Fiction.   I. Title.
  PS3612.E69P56   2008
  813'.6—dc22
2007014173

Henry Holt books are available for special promotions
and premiums. For details contact: Director, Special Markets.

First Edition 2008

Designed by Victoria Hartman

Printed in the United States of America

1   3   5   7   9   10   8   6   4   2

for Sara

PINKERTON'S
SECRET

One

T here was no explanation of who she was or the nature of her business with my Agency beyond her name, *Mrs. Kate Warne,* written in my appointment book for ten o'clock on the morning of August 22, 1856.

At that time the Pinkerton National Detective Agency consisted only of myself, my General Superintendent George Bangs, and three recently hired operatives.

Even though George Bangs has managed to infuriate and exasperate me for thirty years and has never been much of a detective, he has been as loyal and trustworthy a friend as any man could ever hope to have. I gave him his title in recognition of the fact that he saved me from insolvency. I have no idea what possessed him even to apply for a position when I had yet to hire a single suitable employee. He was a banker, one of a whole class of disreputable sons of eastern families of distinction you found here in Chicago back in those days, mostly in the branch offices of commercial enterprises, sent by their fathers to the frontier to spare the family further embarrassment.

That didn't matter to me. He could keep a set of books, which I could not, and get the rent paid, which was crucial at the outset. Over time he helped me build my empire. In return I have always done my best to include him in the activities of criminal investigation, satisfying his appetite for adventure while making sure he never got himself killed.

On the morning of Mrs. Warne's appearance, I had not left the office the previous night. This had become my habit, sleeping only a couple of hours in my chair as I worked to formulate a strategy to crack a difficult case. Lost in thought, I was startled by the brief knock at my door that preceded George's sudden entrance. He ushered her in with a big smile on his face. George has always fancied himself a bit of a ladies' man. Certain women find him attractive. All right, most women do. The man is undeniably handsome. So what? He had nothing to do with it.

These old-family Americans may have been the dregs of England when they first landed, but as is apparent with dogs and cattle there is something to be said for selective breeding. The first men off the *Mayflower* got their pick of the females from each boat that followed. Consequently George is a tall fellow, broad across the chest, his face distinguished by nearly perfect unmarked skin and a square jaw whose bones rise like Greek columns to support his smooth brow. His hair is thick chestnut, like a racehorse, and he carries himself with effortless grace.

George had made this appointment, and in my mood that morning I had little patience for his obvious blunder. As my General Principles clearly state:

The Agency will never investigate the morals of a woman unless in connection with another crime, nor will it handle cases of divorce or of a scandalous nature.

What else could this Mrs. Warne be here for?

What confirmed my assumption of her situation was an ineffable sadness welling behind her dark brown eyes, the sadness of a woman who has lost a man. What she had lost, however, I was not in the business of trying to regain.

George caught the stern look of disapproval on my face and made some inane comment to cover his retreat, leaving me to deal with the unpleasant task of turning her away.

"Mrs. Warne," I said, rising to my feet, "I apologize for whoever accepted this appointment, but it is my strict policy not to accept cases of a domestic nature."

"A domestic nature?"

I detected an unmistakable tone of irony. I hate irony. I am not very good at it, and when others direct it at me I take offense. I stared at her balefully. Mrs. Warne, however, did not flinch from my gaze. The sadness had disappeared from her eyes. She was amused.

"Is that what you have so quickly deduced to be the purpose of my interview with you, Mr. Pinkerton?" As if to emphasize just how mistaken I was, she seated herself without my offer in one of the two chairs across from my desk. "It is understandable that you might arrive at that erroneous conclusion." Her tone was infuriatingly indulgent.

"Then would you be so kind as to inform me precisely what services you wish to employ from my Detective Agency?"

"None, Mr. Pinkerton. I wish to be employed *by* your Agency. I am here in response to your advertisement."

She opened her purse and removed a neatly cut page from the *Chicago Tribune* featuring the cunning logo of my own design, a heavy-lidded, half-closed eye of vaguely mysterious Hindoo origin, which perfectly illustrated the sobriquet that had quickly attached itself to my person: The Eye That Never Sleeps. The advertisement contained the terse announcement, NOW ACCEPTING APPLICATIONS FOR POSITIONS OF EMPLOYMENT IN THE FIELD OF CRIMINAL DETECTION.

I had shown little enthusiasm for advertising for prospective operatives, but George insisted we could not survive with our current meager numbers, no matter how many twenty-hour days I worked. He told me that by placing a notice in a respectable newspaper, next to solicitations for bank managers and industrial supervisors, we would attract a better class of job seeker than those who had appeared at our door to date.

So much for his asinine idea.

"Mrs. Warne, what possible use could a woman be as a detective?"

She smiled, and I realized she had gotten me to pose the very question to which she had already composed her answer. "Isn't it obvious, Mr. Pinkerton, that a woman can worm out secrets in many places to which it is impossible for a male detective to gain access?"

The minute she spoke, I knew it was a damn good idea. Why hadn't I thought of it before? This country has become intolerably prudish since then in its notions of what is decent behavior for a respectable woman. And I am not just a cranky old man glorifying his younger days! There are better times and worse times, and these are terrible times, despite my sons' smug embrace of the era's fashionable hypocrisy, especially in regard to women.

Back in the fifties, however, "widow farmers" were a common sight on Michigan Avenue, rolling into town behind mule-drawn wagons, wearing men's overalls and managing on their own when their men succumbed to fevers and fights or got their brains kicked out by their own horses while defenselessly drunk.

You couldn't spit without hitting a sign advertising the services of mediums, spiritualists, or faith healers, women who were welcome at the finest dinner tables in Chicago. The Women's Suffrage movement was more powerful than the Abolitionist cause. Even more pertinent to Mrs. Warne's argument was the fact that in those days women ran the world's oldest profession, as well as numerous saloons and traveling theatrical troupes, with little of the opprobrium that is now attached to their participation in these enterprises.

When I started the Pinkerton National Detective Agency some thirty years ago, this demimonde was a veritable gold mine of information for my trade. I had from time to time gained nuggets from that mine, but Mrs. Warne was correct in pointing out that a woman could dig even deeper into its hidden veins of precious ore. But was Mrs. Kate Warne the right one for the job?

These are my precise first impressions of her. She was twenty-five. I am never wrong when it comes to assessing men's and women's ages. She was a handsome woman, of slender figure, but not the type who wishes to draw attention to her physical attributes. This was apparent in the plain cut of her dress, which did not blossom in the rear in a full bustle, in the way her hair was gathered in a tight bun behind her head, and in the hat she wore, which was a respectable but by no means eye-catching creation by a decent milliner. A simple brooch was pinned on her right breast. She wore no necklace or other jewelry, except a plain gold wedding band that was revealed when she removed her gloves. The gloves were her only touch of extravagance. They were distinctive, soft kid leather in a fine shade of gray. As she took them off, I noted long supple fingers that hinted at an almost masculine strength.

I had remained standing ever since she entered my office. I am not a tall man, but my build, which some characterize as that of a brick, can be intimidating. When I face an adversary I stand erect, head tilted at an angle. I've known the power of my cold gray eyes since I was a lad. Most people squirm to avoid my gaze. Mrs. Warne, however, had a disconcerting manner of moving her head as she spoke, not to avoid my eyes but to engage them more fully.

Seeking to establish my authority in this interview, I asked her to acquaint me with any details of her personal history she felt might qualify her as a female detective.

Mrs. Warne stated that she was originally from a good-sized town west of Boston, where her father was minister of the Congregational Church. She had two sisters and no brothers, and her father had lavished upon her an education unusual for a female in that society—in part, she had come to believe, out of a wish for intellectual companionship, her mother being a rather dull spirit. In reply to further inquiry regarding the specifics of her educational background, she informed me that she could read Aristotle as well as Ovid in the original and that she was also fluent in French, which, she remarked, would probably be of more use in the business of criminal detection. She also claimed broad knowledge of current views in the sciences of biology, geography, and geology, as well as proficiency in mathematics.

"Mr. Pinkerton." She broke off her narrative to address me. "Would you mind terribly taking a seat? I don't like talking to someone when I cannot look at them, and I am developing a crick in my neck staring up at you."

If any man had spoken to me like that I would have told him to fuck himself. Instead, I muttered some apology and practically tripped sliding into my chair.

We continued our dialogue face-to-face, directly across my desk.

Mrs. Warne told me that her father's eye had fallen on the son of a local farmer, a boy named Alfred Warne, who seemed unusually attentive to his Sunday sermons. With the elder Warne's permission, her father had sent Alfred to Harvard College, to prepare him as his successor as minister of the Congregational Church. To keep it in the family, Alfred would marry Kate.

"Shortly after our wedding, however, Alfred announced to my father that he had no interest whatsoever in the ministry but, instead, wished to take me to San Francisco. I was as shocked by the revelation as my father. You see, even though Alfred and I had been having quite enjoyable sex since our marriage, I hadn't the faintest idea who this man was."

I was familiar with the stratagem of certain females who make casual reference to the activity of sexual intercourse to knock a man's concentration into a cocked hat. I merely nodded and asked, "And what was your reaction?"

"After giving it some consideration, I was thrilled by the prospect of our future in California. My father was furious, however, and I have not spoken to him since we boarded a train for Chicago five years ago. When we arrived, Alfred and I obtained employment, wishing to save enough to reach California with a stake to start our new life." Mrs. Warne stopped suddenly and looked down.

I was furious with myself. How could I have missed it? *Mrs. Warne!* What man would ever allow his wife to apply for a position as a criminal detective?

"How did Alfred die, Mrs. Warne?" I muttered, shaking my head.

"Violently."

I didn't need the details. As I have noted, violent death was a common occurrence in Chicago at that time.

I had to decide whether or not to extend the interview. I had so far discovered little about Mrs. Warne to lead me to any conclusion regarding her suitability as my first female detective. Then, as often happens when I am stymied, my mind leapt to a bold and intuitive strategy.

"Mrs. Warne, do you believe in God?"

"What possible relevance could my belief in God have to my qualifications for employment as a detective?" She looked at me sharply, and I knew that my ploy was working. In fact, I had little interest in her religious beliefs, having none myself. I was only interested in discerning the nature of her mind.

"Mrs. Warne," I answered, in a sharp tone that might well have scared her off right then and there, "I assure you my question regarding your belief in God is pertinent, so please answer truthfully. I can easily detect a false response."

"Really?" Her brows rose, lifting her eyelids, revealing more fully the thin crescent moons of the whites of her eyes, nearly pressed out of sight by the enormity of her luminous brown pupils. "Mr. Pinkerton," she stated, with a touch of haughtiness, "I grew up in a minister's home where that question was posed as frequently as how one preferred one's eggs cooked for breakfast."

"Your answer to the question, Mrs. Warne?"

"Poached."

She smiled. Grimly. Over the course of our years together, I would see many different smiles from her, but I must admit the grim one was always one of my favorites.

"I take it that you do not believe in God, Mrs. Warne?"

"I have declared nothing of the kind," she countered, as if we were at a checkerboard and she had bounced her red disk over three of my blacks. Yet I did not mind; I recall that quite clearly. I was amused, if not charmed, even as a little shrieking squirrel in my head told me to get a grip.

"Then you do believe in God, but you guess that I do not, and you fear that the admission of your true belief would jeopardize your chance of employment."

"Yes, Mr. Pinkerton. I do believe in God."

"Just as I said!" I practically crowed. I am a more insufferable winner than loser.

"Sometimes." She shrugged, seeming to lose interest in the discussion.

I was alarmed. "That is absurd!"

"No more absurd than this interview has become." The corners of her cleanly etched lips pulled back, as if she were gearing up for combat. "I believe in God," she pronounced, "on those occasions when such belief provides immediate fortification, like strong spirits. Otherwise, I am not concerned with life everlasting or eternal salvation, and I tend to ignore the question of His existence."

"I see."

"I'm not sure you do, but perhaps you would be so kind as to explain what this has to do with criminal detection?"

"Everything, Mrs. Warne."

"Then I am all ears." As I have noted, I find sarcasm unbearable. For some odd reason, hers was unquestionably alluring.

"A belief in a Supreme Authority carries the burden of adherence to His laws, does it not? While I struggle mightily to adhere to the laws of this nation, state, and county, any covenant with the commandments of God renders the task of criminal detection impossible."

"Which commandment, Mr. Pinkerton, graven images? I can't imagine that's part of the job. Honoring one's father and mother? Perhaps adultery?"

The woman was mocking me!

"Lie, Mrs. Warne. Lie!" I pounded the table. "Lying is the essential core of our practice. We are deceivers by trade!"

The nod of her head was like the sweep of a swan's neck before the bird takes to the sky. She leaned forward in her chair to listen more closely. No one could listen the way Mrs. Warne could.

"Mrs. Warne, a detective not only lies, but he *steals*. I steal the only thing the criminal has: his pride. I create a false identity to gain his confidence, precisely the way he ensnares his victim. With great stealth I close the distance between hunter and hunted, until my prey is looking me right in the eye, believing he sees a friend. That's a rare thing for a criminal to have, someone to whom he can reveal his art, his craft, someone *he can trust*."

How many times had I tried to explain this to George and the others? They simply enjoyed our business and didn't care about the *why* or *how*. But I did. I went on in a low, secretive tone.

"The only way to gain that trust is to so thoroughly disguise myself that I actually forget who I really am. I know no man named Pinkerton; I am Morley, the forger of bonds, or Banish, a sly clerk at the packing plant who can duplicate the keys to the payroll offices. This cannot be feigned, Mrs. Warne. You must live it—right up until the moment when you rip away the disguise and the detective reappears. Then your recent comrade in crime looks you in the eye, and it is not his outrage that moves you. It is his sadness at your betrayal."

She pursed her lips, a ploy many women use to elicit even greater attention to their person than a man is already paying, but Mrs. Warne's face was a study in contemplation. I was shocked by the realization that she was judging what must have sounded to her like a confession! How in the world had I entrusted myself to this total stranger? I had to get her out of my office immediately.

With great effort I maintained a matter-of-fact tone. "Mrs. Warne, I do not think that you are suited to this type of activity."

"I beg your pardon!"

She wasn't begging anything. She had been sitting before me in some demure disguise that she now cast aside. She rose slowly out of her chair, radiating a physicality that was palpable, her eyes shining like polished stones. Her body seemed to press outward against her dress, her female form demanding my attention. Her smile was both beguiling and commanding as she murmured, in a shimmering tone, "Mr. Pinkerton, how can you possibly conclude that I am incapable of these acts of deception?"

Before I could reply, George Bangs barged into the room. Whatever urgent matter he had to report, he seemed to forget as he stared in amazement at the startling sight of Mrs. Warne leaning across my desk, fixing me in my chair with her mesmerizing gaze. George must have thought the order of the universe had been upended, and the Earth now revolved around the Moon.

"What is it, George?" I asked, not taking my eyes off Mrs. Warne.

"Sorry, Allan, it can wait. You seem to be still . . . *engaged*." He shrugged smugly. George has always tried to penetrate my mind and uncover the unsavory.

"I do apologize, Mr. Bangs." Mrs. Warne turned away from me, breaking the trance as she resumed her prior demeanor. "I have already taken much too much of Mr. Pinkerton's valuable time. I will be going." She was nearly out the door before I regained my wits.

"Will you kindly wait, Mrs. Warne?" George, the jackass, was grinning. "I will be with you presently," I told him.

He half bowed to Mrs. Warne and walked out, leaving the door open, so I had to come close to her because I did not want George to overhear what I was considering. "Mrs. Warne," I said, as nonchalant as I could manage, "I will give honest consideration to your application and inform you of my decision within a week."

"Thank you, Mr. Pinkerton. I could not ask for anything more." She reached out to shake my hand. A good firm handshake.

I STEPPED DOWN from a lake steamer onto the docks of Chicago in 1843, forty years ago now, a penniless Scot arriving via Canada with my young bride, Joan Carfrae Pinkerton, in tow, joining the boisterous, chaotic crowd of other recent arrivals—Germans, Swedes, Englishmen and Frenchmen, Italians and Spanish types, Negroes and Indians—all of us drawn to this new American frontier metropolis. There had never before been anything like this place. As Joan and I made our way from the docks into town, the streets hummed with the sound of homemade sawmills, and the steady pounding of nails was the drumbeat of growth. Back in the city's bawling, screaming infancy, there were only thirty thousand inhabitants, but you had to count again every day as the population kept swelling.

Chicago was the transit point for the livestock from the plains that fed the insatiable appetite of the populace back east, and the veins and arteries of the city flowed with the blood of cattle and pigs. Michigan Avenue was thickly paved with manure, dropped by the herds driven to the slaughterhouses by the lake. Joan and I stood on the raised wooden sidewalk beside the broad thoroughfare, staring in amazement at a heavily laden wagon sinking in muck right up to its hubs. As the teamsters jumped down to haul it out, some locals leapt off the sidewalk to help out, as our fellow bystanders cheered them on. This was their town booming. I joined heartily in the applause.

Standing beside me, Joan pinched her nostrils closed.

"It stinks awfully" was my young wife's first judgment of our new home.

I CAME TO America from Scotland as a journeyman cooper, a skilled maker of barrels, and I have no doubt whatsoever that if I had stayed with it I would at this time be writing an entirely different memoir, "The Recollections of Allan Pinkerton, Founder of Pinkerton's National Cooperage Company"—an enterprise that in today's Gilded Age would completely monopolize the trade in wooden casks across the entire country. I had, however, no ambition for the wealth, power, and peculiar social status that such an achievement would confer, because to me the greatest opportunity America offers a newcomer is the chance to discover what you are really made of. I took full advantage of that.

Just imagine, it was in the bucolic paradise of Dundee, a hamlet to the west of Chicago, where I had taken my wife and built for us a comfortable home and country cooper's workshop, that I discovered my innate gift for, of all things, solving crimes.

In those unlikely circumstances I penetrated to the heart of the problem that had previously baffled every enforcer of the law in history. This is why so many contemporary commentators— though not, I assure you, myself among them—have called me "the Inventor of the modern science of criminal detection." I cannot deny, however, that my revolutionary insight, since copied by legions of imitators, now defines the method of apprehending perpetrators of theft and fraud. I established the fundamental principle that you must first amass the clues that enable you to pick out the actual wrongdoer from a crowd of innocent suspects, and then you must methodically gather sufficient incriminating evidence to obtain his conviction in a court of law.

I am not so naïve as to be unaware that today, in 1883, when so many things are taken for granted in our modern age, some readers of this memoir will jump to the conclusion that I am merely taking credit for the obvious and living up to my detractors' charge of grandiosity. In point of fact, my method was not at all obvious back then, and only seems so today because it was obvious then to me alone, and over the course of my long career I have succeeded, in the face of incredulity, in making it obvious to one and all. And if I have repeated the word *obvious* too many times and tried the reader's patience, I remind you that sometimes repetition is the only appropriate tool for hammering home a point that challenges the pathetic prejudices of popular wisdom.

My technique of criminal detection was so original and successful that I was soon appointed deputy sheriff of Kane County, a job I executed in my spare time while still working as the sole cooper of Dundee. It did not take long for word of my expertise to spread as far as Chicago. Sheriff Walter Church invited me to give up barrelmaking and enter his employ full time in the highly sought-after position of deputy in the Chicago Sheriff's Office. I accepted his offer.

Back then the city's entertainment district was a vast cesspool of whorehouses, saloons, dirt-floor dispensaries of grain alcohol, animal fighting pits, and floating card games where men got cut to pieces with such depressing regularity that the newly ascendant civic leadership demanded that some order be imposed lest the wheels of commerce became clogged with bloody body parts. Sheriff Church was a decent enough man, I suppose, but he ran his office like a frontier version of the police departments back east: namely, as a protection racket.

When a crime took place, he unleashed his pack of uniformed bullyboys to round up the unfortunates who'd been snitched out and apply their clubs until a confession emerged. If the guilty party turned over the stolen loot as a bribe, he was sent packing. The victim then paid a steep gratuity to recover a mere portion of his property. If the police failed to quickly apprehend the real perpetrator, some poor bastard who had nothing to do with it got locked up anyway. The case was closed, and the victim was completely out of luck. While this system was highly efficient and lucrative for the sheriff, it did nothing to reduce crime.

Out in Dundee I had first established my unique modus operandi of beating the criminal at his own game. In this contest, the detective must be the Master of Deception! I lost no time applying my methods in Chicago, with predictable success.

My very first case involved a gambling establishment frequented by a particularly violent breed of predator who would lure a greenie immigrant into a back alley with a smooth offer of some fantastic deal, then strip the man of all he was worth, often leaving him for dead. I strolled into this unsavory den, not as deputy sheriff but disguised as an Olaf just off the boat, a Swede in cap and rough clothes, with money stuffed in my shoes. After a run of luck, one of the slicker gamblers invited me outside to inspect a fine watch he was willing to sell cheap. I followed him enthusiastically. When he drew a knife, I was ready with my Navy Colt.

I quickly availed myself of the resources of the city and frequented the shops where ladies purchase their makeup. I made false beards and mustaches. I listened to the babel on the streets and set myself to perfecting all kinds of accents. Soon the predators became my prey, as they tried anxiously to guess if their innocent mark was Pinkerton in some brand-new disguise.

Even though it took me a mere six months to clean out the entire district, Sheriff Church was not pleased that I hadn't collected a single dollar in bribes which another deputy customarily would have split with him. When I told him I could not achieve my ends through corruption and was content to draw my modest salary and forgo the bribes, Sheriff Church thought I was telling him I was a better man than he was. This was not the case at all.

At this early juncture in what I am confident will be a full, comprehensive, and entirely truthful account of the events and circumstances of my life, I wish to clarify for the reader an aspect of my nature that has been frequently distorted, not only by my Enemies but by certain members of my own family as well.

Contrary to their smears, I judge no man—or woman, for that matter—by the high standards I impose upon myself, and thus I would never consider myself to be better or worse than any man. That does not mean I will ever suspend my judgment regarding what is right and what is wrong. On the contrary. Unswayed by adherence to creed, cant, or callow self-interest, I forge my path guided solely by the voice within me that unerringly discerns right from wrong. When my course of action brings me into collision with those whose ignorance has convinced them that wrong is right, I never hesitate to do everything in my power to defeat them.

If the reader fails to grasp the logic of my position immediately, I urge you not to wrestle strenuously with the proposition but, instead, proceed with my assurance that everything will become as clear to you as it is to me by the conclusion of this memoir.

Returning to the situation with Sheriff Church. While I did not believe myself to be the better man, I was right and he was wrong. When it became apparent that I could not conduct myself in a manner I deemed right, I quit, and in 1853 I went into business for myself. The fact that there had never been a private detective agency anywhere on the face of the earth would have given most men pause, but the chance to do what has not been done before always fills me with confidence, given the pathetic results most people achieve by repeating the idiocies of their predecessors.

When I opened the Pinkerton Detective Agency right here on Michigan Avenue, the first thing I did was nail the General Principles—of my own composition—to the front door. These dictums define to this very day what my Agency stands for and what conduct on the part of my employees I will and will not tolerate!

The Agency will not represent a defendant in a criminal case except with the knowledge and consent of the prosecutor; its operatives will not shadow jurors or investigate public officials in the performance of their duties, or trade-union officers or members in their lawful union activities; they will not accept employment from one political party against another; they will not report union meetings unless the meetings are open to the public without restriction; they will not work for vice crusaders; they will not accept contingent fees, gratuities, or rewards. The Agency will never investigate the morals of a woman unless in connection with another crime, nor will it handle cases of divorce or of a scandalous nature.

Despite the unmistakable clarity of my words, the first day I opened for business every violent ignorant miscreant in Chicago who lacked the political connections to obtain employment in the sheriff's office showed up looking for a job.

When I read my General Principles aloud to them, half fell asleep, while most of the others could not even comprehend my words. One clever fellow mockingly asked if I was looking for coppers or pansy missionaries. I escorted him to the door and pushed him down a full flight of stairs, my office then being on the second floor.

Even though I desperately needed a force of men in my employ, I would not abandon my Principles in the face of bankruptcy. Instead I worked harder, alone, until I found the right men, one by one, who had the requisite character, discipline, and imagination to join my organization as *operatives*. That is how I built the Pinkerton National Detective Agency!

Two

I go to church to hear my wife sing.

Otherwise, I would never attend services. Biblical religion is not merely farcical, it is the prime cause of the earthly evils it claims to ameliorate: namely, human greed and depravity. The so-called Word of God springs from a fountain of intolerance toward any person who does not accept the believer's particular and peculiar creed.

As for God, He is a pathetic crutch for those without the strength and imagination to determine right and wrong on their own and act accordingly. Hence the need for His commandments, as well as regular updates on His will as promulgated by church authorities behind closed doors, like a bunch of aldermen drafting new legislation to tax and police the citizenry.

Given my opinion on this matter, imagine the power of my wife Joan's voice if it can lure me time and again into church on Sunday mornings.

Over the years I have perfected the art of sitting upright in a pew, eyes wide open, rising to my feet and returning to my seat on cue, all the while completely deaf to the words of scripture, sermon, and prayer. Instead, I make good use of the time to ponder important matters, as I was doing this particular Sunday morning, weighing the pros and cons of hiring Mrs. Warne. My ruminations were interrupted by the blast of the pipe organ and the sound of Joan's crystal-clear soprano rising above the chorus in her customary role of first soloist. I was transported, just as I had been the very first time I heard her sing.

"I'VE GOT TO have that girl!"

Those were the exact words that popped out of my mouth when Joan Carfrae opened hers in the parlor of O'Neill's public house back in Glasgow, Scotland, on a summer evening, a Thursday to be precise, in the year 1841. I had just turned twenty-two. My good friend Robbie Fergus, who was sitting right beside me then, has been devilish enough to remind me of those words on many occasions since.

The three of us—me, Robbie, and Joan—all came out of the same hellhole. To this day when I tell a man where I was born, I get a look that is half disbelief and half awe: *the Gorbals*! It was without question the most god-awful slum in all of Europe when I was born there in 1819. By the time I was eleven, I was among the lucky ones because I was still alive. That is a young age to understand depravity. I lived in a small room with two half-witted half brothers. My mother did her own calculation and chose me for the saving. I wasn't going to the mills or to the streets. I don't know why, but she was owed a favor, a family debt, and I was apprenticed to a cooper. It was not a ticket out of the Gorbals, but a man with a trade was as high as you could hope to rise within.

Robbie Fergus had finished his apprenticeship as a printer, and Joan Carfrae, a younger friend of his family, was a year away from finishing hers as a bookbinder. But her real talent, her genius, was singing. She was the featured soloist of the Union Street Unitarian Church, performing that Sunday afternoon in the public house. I don't think Robbie Fergus ever imagined the effect she would have on me, but by the time Joan finished her first song, I was lost.

"I've got to have that girl," I croaked once more.

Robbie poked me hard in the ribs and tried to muffle his laughter. "Are you out of your mind? She's *fourteen years old*!"

THREE YEARS BEFORE that fateful afternoon, I had completed my apprenticeship to my master, the cooper William Larkin, and stood before him in his cooperage, awaiting his pronouncement that I would enter his employ as a journeyman.

Instead, Larkin stood in a pile of sawdust with his arms folded across his chest. "Ye know what times are. I dinna need two journeymen, only one," he informed me. Seven years of indentured servitude had produced nothing except my dismissal, because Larkin's son Peter, who had apprenticed alongside me, a dolt who would have shaved off his own fingers a dozen times had I not shown him how to handle the tools, was the only journeyman he needed.

I tried desperately to keep my twitching fingers glued to my sides so I wouldn't wrap them around Larkin's neck and shrink his air pipe the way a metal hoop shrinks the barrel staves tight.

Today, over four decades later, my spirits still rise just recalling that first experience of wanting to kill a man because he has committed a gross injustice. Of course I have experienced the emotion countless times since but, like other things, the first time is special.

Without remorse, Larkin broke the compact that had bound us together since I was eleven years old, because he knew he would suffer no consequences. His actions were not prohibited by any law of crown, town, or church, and therefore no penalties were prescribed for him, in this world or the next. In his mind he was entirely within his rights.

Yet his actions were wrong, and thus I do thank Master Larkin for teaching me the very definition of injustice.

That's why I wanted to kill him. It is perfectly logical, yet I have wasted a huge volume of breath over the course of my life trying to explain this to those who condemn me for reacting in a murderous rage when provoked by the unjust actions of others.

In case the reader is wondering, I did not kill Master Larkin or I would not be sitting here today writing this memoir.

FINDING MYSELF UNEMPLOYED, I went on the tramp across the countryside, seeking temporary work at distilleries or in the seacoast towns during the season when the herring was salt-packed in new barrels for the winter.

The Scots countryside in 1838 was filled with self-proclaimed "political men": union organizers, followers of the German radicals Marx and Engels, evangelists, temperance men, and antislavers who spoke on public commons or in crowded pubs.

They had diverse causes but were all in agreement that the right to vote could no longer be restricted to those who owned property. A grand scheme was brewing to draw up an official charter, signed by thousands, a petition to Parliament calling for the enfranchisement of every man—and woman too—throughout Great Britain. Later they called it the Chartist movement.

I went to hear them all, but when the audience erupted in

cheers, I remained mute. Even as a young man I already had an uncanny knack for distinguishing between hard truth and hot air.

One night in 1840 I wandered into a packed hall where the featured speaker was a man named Julian Harvey, all the way from Liverpool. I thought he was a poncy little fellow, a natty dresser with a London accent who could have been an absentee millowner. When he spoke you could barely hear him. The crowd grew restless until Harvey quietly proclaimed that every effort to date to effect change had been a total failure because it was based on what he called "moral persuasion." That was the twaddle I'd been hearing all this time. Then, without raising his voice, he informed the audience that you could not apply moral force to a class of men who had no morality. Such men only understood physical force, and the time had come to apply it.

Like the sound of a well-forged bell ringing in the New Year from the tower of town hall, Harvey's words had the unmistakable resonance of truth in my ears.

All the same, Julian Harvey was preaching treason. There was an uproar in the room directed at the little man standing at the podium. The coppers, not to mention a squadron of redcoats, could burst through the doors at any minute and arrest everyone for sedition. As the crowd pushed forward, drowning out his words, the thought seized me: *This man cannot be silenced!*

I leapt out of my seat and bounded onto the podium, protecting Harvey with my broad body. The surging crowd paused in confusion and went quiet. I had never spoken in public before, but that night I discovered that I am never at a loss for words. "Thank you for your silence," I said, "which I'll ask you to maintain until the speaker has finished what he has to say."

Someone in the audience taunted me: *Who the fuck are you, telling us—*

My voice rose. "And if some here have trouble keeping their traps shut, I'll come down to you and you'll not make a sound again." My threatening tone and glowering visage restored order for the rest of the meeting. I was quite pleased with myself.

I tramped over a thousand miles with Julian Harvey. He took me into his confidence, made me his true apprentice, and taught me everything he knew about politics and organizing. When Tory bullyboys tried to break up our meetings, they were met by my fists and heavily shod feet. I became a leader among those known in Scotland as "the physical force men."

One of the baseless slanders of my character that must be laid to rest right here is the oft-repeated canard that I am a violent man. This wounds me, despite my general imperviousness to criticism.

Regarding my so-called violent nature, I simply ask the reader, *What man is not violent by nature?* Not a one. I don't give a damn what those pious Quakers say, they don't love their neighbors any more than does a heathen savage. They simply manage, through arduous practice, to squeeze their sphincters tighter than most to contain their rage when someone crosses them. That's why they quake in prayer: holding it in.

Well, without the slightest tremble I contain my rage in the face of insult, injury, theft of all kinds, and betrayal of my person. I will not be baited!

On those occasions when I have freely chosen to unleash my considerable physical abilities against another man, it was never personal, nor was it, like the truly conscienceless killers I have confronted, for the perverse pleasure of taking another man's life.

I only fight for a cause and make no apologies for that.

One time I was sitting with Julian Harvey in a tea shop after a particularly bruising encounter with our adversaries, holding a bloody rag over a gash on my forehead, a minor wound compared to those I had inflicted on our opponents. After a thoughtful silence, Julian Harvey remarked, "Got quite a taste for this sort of thing, haven't you, young Mr. Pinkerton?"

It is praise I treasure to this day.

The ends justify the means. That has been my life's creed, which I learned from Julian Harvey when he made me his operative. Some may call me blasphemous for saying it, but I believe it to be a more useful creed than any offered to mankind by the Christian church.

Once I was firmly established in the movement, I got Robbie Fergus involved because he was always game for adventure, and there was money to be made printing pamphlets and such. I was now speaking regularly at our meetings. It was his idea to add a bit of entertainment to increase the crowds and donations at the door.

That was why Joan Carfrae was singing at O'Neill's the day I first laid eyes on her.

AS THE READER has probably grasped by now, I am a man undaunted by any obstacle. Even though she was technically still a child, I pursued Joan Carfrae relentlessly. In my campaign to win her I enlisted my dear ma as a chaperone for our weekly walks around the tiny green enclosure that passed for a park in the Gorbals. Joan Carfrae would sing as we strolled. Enraptured by her voice, she appeared to me as a celestial apparition, with her fine brown wavy hair hanging long in the style of a child over the pure whiteness of her cheeks.

She was bewitching.

After a month I got her to sit beside me on a bench in a secluded corner of the park. A month later I dared rest my hand on her knee. For the next month I moved my palm back and forth across the cloth

ERIC LERNER

that separated her skin from mine, as she sang all the while. But how much rubbing of skirt can a man endure? I finally got up the nerve to slide my hand under the folds of cloth and touched flesh.

Without pausing in her rousing hymn, she reached down with those deft bookbinder's fingers, removed my hand, and held it in hers. "We cannot," she pronounced. I stared at her fingers, my eyes bulging like a hunting cat examining some tender prey within its grasp.

"I beg you, Joan, please forgive me."

"It would be wrong."

"It is true." In those days I often rushed to agree with her before fully knowing what she meant. "It would be a sin," I blurted out, believing no such thing.

"God would forgive us, Allan, but my master would not, and that would be the end of my apprenticeship." Her assessment of the risks and rewards was only too accurate. Joan has always been good at such calculations.

I hung my head and nodded. "Then it cannot happen."

"No," she replied, with unexpected good cheer. "Not unless we are married."

She had recently turned fifteen, a full three years shy of the age of legal consent, and there was no chance that such consent would be forthcoming from her parents. The problem was solved by Robbie Fergus, whose artfulness with a printing press produced a phony birth certificate that was good enough for the drunken minister of a certain church, since it was accompanied by a generous donation to his ministry. That's how we were married three months later.

Until now I have acquiesced to Joan's slavish devotion to propriety and obfuscated the true date of her birth and our marriage, when all the while I have been quite proud that our union was

· 26 ·

forged, literally, in defiance of the law because it was the right thing to do.

FOLLOWING OUR HURRIED wedding, I finally found myself alone with Joan in a tiny attic whose slanted ceilings kept bumping my head. Despite months of feverish imagination, I was quite unprepared for this encounter.

Fortunately, my new bride began to sing, and it lifted my cock like a tree branch in the wind. It also enabled her to depart this world for some other place where all is harmonious and melodic, which was not a bad thing, considering what I was inflicting upon her person in my unpracticed manner. She didn't seem to mind as she kept on singing with a bit of gusto, even tapping out the rhythm on my back. She sang her song while I madly played my instrument to accompany her. Thus began the marriage.

Within a few short months a warrant was sworn out for my arrest, as one had been for Julian Harvey the year before, and we fled in the night to America.

JOAN BELIEVES HER primary mission as a servant of God is to prevent Allan Pinkerton from ending up in Hell. In order to impress His bounty upon me, we have sexual intercourse on the Sabbath. To my chagrin she somehow believes the lesson will burn deeper if she religiously rebuffs my midweek advances. Yet how have I responded over the years to her idiotic beliefs intruding in our bedroom? I have submitted, as meekly as the good Christian she still hopes I will become.

What greater proof can I offer to refute the oft-repeated charge that I am a brute?

If I were, I'd have done what I've heard many men describe in barrooms as the proper way to deal with a balky wife who refuses to fulfill her marital obligations—by tossing her on her back, grabbing her ankles, raising her legs high, and taking what is her husband's rightful due.

As a detective I long ago learned to discount claims made by men standing at a bar. Even if these tales were true, though, I would never have resorted to such actions. I repeat: I am not a brute. On the contrary. Due to the influence of my dear ma, I am excessively eager to please women. It is a desire that I rarely experience toward men, but I want to make women happy. Happy with me! And now I sound like a pathetic mama's boy and will probably delete these lines at a later date.

For now I will simply record the fact that Joan and I did have sex regularly. It is with a sense of nostalgia that I recall those Sundays in the early years of our marriage. I would wait outside the church after the service ended, smiling amiably as I mingled with the hypocritical small-minded immigrant Scots churchgoers, because *I was going home to fuck my bonnie lass!* When Joan emerged, glowing, I felt as proud as any man alive to offer her my arm.

Could every Sunday afternoon have been sunny, light streaming through the windows, her music trilling over the blood pounding in my temples?

Naturally, these regular encounters produced a family.

William was our firstborn and Robbie followed some two years later. At the time I am recounting, Little Joan, named for her dear mother, was our most recent addition.

As I never had a real family myself, it took awhile for me to understand that a family is more than the bond between a man and a woman or their bond with their offspring or the unique ties between children of the same seed and womb. All these bonds are woven into a thick cord that is wrapped around and passed through each of the individuals in ways that cannot be fathomed.

While our household of demanding little souls ended our Sunday-afternoon idylls, Joan remained devoted to her mission, so we continued my religious education in the dark, as it were, during the early hours of the Sabbath before church. On the particular Sunday morning I am recollecting, however, I had to forgo the pleasure because we were up well before dawn to take care of our guests.

You see, Allan Pinkerton's house was the main station in Chicago on the Underground Railroad.

HOW HAD I gotten involved in this dangerous business?

Robbie Fergus was already settled in Chicago by the time Joan and I arrived from Scotland, and he had a profitable printing operation going, publishing tracts and political broadsheets. His best customers were the Abolitionists.

One Saturday night shortly after our arrival in America in 1843, Robbie led me through the crowded streets to the Orpheum Theatre to hear Henry Ward Beecher, the famous Abolitionist preacher from Boston. Beecher had probably given the speech I heard that night a hundred times before, but it was new to me. In a calm clear style, he detailed the history and current state of slavery in America, where four million men, women, and children lived as chattel. I spent the whole night trying to imagine that number of human beings.

Beecher wasn't one of those thundering, fiery speakers. His act consisted of what we'd called back in Glasgow *fine talking*. He quoted scripture and law, Jesus and Jefferson, as he described the horrors of the dank holds of the slave ships, the auctions of human beings, and the breeding farms of Virginia. This was the "peculiar institution" of human slavery in the United States of America, one of the greatest abominations in history.

Still, I had no idea what it had to do with Allan Pinkerton.

To the astonishment of all, Beecher introduced a special unannounced guest speaker, "My good friend, Mr. Frederick Douglass." There were gasps from the crowd as the escaped slave from Maryland, the most articulate spokesman of the era for his race, strode onto the stage. The man looked like a lion. He was the color of a lion, and his hair was like a mane, but most unsettling to the white audience was the way he carried himself, like a lion, the king of beasts.

Later that night I shook his hand for the first time when Robbie Fergus took me to a gathering at the home of the sponsor of that night's lecture. I felt out of place back then in the formal parlor among those fine gents, but Robbie was well known to them. He introduced me to Douglass, who smiled as if he'd been waiting for this opportunity.

"Ah, Mr. Pinkerton! Mr. Fergus has informed me that, like myself, you too are a fugitive from the law."

"Well, sir, true to an extent."

"Welcome to America. And welcome to a cause worthy of your political convictions and talents." Oh, Douglass was a smooth operator. He knew right where to get me. Robbie saw the look on my face and laughed and slapped me on the back. He knew politics was in my blood and I'd only left Scotland to spare my young wife the hardships she would have had to endure if I were imprisoned. Now, in America of all places, I'd found the greatest cause of my life.

Three

As we approached our house after church that Sunday, I scanned the streets, alleyways, and neighboring structures with my detective's eye for anything amiss. Joan practically bounded up the small porch, impatiently waiting for me to unlock the door.

Siobhan, the young Irish girl we hired on Sunday mornings, was standing in the parlor holding our infant daughter, Little Joan, smiling dreamily, as if she were imagining one of her own in her arms, which I'm sure she would soon have, since these Irish multiply like rabbits. Siobhan got up early to go to mass before coming over to mind our children. She was a tad dull-witted, which was a cause of alarm to Joan, but I explained that was preferable to some sharp-eyed busybody who might notice certain things amiss in the Pinkerton house and make improper inquiries.

Joan took the baby from Siobhan's arms, as if amazed to find her still breathing.

"She's doin' jus' dandy, Mrs. Pinkerton. Tha's only a bit of a summer snuffle she has an' nuthin' t'worry about."

Joan looked at the girl as if she were mad or worse. Not two years earlier our first daughter succumbed to what they'd called at the time *only a summer cold*. Her death had cast a dark mood over Joan that had not lifted with Little Joan's birth. The mother could barely leave her baby to go to church.

I handed the Irish girl a silver quarter, sent her on her way, and locked the door behind her. While Joan cooed over her daughter, I took my boys aside, Willie, now ten, and his little brother Robbie, age eight.

I knelt down and lowered my voice, addressing William. "Assistant Station Master, what's your report on the condition of our consignment?"

Willie used a similarly hushed tone. "All's well. Siobhan didn't suspect a thing."

"Excellent." I could count on Willie. He beamed, then shot Robbie a look. Robbie scowled at him, and I detected a warning in his glare. "Robert, does the Sub-Assistant Station Master have anything to add to the report?"

"No," he replied sullenly, then exploded, as he does to this very day, with an aggressive defense of his misdeeds. "All I was doing was *assisting.*"

"You were not, Robbie." Willie practically bit his tongue. Even at that age he hated snitching on his brother. I looked at Robbie and nodded serenely, a tactic I routinely employ to obtain confessions from miscreants.

Finally, Robbie came clean. "I just went up to see if they were all right, and I took my marbles. The little boy did good. I let him keep the cat's eye he won."

They had explicit orders to stay out of the attic until I returned home. They were supposed to check on the fugitive slaves by using a series of coded knocks on the secret trapdoor. There is some peculiar part of Robbie's mind, however, that simply does not comprehend orders. At that age I was not too hard on him. Maybe I should have been.

"Willie, did you burn all their clothes?" Joan interrupted, with unsettling urgency.

He looked at me in alarm. Had he forgotten some important assignment?

I quickly interposed. "I'll attend to the task in due time, Joan. It wouldn't have been wise to do it earlier."

"They're filthy with disease!"

Robbie, of course, thought this was funny. "They stink like dead varmints!"

I cuffed him on the side of the head. "Get a sack and take it up to the attic. Willie, fetch our guests fresh clothes, a bucket of water, and soap. Tell them we'll be having Sunday supper in an hour."

The boys scurried to their tasks as Joan stood there, holding her baby girl so tightly I feared she might smother her.

THE WAGON HAD arrived late the night before. Joan and the children were already in bed while I waited at the back door until I saw a lantern raised three times at the end of the alleyway. I made a low whistle to signal that it was safe to approach. When the team of horses pulled up beside the house, the driver, a white man wearing a slouch hat that hid his face, got down and shook my hand. His voice was low and steady. "Mr. Pinkerton? Josiah Rook."

"Pleased to make your acquaintance."

I helped him untie the heavy tarpaulin that covered the big freight crates in the bed of the wagon. Little trap doors popped open and five people emerged like shadows, barefoot and dressed in rags, each clutching some kind of bag or satchel. I quickly ushered the Negroes into the house and whispered instructions to Rook as to where to hide the wagon, waiting for his return with a loaded shotgun pressed against my leg and my pistol in my other hand. I did not consider these precautions unnecessary.

The Federal Fugitive Slave Act decreed runaway slaves to be stolen property. Even if they managed to reach the free soil of a state where slavery had been abolished, their owners had the right to pursue them into that state to recover their property or hire agents to do so. If the slave catcher couldn't bring the fugitives back alive to collect his full bounty, killing them to serve as an example earned partial payment, as long as the hunter delivered a body part for proof.

Chicago was the last stop on one of the main lines of the Underground Railroad. From here, fugitive slaves only had to cross Lake Michigan to freedom in Canada. When I began aiding the cause, Chicago was hostile to slavery and did not welcome southern bounty hunters entering the city. By the mid-1850s, however, the growing national conflict between North and South had given rise to a strong faction of Northerners who supported the institution of slavery. These men were known as Copperheads.

Now I have to ask the reader to consider something you surely have never considered before: namely, why the fuck would a man residing in a state where slavery had been abolished, a man who had no chance whatsoever of owning slaves himself, be so sympathetic to this monstrous institution that he would base his political affiliation on it?

The answer is perfectly obvious to anyone with the spine to wade through the ocean of horseshit that has drowned out a rational discussion of slavery in this country for two hundred and fifty years.

The benefits of owning other human beings are not just economic. A slave owner sleeps better at night knowing that not far from his bed lie men and women who are his property because they are *inferior creatures,* according to the law of the land and some perverse interpretation of the law of God.

This belief is so intoxicating that men all across the North fervently embraced it. Just knowing that somewhere in this great land of America the inferiority of black people was undeniably proven by their condition of enslavement made any mediocre white man better than he really was—at least in his own pitiful mind.

That's what a swamp-dwelling, poisonous, copperhead snake believes.

Copperheads had become a powerful political force in Illinois, a state whose southernmost counties bordered the slave state of Kentucky, and Chicago's new mayor was an unabashed Copperhead. He declared that any Abolitionist caught harboring fugitive slaves would be arrested at gunpoint. I only wished he tried it with me.

WILLIE AND I set out the afternoon Sabbath meal for our family and guests. Joan had prepared stew the day before in the big cast-iron pot, and Willie had kept it simmering on the stove all morning while we were in church. When I lifted the lid we exchanged winks over the tantalizing aroma.

I tilted my chin toward the ceiling. Willie took the signal, and in almost no time he was leading five fugitive slaves in silence down the stairs to the kitchen. I introduced them to my family as Josiah Rook had introduced them to me the night before.

Their leader was a big coal-black man in his early thirties named Joseph. His wife, a woman of the same age and color, was named Lizbeth, and the boy and girl were their children. There was also a lighter-skinned young man of about twenty whom Joseph referred to as his cousin.

Even though they might have to return to hiding at any moment, I insisted that we sit together around a proper dinner table. I had taken the precaution of installing stout wooden bars on the doors, heavy curtains masked the windows, and my holstered Colt was always within sight, hanging from a peg on the wall.

In deference to Joan, I said grace before we ate, as she held the baby on her lap. The boys sat smiling on either side of the young colored boy, whose name I recall was Samuel.

The shared communion of a Sabbath meal seemed to calm everyone's nerves. Joan accepted our guests' thanks and their praise for her stew, even detailing to them her methods of preparation.

"And who would like a second portion of Mrs. Pinkerton's famous mutton stew?" I asked. "Please, do not be shy in our house."

"I want more, Da," Robbie announced, holding out his bowl before I could remind him yet again that guests went first.

None of the guests asked for more, even though I knew they must be famished. They had been on the road for nearly a month since their escape from Tennessee.

"Joseph." I reached across the table for his plate. "I'm sure you'd like some more."

Joseph hung his head, and I heard his sigh of relief. "Yassa, Massa Pinkaton."

When I'd filled his plate again, I held it in my hand until he lifted his head so I could look him squarely in the eye. "Joseph," I said quietly, "I am no man's master."

"Yassa, Marse Pinkaton."

"Joseph, did you hear me?"

"Ah did"—and then, with great delicacy—"suh."

"I would prefer *Mr. Pinkerton*, but whichever suits you. It would please my wife if you addressed her as *Mrs. Pinkerton*."

Joseph's eyes darted so quickly to his wife, children, and cousin that no one, he assumed, could have possibly detected the coded information that passed among them in a split second. I sensed a sudden palpable fear in the room. Lizbeth acted quickly, saying "Missus Pinkerton" in the most soothing voice imaginable and giggling as if *What fun to follow this white man's orders.*

Even though I harbored hundreds of fugitive slaves over the span of more than a decade, I never succeeded in penetrating the masks they clung to for their survival. You see, both the men who enslaved them and the Abolitionists who proclaimed their wish to free them were inspired by the same self-serving ignorant belief. The Negro's mask of servility deliberately confirmed the white man's belief in his superiority, and thus protected black people from any accidental but potentially fatal challenge to this specious myth of their own inferiority. I have bitten my tongue for more than thirty years now, but this ignorant belief continues to rule the nation to this day, as if the War of the Rebellion was fought for nothing.

Josiah Rook, the man who guided Joseph and his family to my door, was not free from this ignorance, no matter how good-hearted he may have been. Upon their arrival the night before, I had brought out a cold supper for Rook and his *consignment.* As we huddled by candlelight, the fugitive slaves would not touch a morsel without getting a sign of permission from Rook that they could eat. During the meal they did not speak a word to each other, addressing all speech instead to "Massa Rook." When he recounted their adventures in reaching Chicago, the slaves laughed heartily. When he complimented the quality of the food, they all chimed in.

Finally, when Rook rose and announced that it was time for him to be leaving, they joined in a singsong hymn of gratitude for everything he had done on their behalf.

Rook smiled benevolently, accepting the garlands. The poor dupe was totally unaware that it was all an act, a play for his benefit. The obsequious humility and expressions of eternal gratitude to the kind and noble white man were meant to convince him that they really were the harmless, dumb, friendly house dogs he believed them to be. That is how the Negro had survived slavery—by successfully reassuring Massa that there was nothing wrong with owning another human being because they weren't really human beings at all!

Having escaped bondage, they were not about to risk their lives to find out if men like Josiah Rook thought any differently of them. For the most part, their fears were justified. While white Abolitionists fought passionately for the abstract principle of ending the institution of slavery, most of them never accepted the Negro as an equal: not then and not now.

JOAN SEEMED GREATLY calmed when the fugitive slaves returned to the attic after dinner. I sent the boys out to play, wishing to seize this opportunity to air what had been on my mind since church that morning. "Joan, I am making tea. Would you care for some?"

She was seated in the stuffed rocker, holding the baby. Little Joan was in remarkably good spirits, and when I went over and chucked her under the chin she gave me a wide-eyed smile. Her mother seemed to take this as a sign that, for the moment at least, the dark clouds of imminent danger had passed.

"I would like some tea, yes, thank you."

I got busy boiling the water and measuring the leaves. "Joan, your idea to place an advertisement for new employees has produced promising results."

"And have you hired anyone yet?"

"I am considering an applicant. She seems exceptionally well qualified."

"A woman." Joan said it matter-of-factly, not giving away her opinion on the matter one way or the other.

"Yes. At first I thought it was out of the question, but on closer reflection I realized that certain tasks in the enterprise of criminal detection are better suited to a woman than a man. This applicant is experienced in matters of commerce and is well educated. She even speaks French."

"French."

"Yes."

There was a long silence as the tea steeped. I poured a cup and took it to her. With some reluctance she exchanged it for Little Joan, who was quite content to rest on her father's shoulder. Joan sipped her tea and nodded approvingly. "You wouldn't have to pay a woman half as much as a man."

I smiled in agreement, marvelling at my own stupidity. I had anticipated opposition based on Joan's fear that her fellow congregants would be scandalized if her husband employed a female detective. I had completely forgotten that the God of the Scots imposes a more precise measure of moral rectitude: the accumulation of money.

You see, that is why Joan was appalled when I quit my job as deputy sheriff to become a private detective. I had turned my back on God's grace—namely, monetary reward—in exchange for some abstruse principle mentioned nowhere in scripture.

That made me a blasphemer.

When she finished her tea, Joan gave me the opportunity to report any encouraging news about the current dismal financial state of my business. My silence indicated that I had nothing to offer, so she rendered her judgment. "You know, Allan, Sheriff Church would take you back like *that*."

She emphasized the point with a snap of those bookbinder's fingers as loud as a pistol shot. When I first met her and she snapped them, I was entranced, as I was with all things about her person. But that was a long time ago. The woman sitting in the chair this Sunday afternoon bore only scant resemblance to the creature who had bewitched me in the public house back in Glasgow.

If this sounds uncharitable to some readers, I will clarify my position. First, I did not find my wife's matronly roundness unattractive. On the contrary, I still entertained hopes of fucking her during the week as well as on Sundays, even though she insisted on hiding her delightful hair beneath a tight black skullcap! The girl who once loved finery now covered every inch of her body with the drab dark frocks that all the women in her flock wore like uniforms in God's army! Why? Because Joan was making a point.

She had concluded that her missionary work on my behalf had borne so little fruit in the fallow field of my soul, that rather than lavish more attention on this barren ground she would instead parch the soil. When she sneered at my efforts to earn a living on my own terms, she was punishing me!

Still, I said nothing. I consider domestic tranquillity a manly goal for which I will endure infinite abuse, even Joan's telling me that Sheriff Church would give me my old job back, when I knew that perfectly well. Lately, citizens of means in Chicago had started bringing their cases to the private detective rather than the sheriff, and they were getting better results. He would gladly welcome me back, and I wouldn't even have to take bribes. He'd pay me hand-somely out of his own pocket.

All I would have to do was stop harboring fugitive slaves.

You see, that is the real reason why I quit my job as deputy sheriff. The Copperheads had put pressure on Sheriff Church, and then he put pressure on me to stop my Abolitionist activities. But I wouldn't.

They couldn't make me abandon my cause in Dundee, out in Kane County, and for damn sure they weren't going to intimidate me here in Chicago!

That's right. I was harboring fugitive slaves at my country cooperage almost from the day we arrived there. I became deputy sheriff of Kane County for added protection against any slave catcher who might be foolish enough to try sneaking up on me in the night.

But that wasn't protection enough from the hidebound religious fanatics who ran the local Scots church where Joan sang, prayed, and had her head filled with pernicious shit. Those people were notorious Copperheads, and they tried to exert their will over me by bringing me to trial in an ecclesiastic court, if you can imagine such a thing in America. They not only convicted me of blasphemy but of the bogus charge of intemperance, and I'm a goddamn teetotaler!

I told them to fuck themselves, and that night I packed up Joan and little Willie and all our belongings to return to Chicago and take Sheriff Walter Church up on an offer I had been turning down *for a whole year* because Joan loved life in the countryside among those dwarves. Too damn bad. And while it was not my original in-tention to reveal this sordid disagreement between my wife and myself, I will not be misunderstood! I went to work for Walter Church because he was fully aware of my political activities and just winked at them. He was secure in his power in the city back then. It was when the Copperheads took over that he didn't have the nerve to stand up to them for me.

I did not return to Chicago to abandon my beliefs. I wouldn't give in back in Dundee, and I wouldn't give in to Walter Church and the Chicago Copperheads. So I quit!

"Allan."

"Yes, Joan."

"How long do you think you're going to get away with it, upholding the law with your right hand and breaking it with your left?"

It seems to me that the longer a man and a woman cohabit under the same roof, the terser the dialogue between them becomes.

Four

Each morning at seven my staff gathered in my office to report on their cases for my comments and further instructions. George and Timothy Webster, the very first operative I hired, an Englishman whose family had emigrated to New Jersey when he was only a lad of twelve, sat in the chairs across the desk from me. My two other operatives, whom I'd hired the year before, John Fox and Adam Roche, slouched on the windowsills or paced about. It didn't take long for the shroud of tobacco smoke in the room to grow so thick we could barely make one another out. I smoked a cheroot. I like the tough wrapper and dry filler because my activities during the day frequently cause me to extinguish and relight it. A cheroot can take such treatment, whereas the big fine-leaf Havana that George favored suited his sedentary activities. Timothy had adopted my preference, while Fox, always interested in new things, twisted little pieces of white paper around loose leaf. Adam Roche, a stolid German, was constantly at work with a small entrenching tool on his curved-stem meerschaum pipe.

Recently I had taken on the first major case offered to my Detective Agency by none other than my old friend, Sheriff Church. He convinced me that we would be doing each other a great favor if I solved it, since the stolen goods were U.S. Post Office packets containing large-denomination bonds and certificates en route to the city's biggest commercial concerns, who would then be in both our debts. I methodically employed my undercover methods until I identified my man. When I revealed to Sheriff Church that the thief was Charles Dennison, the ne'er-do-well son of one of Chicago's most prominent families, Walter shook his head, clucking like a chicken in sympathy for my predicament. Unless I could back up my accusation with ironclad proof, he told me, the Dennisons would run me out of town. He walked out of my office laughing. The son of a bitch knew it was Dennison all along, but he had no idea how to get the goods on him. Now I had to catch his man, or my Agency was dead. Walter Church came out ahead either way.

I instructed my operatives to tail Charles Dennison night and day. We discovered that his wife's father had died only a year ago, leaving her a sizable inheritance. From my connections at her bank, I learned that the inheritance had shrunk to nearly nothing. Meanwhile, our sources in the realm of high-stakes gambling revealed that Mr. Dennison was a man well known for his willingness to wager on anything from a horse race to a bare-knuckle fight to the hour of the sunrise, and in the past year his bets had been mostly losing ones.

That morning, before my men could present their latest reports on the case, we were interrupted by a soft, almost shy knock at the door.

I feigned surprise. "Come in," I sang out.

Mrs. Warne opened the door and peered through the smoke until I waved her in.

I had requested her presence by letter, informing her that as a prerequisite to my decision on her employment I had to evaluate her abilities in an actual case of criminal detection.

In truth there was another, equally important test I had to conduct. I needed to determine how hiring her would sit with my male operatives, on whose complete faith in my judgment rested the foundation of the Pinkerton Detective Agency. I could not ask their opinion directly. I never consulted them in my decisions. This carefully designed system of management has over the years occasionally come under attack from disgruntled employees, primarily my sons, who denigrate it as "arbitrary and dictatorial," and I am only mentioning their nonsensical whining in order to paint a complete picture of the complex issues I was grappling with in deciding whether to hire Mrs. Kate Warne.

I had to consider the possibility that one of my men might not accept Mrs. Warne in our midst and quit without daring to tell me the real reason why. Therefore, not only did I have to devise a way to gauge her abilities as a detective, I had to ascertain the ability of my men to work alongside a female. That is why I had not revealed to any of them, even George Bangs, that I was considering hiring her on a permanent basis. I wanted to observe their uncensored reactions.

I had correctly anticipated that Mrs. Warne's entrance would catch them off guard. They leapt out of their seats and started to extinguish their smokes. "Goddammit, sit down!" I barked irritably. While I often uttered profanity in the office, they were shocked that I did so in front of a woman. If I were to hire her, however, nothing in our routine could change simply because of her femaleness.

They obeyed in reluctant confusion. I pointed to a small stool in the corner behind my desk, and Mrs. Warne seated herself with not so much as a pinched nostril of distaste for the smoky atmosphere. "Gentlemen, this is Mrs. Kate Warne. Mrs. Warne, you've met Mr. Bangs. This is Mr. Webster, Mr. Fox, and Mr. Roche."

She gave each of them a nod and a smile and then listened carefully, interjecting nothing, as Fox and Roche read from their logs, detailing Dennison's recent activities.

While they had little new to report, Timothy Webster announced that he had managed to slip up boldly on our quarry. Establishing his cover as a visiting scion of a prominent East Coast family, he'd gained entrance to the upper echelons of Chicago society and procured an invitation from Mrs. Dennison for tea just the day before. He reported that Elisa Dennison had confided to him how upset she was over matters she could not possibly reveal.

"Nevertheless, she unknowingly revealed much, Mr. Pinkerton."

I have to digress briefly to explain that one does not meet a man like Timothy Webster more than once in a lifetime. I say this, having met many extraordinary men of power, ambition, and courage. I pride myself on being a man who fears nothing, but I understand what fear is. I don't think Timothy really did. He was reckless, but he was not like other reckless men. He never tried to prove anything. If attention was drawn to his exploits, he would just smile his dazzling, unconscious smile and shrug. "Only trying to get the job done." Then he would embark on some new course of action no other man would consider prudent.

One time we were riding a train—I cannot recall where or when but the sun was setting and our spirits were high. Timothy spoke as casually as if he were commenting on the fine sunset over the far edge of the empty field that our train was racing through. "I'm glad for this life you have created for us, Mr. Pinkerton. I can't imagine what my life would have become had fate not brought me to you. There is no world quite like ours, is there?"

He was tall with a broad chest and wide shoulders, yet he had the grace of a much slighter man. His features were strong: square jaw, high cheekbones, and wide forehead. His blue eyes were not gray and forbidding like mine. They were blue like the sky, eyes that embraced life totally.

Timothy smiled slyly as he teased me with the prize he had so masterfully obtained. "Mr. Pinkerton, by great coincidence, who do you think Elisa Dennison devotedly confides in, on a regular paying basis, and who surely possesses the information we need to make this case?"

This was a game we both enjoyed. "Might it be Victoria Claflin?"

Timothy smiled broadly, having anticipated my correct reply. "Exactly."

I have developed the ability to see out of the corners of my eyes and was aware that Mrs. Warne was intently observing our interchange. Only now as I recall it do I realize that Timothy and I had both been performing for her.

VICTORIA CLAFLIN WAS the foremost psychic medium in Chicago. She lived with her husband, the dissolute and utterly contemptible Lieutenant Claflin, on the outskirts of the city, in a rambling dwelling whose residents included all of Victoria's family and many of Claflin's. Their sole means of support were Victoria's extraordinary gifts in the psychic arts. She traveled as far as New York, Boston, and Philadelphia, where her mesmerizing performances filled not only large public halls but also the drawing rooms of prominent citizens. They paid top dollar for the private sessions Victoria conducted where the bereaved made contact with their dearly departed.

I met Vickie when the Chicago cops first tried to run her out of town as a whore. She had the temerity not only to deny the accusation but refuse to pay the going rate for police protection. I called the cops off, and she repaid the favor over time with occasional discreet bits of confidential information she obtained in her séances. I also attended a couple of her public lectures to learn more about illusion and gullibility and found them entertaining and instructive.

Timothy leaned back in his chair now, and I noticed he shot Mrs. Warne a look as he announced, "For a modest fee I'm sure Victoria will reveal to us just how Mrs. Dennison's husband steals from the United States Post Office to pay his gambling debts."

I was sure Victoria would. However, that would not achieve all my ends. So instead of congratulating Timothy, I sighed in disappointment and shook my head. "Unfortunately, Timothy, whatever we offer, she can get more from Mrs. Dennison for alerting her that the Pinkerton Detective Agency is on her husband's tail."

This brought forth a chorus of denunciations of Victoria Claflin, which was my intent, so as to open the way to the stratagem I had formulated.

"Gentlemen," I announced, "we must shepherd Mrs. Dennison to another spiritual medium who will share her confidence with us."

As I anticipated, George provided the line I needed. "Who else could we possibly trust?"

I turned to her for the first time since she had taken her place in our meeting. "Mrs. Warne, do you think you could pose convincingly as a spiritual medium?"

"Of course, Mr. Pinkerton," she replied, without the slightest hesitation, unflustered by a proposal I had only just revealed to her.

George objected. "Is it wise to base the success of our entire operation on the ability of Mrs. Warne, about whom we know little—"

"Mrs. Warne is a highly accomplished actress," I shot back. "Why else would I have brought her here, Mr. Bangs?"

He was astonished. I nodded sagely at my patent lie. If the reader thinks the deception of my most loyal employee to be cruel, you are simply missing the point.

George and the others looked at Mrs. Warne with new respect, and she tilted her head slightly to one side, as if acknowledging applause as the curtain rises.

LATER THAT DAY Timothy Webster walked up to the Dennison house at the very moment Vickie's errand boy was arriving with a missive containing the time of Mrs. Dennison's next appointment.

Announcing to the boy that he was just on his way in, Timothy offered to deliver it, saving the lad some time. Mrs. Dennison was delighted at the unexpected call from Mr. Webster. As she invited him in for tea, he handed her Victoria's letter—or, rather, a letter that our excellent forger, Adam Roche, had composed, perfectly copying Victoria's elegant stationery on our office press. This letter informed Mrs. Dennison that Victoria would be unable to see her for several days because she had been called out of town on urgent business. Instead she *insisted* that Mrs. Dennison meet with the eminent Madame Fouget in her stead at Victoria's Spiritual Parlor on Michigan Ave. at the usual hour.

Victoria's urgent business was an offer of $500 in cash from a wealthy family in Cincinnati who wanted a private séance. The family did not, in fact, exist. I had composed that request and sent it by telegraph, and Victoria quickly hopped a train for Cincinnati.

The next morning, before Mrs. Dennison's rendezvous with Madame Fouget, Timothy came calling at Victoria's Spiritual Parlor. The messenger boy also served as Victoria's watchman and recognized him as the man who had delivered the letter to Mrs. Dennison. He told Timothy that his mistress was out of town, so Timothy cheerfully left his card with a scribbled note and proffered a gratuity to the boy. Not the usual nickel. Instead, Timothy drew from his pocket what every boy craves: a chocolate, wrapped in foil, all the way from New York. He watched the street-hardened fourteen-year-old turn into a greedy child, tearing off the wrapping and popping the whole chocolate in his mouth—along with a full dram of laudanum, whose taste the chocolate masked. Timothy waited on the street for precisely twenty minutes, then casually went back up the stairs of the clapboard building. Using his lock pick, he found the boy lying flat out on the carpet of Victoria's séance chambers and deposited the unconscious lad in a back room.

He left behind a satchel containing Mrs. Warne's disguise and snuck out. I was waiting across the street, and when I saw him leave, I immediately entered Victoria's building. Once inside I had no trouble finding the secret hiding place that Victoria once told me she used to spy on her own clients. It was a broom closet in the hallway adjacent to her séance room, outfitted with a secret peephole covered by a daguerreotype that Mrs. Warne would remove just before her séance with Mrs. Dennison began.

So far the plan had been executed to perfection.

That is when I experienced one of the few moments of genuine doubt in my entire life, entertaining the slim possibility that George might be correct. I was wagering the outcome of the most important case in my Agency's brief existence on the ability of this woman to give a performance that would have challenged Sarah Bernhardt, simply because she said she could do it!

I lurched out of the broom closet. Too late. Mrs. Dennison was already coming down the hallway. I quickened my pace to somehow head her off when Victoria's door opened. My heart sank as Mrs. Warne called out, "*Ah, Madame Denneeson. Quelle plaisir! Entrez, entrez, s'il vous plaît.*"

She stepped out into the hallway, and I stopped dead.

With her bun loose, her thick hair cascaded wildly to her shoulders. She had painted her face in a manner neither cheap nor tawdry, but rather stunning. The lines of color on her lips were razor sharp, her eyes were outlined in black, her cheeks were subtly rouged. In the recounting, the reader might get the wrong impression that it was *Mrs. Warne* who ensnared me in a rather vivid sexual trance. It was, of course, *Madame Fouget.*

"Monsieur!" Her voice was stern and disapproving, as if she were facing down a trespasser. "What is your business here? *Je demande—*"

"My apologies. I took a wrong turn. The law firm is . . ."

"Downstairs."

She ushered Mrs. Dennison inside, turned on her heel, and shut the door. I raced back down the hall and returned to the broom closet. Mrs. Warne had removed the daguerreotype from the wall, and I watched through the peephole as she held Elisa Dennison's hands across the table. She peered into her eyes and spoke in a low voice, forcing Mrs. Dennison to lean closer across the table to hear Madame Fouget's words and stare into the captivating eyes of this magical Frenchwoman, who solemnly informed her that she was about to open a channel to the departed soul whose advice Mrs. Dennison so desperately needed.

"My dear father!"

"*Bien sûr.* Your father."

"Daddy, speak to me!" Mrs. Dennison was practically panting.

"I have spread back the folds and opened you so he may penetrate your mind, your heart . . . your flesh itself." Madame Fouget smiled wickedly.

Mrs. Dennison's eyes went wide with fear, terror, and delight, as if she were tied helplessly to a tree, awaiting her ravisher, incapable of resistance to whatever unholy acts were about to be perpetrated upon her.

Madame Fouget closed her eyes. "He knows you are deeply troubled by someone close to you. He is enraged that you are treated so, by . . . your husband."

"Yes, oh, yes, he knows! You have . . . I . . . even Victoria could not . . . what does Daddy want me to do?"

Suddenly Madame Fouget gasped as if stabbed. "Tell him, tell him *now*! What has your husband done?"

"Daddy, my husband has brought filth and shame into our house."

"How? Tell me!" Madame Fouget, Daddy, and Mrs. Warne demanded, in a spooky, otherworldly, masculine voice.

"Right beneath your eyes, Daddy! Don't you see?"

Madame Fouget was possessed. "Daughter, purge yourself! Where is the stolen money?"

"Right beneath your eyes!" Mrs. Dennison screamed, unfortunately awakening the drugged boy in the other room. He moaned loudly.

Mrs. Dennison leapt to her feet. "Who's that?"

"No one. Please sit down."

Mrs. Dennison, no longer entranced, suddenly looked sharp-eyed and suspicious. How was Mrs. Warne going to handle this?

"Madame Denneeson! I command you to sit down. Your very being is in mortal danger, and I cannot protect you unless you do exactly as I say!"

Mrs. Dennison went pale and sat down docilely. Mrs. Warne

wisely knew when to quit. She held Mrs. Dennison's hand and gave the explicit instructions upon which her life depended. She was not to say a single word to her husband about anything that had just transpired. A channel to the other world was now open, and it had to remain so. They would meet again soon, perhaps tomorrow, and contact Mrs. Dennison's departed father for further instructions.

Even though the boy was groaning loudly in the adjacent room, Mrs. Dennison couldn't hear a thing. She was clutching the hand of Madame Fouget, who ushered her out the door.

A short time later Mrs. Warne was waiting for me down the street. Or Madame Fouget. I couldn't tell.

"*RIGHT BENEATH YOUR eyes!*"

That was all I needed. I searched the Dennison house as Mr. Dennison irately cursed me and Sheriff Church looked on, laughing the whole time. People hide things in places they think are ingenious, but the fools don't realize something weighs a lot more when you've hidden something in it. Like the portrait of Mrs. Dennison's father hanging on the wall, staring balefully down at us all. I lifted it and felt its heft.

Ignoring Dennison's protests, I placed the painting face down on the carpet, whipped out my pocket knife, and neatly slit open the backing. The packets of stolen bonds, letters of credit, and other negotiable securities that had disappeared from the Chicago Post Office were there, *right beneath his eyes.*

EVEN THOUGH MRS. WARNE'S performance had exceeded my highest expectations, I had reluctantly concluded, after witnessing her terrifying transformation to the polymorphous sexual predator

Madame Fouget, that I could not unleash this enchantress in my office or I would soon be retrieving my operatives' body parts—which they would remove from each other in fits of deadly competition for her charms.

When I returned to my office later that afternoon, she was waiting for me as I had instructed. She inquired about the outcome of my search of the Dennison house. I felt it would be uncharitable to simply dismiss her then and there, so I invited her to join us as I gathered everyone to relate the details of Dennison's arrest. The case was nailed shut tighter than a coffin, and as we often did once the body was in the ground, we conducted a kind of postmortem. Everyone took turns recounting their roles, and I graciously gave Mrs. Warne the opportunity to present a condensed version of the climactic confrontation between Madame Fouget and Mrs. Dennison. She alternated voices, even bringing Daddy back from the dead.

As I had predicted, the men were completely in Mrs. Warne's thrall. To my utter amazement, however, Mrs. Warne produced a type of enthrallment I'd never encountered before, much less imagined was possible from a woman.

As a detective, I had long ago observed that females don't much go out of their way to express interest in anything a male has to say, except as an opportunity to fix him with their eyes and make it clear that they are the only suitable object for his attention. Men accept this as a perfectly natural state of affairs. When a woman is present, the conversation quickly turns to banal compliments of her garb, earnest inquiries into the state of her mood, and inane solicitations of her approval on all aspects of the surroundings, including the weather, the food, and the very chair she's sitting on.

Mrs. Warne demanded no such attention. On the contrary, she

exchanged compliments, jokes, and clear insights with every man in the room as we discussed and dissected the case.

Mrs. Warne acted as if she wasn't a female! I was dumbfounded.

She rested her chin on her hand, something men do all the time, but she made it more feminine by holding her thumb all the way back, balancing her chin with her index finger extended up across her lips, indicating her interested silence when someone else spoke. I had recently seen her brown eyes catch fire in Madame Fouget's skull. Now she rested them only lightly against the look of every man in the room, reassuring them that they had, somehow, the good fortune to be in the presence of a woman who, while quite pleasing to the senses, had no interest in grabbing hold of their balls.

While this was entirely a role of her own devising, it was of such superior invention that the artifice was undetectable to the others. She had quickly absorbed the cocky, confident attitude of the detective. I noted how each of the men experienced a pleasant little physical jolt when she addressed them by name. *Of course, Mr. Bangs. . . . Now, Mr. Roche. . . . Mr. Fox, how insightful! . . . Timothy, don't you think . . . ?*

Timothy.

He was the only one she called by his first name.

How did she apprehend that it was Timothy whose reaction mattered most to me and whose ease with her presence she had to acquire? Which she did, and in such a manner that it did not elicit any jealous pawing of the ground among the others.

"Well, I'm sure you gentlemen have many important matters to attend to," she announced, as she rose and put on her cape, hat, and, finally, with great deliberateness, her gray kid gloves. "It has been a great pleasure to have been of service to you, Mr. Pinkerton."

She held out her hand for me to shake, just as she had after our interview.

There was a confused silence in the room. She was leaving! The others could not hide their disappointment. I recognized this as a clever bit of improvisation on her part, to set the stage for my next line, if I chose to utter it. Unlike most men, when I am confronted with compelling new evidence that contradicts my former opinion, I can change my mind in an instant.

"Mrs. Warne, I believe that employing you on a regular basis could be of great value to the Pinkerton Detective Agency."

"Mr. Pinkerton, I don't know what to say."

With her back to the others, only I could observe her slightly raised eyebrow, a nearly imperceptible signal that she considered it unwise for me to present the matter of her employment to my subordinates as a statement of fact not open for discussion, which, as I have indicated, was my tried and tested manner of running my own goddamn business!

Her presumption infuriated me, and I was about to reconsider my decision to hire her. But I never let emotions cloud my reason, and I quickly realized that she was correct.

"What do you gentlemen think?" I am not sure if they were more shocked by the nature of the proposal or by the fact that I was soliciting their opinion. Then Timothy leapt to his feet.

"I think it is a damn good idea. We are in the business of unpredictability and stealth. Why not a female detective?"

I smiled broadly, feeling positively magnanimous. "George?"

"While the idea is confounding, Allan, it is no more confounding than Mrs. Warne's estimable skills." She gave George a genuinely grateful smile that I believe cemented their relationship forever.

"There you have it, Mrs. Warne. Do you accept?"

She gave me a look of such layered meaning that it took my breath away. She was amused, of course, but, she wished me to know that she was agreeing to an intimate pact of secrecy that would require the utmost discretion on both our parts.

"Mr. Pinkerton, I am honored to accept your offer."

Five

"Allan, we are going broke."

Despite my attempts to wave him off, George placed in front of me one of those annoying green-bound ledger books whose contents look like Chinese gobbledygook.

"What are you talking about, George? We have more business than we can handle. How many cases did we turn away last week?"

"Allan, you do not make a profit on the cases you turn away. You lose money by turning away business."

"We just hired two new operatives."

"Bringing our number to six, counting Mrs. Warne."

"Of course we count Mrs. Warne. But we only pay her half salary."

"Not since you agreed to the raise she asked for last month."

I had forgotten about that. "She has certainly proven her worth."

"That is not my argument, Allan."

"I'm glad for that, George."

Mrs. Warne had not just proven her worth, she had transformed the Agency. Though we had previously utilized the artifices of disguise borrowed from the theater, we were now an accomplished troupe with a leading lady.

We filled an entire room with costume closets and another with steamer trunks overflowing with props. All the tricks of the carnival and circus illusionists were at our disposal, from disappearing inks, to hollowed-out canes and table legs, to elaborate hidden mirrors for secret observation. Still, Mrs. Warne understood as well as I that a convincing disguise requires more than clothes and face paint. A totally believable persona must inhabit the costume. She began tutoring the men in matters of contemporary and historical culture to help them play their various roles more credibly.

Webster became her most avid pupil, eagerly gobbling up the books and articles she brought him. He began accompanying her to the theater and serious lectures. I heartily approved. We needed the greatest sophistication to take on the entirely new breed of vermin that was feeding on the nascent commercial enterprises of Chicago and the West.

THESE DAYS PEOPLE may forget that, back before there was a National Mint, local banks printed their own currency, whose reliability was vital to the institution's survival. Forgery had always been a problem, but as men like Armour and McCormick built their packing plants and manufacturing facilities, payrolls burgeoned and the amount of cash in circulation grew so large that it attracted skilled artists of forged currency from as far off as France and Switzerland. The lax law enforcement on the frontier was much more conducive to their schemes than the tightly run old cities back east.

The best of the con men lured their victims into large transactions that left the suckers holding sacks of worthless paper. Other poseurs dealt in bogus bearer bonds and letters of credit netting huge profits on a single swindle.

Still others worked in teams to concoct elaborate inside jobs, preying not only on banks and post offices but such brand-new enterprises as Henry Wells's American Express, that conveyed large amounts of currency, bonds, and even gold in locked boxes.

The Pinkerton Detective Agency now had the means to smash these crime rings. We could disguise ourselves as a group of wealthy investors, rich fat pigeons eager to make an outrageous profit from a new financial offering. Or we could set ourselves up as the fictitious management of an industrial enterprise, ripe for fleecing. We could even pose as a competing gang of crooks, inviting the real thieves to join us in a huge con of our own invention, until we ensnared them with the stolen goods.

On those early mornings when we left town for our next big case, we arrived at the platform of the Chicago rail station in character, wearing our costumes, ready to set forth in high spirits for destinations as far away as New York, Philadelphia, and Atlanta.

Yet even as the cases grew more complex, Mrs. Warne never failed to remind me of her own fundamental principle of criminal detection: When a crime occurs, *cherchez la femme*. Mrs. Elisa Dennison had been the first; there would be many more. Sometimes it was the woman for whom the con man played his con; other times it was the woman he used unwittingly as his accomplice. It could even be that the woman he believed was his loyal co-conspirator was, unbeknownst to him, planning on double-crossing him and escaping with the loot. Mrs. Warne could sniff them all out. She was like one of those sleek hounds that will lope easily in pursuit until their prey collapses from exhaustion. Then she would pounce and tear them to pieces.

I HAVE STRAYED from my narrative.

Despite my attempts to drive him out of my office, George insisted that I examine our ledger books. I may be slow when it comes to figures, but it is hard to ignore two numbers, one representing EXPENSES and the other representing INCOME, especially when the former is far greater than the latter.

"All right, George. Advertise for more detectives so we can take on more cases." I wanted to be done with the damn discussion.

"Allan, that will only compound our losses. The time and personnel you require for each case exceeds the amount we can charge. The only solution is to change the way we do business."

Oh, that lit a bomb under my ass! "Are you suggesting, Mr. Bangs, that we abandon the General Principles and work for a cut of the loot?"

"Will you get off your high horse and listen to me for once?"

"What have you got to say?"

"Our greatest source of profit, Allan, is the railroads."

The man can be insufferable at times. I knew that! The railroads were now transporting goods, foodstuff, and passengers across the ever-expanding country at a heretofore unimagined rate of speed. But they were fragile spiderwebs, spun out over distances so great it was impossible to guard every thread. Depots, storage yards, and payroll offices were easy targets for stickup artists. Worse, the sheer number of employees involved in loading and unloading freight, selling and punching passenger tickets, and handling locked boxes afforded endless opportunities for inside operators.

The managers of the Illinois Central Railroad headquartered in Chicago brought me one case after another. I rooted out crooked terminal managers; I collared conductors pocketing fares; I was waiting when masked men who had obtained passkeys walked into a payroll office to make off with ten thousand in cash.

Still, as George insisted on reminding me, for every case I solved, ten went unsolved because I simply couldn't take them on.

The thought did not please me one bit. George could tell that by my look of visible displeasure. Over the years this look has, I must admit, made me more than my share of enemies. I suppose most men go to great lengths to disguise their anger to avoid conflict, but I don't have time to waste on the effort, especially since my face seems set in a look of perpetual menace that gives quick offense to many. My forehead has several permanent creases above my brows that are somewhat pinched together. I look terrible with whiskers and, instead, cut my beard close to my face, an effect some consider sinister. The corners of my mouth naturally turn down and my jaw juts defiantly. Many times Mrs. Warne would ask why I was scowling when I was perfectly content. Damn it, I don't do it on purpose!

I drummed my fingers impatiently, waiting for George to reveal his brilliant plan to run my business.

"We will make the Illinois Central a proposition. For a fixed yearly sum that will generate a healthy profit, the Pinkerton Detective Agency will police the entire length and breadth of its lines, as well as its depots, yards, and stations."

"Where the hell are we going to find an army of operatives for that?"

"These men will not solve crimes but prevent them from occurring. They will approach ticket sellers, freight managers, and payroll masters with criminal propositions, and when a crooked employee takes the bait, they'll arrest him on the spot. Once word spreads that Pinkerton guards are anonymously riding every route, criminals will be looking over their shoulders, unsure if the passenger beside them might be one of us, ready to slap on the cuffs if they make their move. But the beauty of the plan is that no one except us will know *how many men are on the job,* not even the guards themselves! With a relatively small force, the Pinkerton Detective Agency can be everywhere at once!"

I got a headache trying to do the multiplication of trains and men and lines and miles. "Why the hell would I want to get mixed up in that business?"

"To allow you to pursue your other interests."

That got my attention like the crack of a pistol shot at my back. I had never discussed my political activities with any of my employees, even George Bangs. I was committing a federal crime. If confronted, they could truthfully deny any involvement or even knowledge of my activities.

"What are you referring to, George?"

"Allan, I have no idea why it suits you to treat me like an idiot. My father tended to speak to me as if I were dull-witted. I assure you I am not, and I intend to prove it by making the Agency a profitable commercial concern."

"So that's your only interest? Making a profit?"

George is a cheeky fellow, but I could not mistake a look of wounded offense on his face. "If that is what you wish to think."

"I asked a question, that's all."

But I really didn't want to know the answer. I wasn't sure I could employ a man who believed in slavery, and George Bangs, like many men of his background, could easily have cousins or uncles with plantations in Virginia or the Carolinas.

"The answer, Allan, is that while I am greatly interested in making a profit, I also wish to do whatever I can to further the cause for which you personally risk so much."

I didn't know what to say. I just nodded thoughtfully. I probably should have said something. There were several occasions over the years when I should have thanked George. Dammit, though, he must have known how grateful I was!

"Allan, think about it. Right now a railroad crook needs only to stay aboard a moving train, and he will soon be out of the jurisdiction of the local law enforcement where he committed his crime. The Illinois Central will grant us the power to protect it *wherever its tracks run.* We would become the first *national* law enforcement agency. And if it works for the Central, every other railroad will be clamoring for our services." George gave me a chance to consider that before delivering the clincher. "Think of the opportunity you'll have to advance your views if you become the most powerful lawman in the country."

George's idea had implications I am dealing with to this day. By agreeing to his plan, I soon found myself negotiating a contract with the lawyer who represented the Illinois Central Railroad at the time.

That ninny Abraham Lincoln.

I WAS ALREADY familiar with the class of successful self-made men in Chicago like Lincoln who lost no time telling you all about their humble origins. For many it was the gangplank of a boat; for him it was that dirt-floored backwoods cabin. He amused a lot of folks with his nonsense. I recognized that he was a snake oil salesman and a damn good one. He wasn't holding up a bottle, though; he *was* the bottle—and it contained a phony patent remedy of his own concoction. Lincoln was not self-made, he was entirely self-invented.

I have been accused of having no sense of humor. That's shit. I like a good joke as much as any man. Lincoln told a lot of jokes; some were good ones. He had an excellent memory and was always eager to hear a new story to add to his repertoire. What annoyed me to hell was that half the time he was being serious, he was still joking. Mrs. Warne called it his sense of irony, which she greatly appreciated. It was why they got on so well.

Well, to me irony is just another con game. If you cut through Lincoln's twaddle, you found nothing except a cauldron of ambition. The Great Emancipator, the Savior of the Union, was driven by the fear that he might wake up one morning back in that dirt-floor cabin.

Still, he was likable. That was the problem. I always liked him. There was a lot about him I even admired. He was blind half the time, but he chose to be. He couldn't stand the sight of certain things, so he closed his eyes. He was deaf too. He didn't really listen to anyone, and that was his best con. It was amazing how many men swore they had Lincoln's ear—maybe because those ears were so damn droopy. Droopy and deaf. He always ended up doing exactly what he wanted to do. He listened to me once, and I saved his life. But I'm a hard man to ignore.

The rest he made fools of. How could I not like him? He never tried to make a fool of me—until the last time, when he made a complete ass of me and got his head blown off.

WHEN HE STROLLED into my office for the very first time and proudly presented me with the draft of the contract he'd drawn up, Lincoln had been active in state politics for several years. Everyone knew he was going to take on that miserable Copperhead Stephen Douglas for the United States Senate. Lincoln was antislavery, and that was no small thing for a politician in Illinois.

As I read over the contract, he tried to distract me. He was always a good poker player. "So, Mr. Pinkerton," he remarked casually, as if commenting on the weather, "I have heard your expertise in railroads extends to a working knowledge of lines whose tracks lie *beneath* the ground."

I couldn't think of a good riddle in return, so I spoke plainly. "Are you genuinely opposed to slavery or not, Mr. Lincoln?" He'd succeeded in turning my attention away from the legal document that outlined the terms and conditions of the Agency's employment by the Illinois Central.

"An old farmer once told me," he began with that crooked smile, "when you're fencing a pasture, if you come upon a rock that's too big to move, you've got to run your fence around it." He grinned, pleased with his homily. I knew then and there he had made it up.

"In that case," I sniffed, picking up the contract, "we should confine our discussion to railroads with tracks you can see, the lines your employers wish me to protect."

He was disappointed that I wouldn't join in his fun, so he turned serious, or at least as serious as he could manage. "Mr. Pinkerton, would you just completely abolish slavery if it were in your power to do so?"

"In two blinks of your eye. Unlike some men, I do not equivocate over what is right and what is wrong."

"And after you abolished slavery, what would you do with the slaves?"

He asked me what I thought about shipping them all back to Africa. I was sure he was joking, but that may have been one of the few times in his life he was dead serious.

"Mr. Lincoln," I replied, "it took two hundred years to bring them over here. Even with our fast clipper ships, how long do you think it would take to take them back?"

Years later Frederick Douglass told me when Lincoln invited him to the White House he had the feeling as they shook hands that Lincoln was as amazed as if he were beholding an exotic animal in the circus. I don't think the Great Emancipator ever personally knew a Negro. His wife did, because the crazy bitch used to own slaves. They had free blacks waiting on them in the White House, but I heard Mary gave the orders, because she knew how to "deal with the darkies."

Secretary of State Seward told me that the day before Lincoln wrote out the Emancipation Proclamation, he had several military men calculate the number of ships and voyages it would take to relocate four million freed slaves.

Slavery was just an idea to him. Everything was just an idea. Still, he was a good man. He wanted the best for everyone, but most of all for himself. His ambition suited me fine. He was going somewhere, and I wouldn't be far behind.

"COME IN, MRS. WARNE." I was reading over Lincoln's final contract.

"Mr. Pinkerton, it is my understanding that the Illinois Central is prepared to pay the Agency ten thousand dollars a year for its services."

"Mr. Lincoln made it clear to me that they will go no higher than eight."

"Ah." She smiled her cat-that-captured-the-canary smile. "Mr. Lincoln just made it clear to *me* that if you insist on ten thousand the railroad will meet your demand." I eyed her narrowly. "Mr.

Pinkerton, which statement of Mr. Lincoln's would you believe? The one he made to you in order to drive his hardest bargain, or the one he made to me on the stairway, between his amusing anecdotes about his uncle in Kentucky who was a savvy trader of mules?"

"Lincoln isn't stupid. Why would he reveal his bluff to my employee?"

Her grin grew wide enough to swallow a crow, not a canary. "Mr. Lincoln is indeed a shrewd man. He is also exceedingly homely, and most women do not appreciate his convoluted humor. I conveyed to Mr. Lincoln how charming I find this quality." She lowered her voice to a whisper. "If a man believes he has gained a woman's admiration, he will trust her with any confidence."

It seemed unfathomable at the time that any man could be that stupid, but I would find out just how correct in this matter she was.

"And you feel that you have conveyed such a sense to him? Of admiration?"

"Apparently." She gave me a frankly coquettish look, lashes fluttering, lips twitching almost imperceptibly.

"Ten thousand?"

"Bank on it, Mr. Pinkerton."

I did. That was the deal we made with the Illinois Central and the beginning of Mrs. Warne's role in my complex relationship with Lincoln.

Six

As George predicted, our new contract with the Illinois Central gave me the power and opportunity to greatly expand my activities in the cause of Abolitionism. One benefit I had not foreseen was that, once the Agency was making a profit, I could move my family into a spacious new house between Fifth and Franklin, whose construction I personally supervised. I finally had proof to offer Joan that I could provide an ample livelihood on my own terms, and for a time she became a more willing host to our guests.

This interlude of domestic tranquillity was blasted sky high by John Brown's first visit to our home. I knew him by reputation long before I met him. The vivid descriptions by my fellow Abolitionists in Chicago were disapproving, even fearful. John Brown had decisively veered from their course of what I would have called, back in Scotland, "moral persuasion."

By the late 1850s the battleground over slavery had shifted to the territories of Kansas and Nebraska. When their populations reached a certain size, the settlers would get to vote not just on the issue of statehood but on whether the new states would enter the Union slave or free. Which way they went could tip the delicate balance that existed between North and South in the Congress and finally decide the future of slavery in America.

The South got a jump in the contest by financing settlers who rushed in from Missouri and grabbed the best land in Kansas, so that by the time the so-called Northern Free Soilers arrived, they were met by well-armed slavers determined to drive them off.

While the respectable Abolitionists debated a course of action, John Brown acted, setting the fire that would ignite the War of the Rebellion. His tactics were simple: to wreak havoc until the Federal Government had no choice but to send in troops, ensuring that Free Soilers would gain control of the territory. Skirmishes between the opposing forces finally led to a bloody battle in which a dozen Free Soilers were killed. John Brown's response was swift and terrifying.

At the Pottawatomie River, there was a settlement of slavers who had taken no part in the previous battle. That was John Brown's point when he and his followers attacked by surprise and massacred them.

It was a prophetic revelation, but he was unlike any prophet seen before in this world. To John Brown, fire and brimstone were not fates awaiting men for their sins in the hereafter. They were punishments that would befall them in this lifetime.

Among the prominent Abolitionists, only Frederick Douglass, a Negro and former slave, could embrace John Brown wholeheartedly. He did not fear John Brown, he loved him. "You and John Brown, Mr. Pinkerton," he told me, "our hopes rest with both of you."

The only other Abolitionist in Chicago who was a friend to Brown was John Jones, another free Negro. He brought John Brown to my door for the first time, along with his closest lieutenants, Kagi and Stevens, and an exhausted band of fugitive slaves they'd led across the battlefield of Kansas.

There was always a fresh supply of meat and provisions on hand in the oversized larder I'd constructed in the new house. Two cast-iron stoves sat in the kitchen for preparing food. Willie was exceptionally excited by this visit. He was an avid newspaper reader, and even before he met him, he knew John Brown as a kind of mythic figure. In person he did not disappoint expectations.

He was of good height, strong build, and, despite his age, which I pegged at closer to sixty than fifty, a man of considerable physical strength. His gunmetal-silver beard came down from his ears to the top of his chest, like some forged plate of armor a knight of the Crusades would wear into battle. His powerful wide brow hung like a cliff above two deep caves that dared you to peer within. I had never looked upon eyes such as his. It was like staring simultaneously into the pit of Hell and the calm of a Heaven so far beyond the realm of human imagination that one was as frightened of this Paradise as one feared the fires of Perdition. He consciously projected an aura of intimidation.

Yes, he was vain, but it was not personal vanity. Every single thing he did was for the cause he believed in so absolutely that it frightened most men.

I observed him closely while he and his band ate the meal Joan had prepared, probably their first hot food in a week. It was clear that his lieutenants revered him. And the former slaves? They did not play the role of servile Negroes with John Brown. They acted like invited guests in my home, their dignified manner announcing that they were human beings. John Brown was the most color-blind white man I ever encountered, and Negroes were as at their ease with him as he was with them.

He had *already* set them free and delivered them to the Promised Land, whether they reached Canada or died en route. Despite my own disbelief in God, I have come to understand that the Negro knows of matters which I do not. In their shattered existence on this earth they have made contact with a realm and power that I cannot see or know but that is nevertheless real and true and perhaps divine. I have faintly glimpsed it in their eyes as they sing, not to Joan's Lord but to a God who is much nearer at hand. He is beside them, and John Brown is His Operative. He made them whole, made their laughter genuine, and made their fate something that mattered.

After midnight, when everyone else had been fed and bedded down, John Brown and I sat in my small parlor in front of the stove. "Mr. Pinkerton," he began, as if his speech were well rehearsed, "Mr. Douglass convinced me to take this considerable risk, seeking shelter in the house of a lawman, even one whose views on slavery are well known."

"Captain Brown," I replied, using the title that John Jones and all the others addressed him by, a rank he had bestowed upon himself as the leader of his righteous army, "you can trust me or not, but I've got small children, and I cannot allow you to reside here with a loaded Colt at your side."

I gestured to the pistol that hung from his belt in a well-worn holster. Despite the man's almost preternatural calm, his hand moved swiftly to the butt of his gun at the slightest unexpected sound within or outside the house. I stood up from my chair and held out my hand. "Besides," I added, "if you can't trust me, that Colt wouldn't be enough protection."

I had intended no humor in the remark, but he laughed heartily.

That annoyed me, and he held up a hand, indicating that I had taken his laughter the wrong way. He rose out of his chair, threw back his coat and with an almost theatrical gesture, gently lifted his gun from the holster with two fingers on the butt and held it out to me.

"If you'd like, Captain, I'll take it to a reliable smith and have it tightened before you leave. I will also obtain several new carbines for you."

In my own vanity I thought I had proved my mettle to the man, but he just smiled indulgently. "Thank you, Mr. Pinkerton, but pray, tell me, how do you intend to arm yourself when this battle is joined?"

"Which battle are you referring to, sir?"

"These little skirmishes, spiriting a dozen slaves at a time to freedom, merely serve to draw the enemy out onto the field. There is only one battle to be fought, and that is the one that will destroy the monstrous enterprise of slavery forever. It is a stain upon our land and an abomination in the eyes of God."

I tried to maintain some manly skepticism. "When and where exactly will this battle take place, sir?"

There was not a trace of humor, pity, or remorse in his eyes. I was staring at the wrath of God.

"Where?" He delivered the single rhetorical syllable like a blow to my head. "Why, Mr. Pinkerton, across this entire nation, on every inch of its soil, and in the breast of every man who, by his actions or inactions, his words or his silence, has allowed the twisted vine of slavery to flourish and spread. We will tear out the vine by its roots and scorch the earth so the vine can never be replanted. When, sir? At this moment the fire smolders, but the time grows nigh when we will fuel it to ignite the conflagration. Then it will spread, out of control, until all that remains of the House of Bondage are ashes."

Listening to the words of John Brown was the closest I have ever come to experiencing awe.

IN THE MIDDLE of the night I was awakened by Joan screaming beside me. I reached for the pistol I kept by my bed whenever we had fugitives in the house. She gave me a fright when she grabbed for the gun, trying to wrench it out of my hands. She was hysterical, and it took a great effort to quiet her, lest an alarm spread through the house. I finally managed to light a lamp. She lay back on her pillow, her breathing shallow, her face pale, her hair lank and sweaty, sticking to her cheeks.

"You're blind, Allan! You think he is righteous, but he is Satan's messenger!"

She sat up slowly, as if in a trance, and then violently puked up her supper all over the comforter, not even trying to put her hands over her mouth, as if she wanted to get some poison out of her. I jumped out of bed and got a towel from the washstand.

"I'll go for the doctor."

"No." She took the towel and wiped her mouth. "It's only my condition."

"What condition?"

She looked at me as if I were dull-witted.

Oh, Jesus, her *condition*. "Why didn't you tell me?"

"I was not sure until tonight. Until he came into our house."

"Joan, calm down. Your condition—"

"Promise me, Allan!" Her blue eyes shone like steel. "Promise me for our unborn child!" She held her hands over her belly, covered in puke, to demonstrate how she would protect the living thing inside her.

"Promise you what?" I whispered.

"Promise me that John Brown will never set foot in our house again!"

How could she ask that? On the night when I finally apprehended some inkling of the presence of God, my wife demanded that I cast Him out and curse him as Satan.

Nevertheless, I promised.

I can practically hear certain readers chortling. *"Aha! Pinkerton makes promises he never intends to keep! That sort of man always does."*

Well, you giggling assholes, you obviously have never been married, much less for forty-three years as I have, or you would know, as I do, that certain marital promises—such as oaths demanded by a spouse in moments of extreme duress to calm totally irrational fears—are not binding commitments. They are not part of the litany of things agreed to in the matrimonial ceremony, certified by the utterance *I do* and sealed by the agreement *Till death do us part.* If the authors of this contract believed that promising not to entertain houseguests your spouse imagines are messengers of Satan was crucial to the institution of marriage, they'd have you recite that one as well before they pronounced you man and wife.

So—big deal—I promised Joan I wouldn't let John Brown visit us again. It wasn't for the sake of my unborn child, but just so she'd let me clean the puke off the bed!

For chrissakes, who would ever believe I meant it?

Except Joan.

LONG BEFORE THIS incident—in fact, only a few months after Mrs. Warne began her employment—I was working in my office well after midnight as I often did, when I heard the door to the anteroom open and close. I rose with a drawn pistol and listened to the soft footfalls.

"It is only I, Mr. Pinkerton; please do not allow me to interrupt you," Mrs. Warne called out, saving me from appearing the fool by leaping out with a gun in hand. I listened as the door to her office closed softly. About an hour later, I heard her leave quietly so as not to disturb me.

The next day she apologized for her intrusion, explaining that she had some files she needed to bring up to date. I assured her that no apology was necessary. She then asked whether I minded if, on future occasions when circumstances required, she might work in her office at the same late hours. If George or any of the others had made the request I would have told them to work outside in the street and leave me the hell alone. Instead I replied, "Of course, Mrs. Warne, it's perfectly all right."

Her periodic late-night appearances become routine, and I came to welcome her silent sensate presence in the office.

Now, on the night after John Brown led his fugitive party from my house without my telling him of my promise to Joan, I rose from my desk and crossed the anteroom and knocked on Mrs. Warne's door.

"Yes?"

"Mrs. Warne, might we speak in my office?"

A moment later, she entered with an inquisitive look, and I motioned for her to be seated. I probably seemed excessively grave; she inquired whether I was feeling ill. I waved off the suggestion.

"We have not had the opportunity to talk of any matters of substance since I interviewed you in regard to your application for employment. If you recall?"

"How could I forget?" she replied, startling me with a smile I had not seen since that first interview. Only that was day and this was night and at the risk of sounding like an old man wallowing in memory, I will say her smile was like moonlight. She was wearing a necklace. It was not extravagant. The small stone in the pendant glinted in the lamplight.

"Mrs. Warne, two implacably opposed forces are on a collision course that cannot be averted and will produce an apocalyptic battle between right and wrong."

She replied with appropriate gravity. "You are referring to the issue of slavery, Mr. Pinkerton?"

"Of course."

"Of course," she concurred.

She was with me! My breath quickened. You'd think I was back in the park in Glasgow, leading young Joan to the far end of the path to surreptitiously put my hand under her skirt.

"I have sheltered John Brown, along with fugitive slaves, under my roof." I needed her to know this.

"I see."

"Do you, Mrs. Warne?"

She nodded with that same affirmative sweep of her swan's neck I had glimpsed at our very first meeting, and I experienced the same powerful sensation of my throat, so long constricted by self-imposed silence, opening wide, and the gratifying sound of my own words spoken aloud instead of echoing in the hollowness of my mind.

"Mrs. Warne, you know I am an exceptionally harsh judge of character. Yet I believe that this man John Brown, who calmly slaughtered five unarmed civilians, is the noblest soul I have ever encountered."

Her brow furrowed as if she had been presented with a puzzle worthy of her deepest consideration. "Mr. Pinkerton, you believe that the ends justify the means if the ends are right. Therefore, you agree with John Brown that the destruction of slavery justifies any means, even cold-blooded murder."

"But do you agree with *me*, Mrs. Warne?" Now you may well ask, What in the world was I doing, practically begging this woman to affirm my strongest convictions? The sad truth is that when it comes to women, men are meagerly provisioned beasts who must beg for the fulfillment of their needs.

"I honestly do not know if I agree with you," she replied, crushing my hopes. "I must ponder it for myself." I nodded, but she must have detected the sullenness in my silence, because she quickly added, "I do not imagine that you or John Brown arrived at your beliefs in an instant."

I was uplifted. There was still hope!

We talked until dawn. It was the most penetrating discussion of morality, political conviction, and the necessity of reforming the world I have ever engaged in. As the sun rose, I seized the moment. "I am about to put a proposition before you whose importance I cannot minimize. However, your acceptance or rejection of it will have no repercussions upon our professional relationship, your position at my Agency, or my judgment of you in any way."

"What exactly are you asking me to do, Mr. Pinkerton?"

"Run guns to John Brown in Kansas."

She pursed her lips thoughtfully. "That would be quite dangerous."

"You will be accompanied by two strong young fellows. Properly made up, you could pass for an older widow, accompanied by your sons, driving a covered wagon into the Kansas Territory loaded with your worldly possessions and tools for farming—underneath which are hidden the crates of carbines."

"You've given this quite a bit of thought, Mr. Pinkerton."

"I have."

"I assume no one else in the Agency would know of this new arrangement between us?"

I nodded, hoping I did not look like a dog panting for a bone.

"And when would I begin this mission?"

"In a week's time."

"Then I'd better bring my cases up to date," she remarked, as casually as if we'd just decided on a plan to catch a common cardsharp. That was how we became secret comrades in arms. Matter-of-factly.

Seven

It was Mrs. Warne who warned me that trouble was coming. While running guns into Kansas, she created a network of informants that was as good as having our own private telegraph line to Topeka from the office of the Female Detective Bureau of the Pinkerton Detective Agency.

Thus I was not surprised by the thunderous knock on the door of my house at three in the morning on March 11, 1859. When I came down the stairs and opened it, Captain Brown, accompanied by Kagi, Stevens, and eleven fugitive slaves, staggered inside. I quickly barred the door behind them, and John Brown embraced me. I felt like a son who had never before felt his father's embrace.

I was horrified by their condition. They were gaunt and exhausted and had unattended wounds, having fought several skirmishes just to get out of Kansas. Even so, Captain Brown looked radiant, despite, or maybe because of, the bloodstains on his coat.

As if he were speaking not to me but to a vast audience, he

announced that his work in Kansas was complete. The territory was engulfed in brutal open warfare. Federal troops were pouring in to do battle with proslavery border ruffians from Missouri. Captain Brown was not only a wanted, but a hunted man, despised on all sides, even by the Free Soil Jayhawkers, who blamed him for the mayhem he had unleashed, which now could not be stopped.

He smiled with grim satisfaction as he recounted all of this. "Allan, it is time to light the fuse to this powder keg we have so carefully packed." The most notorious man in America had come to my door, because only America's most prominent lawman had the power to bend and even break the law to obtain food, clothes, and weapons to enable John Brown to serve our purpose.

When I went back upstairs, Joan was awake and dressed, sitting at her little table, her face an inch from her mirror, sticking pins into her hair as if it were my skull and not hers that she was dangerously close to penetrating.

"I'll go light the fires in the stoves, dear."

"You may do whatever you wish, Allan."

I shuddered. Joan can say precisely the opposite of what she means without a hint of irony.

I watched helplessly as she woke Little Joan, who was almost four years old by then, and quickly dressed her. Then she picked up our new little baby girl, Belle, born the year before, and wrapped her in her woolens and a blanket and a hat, and marched down the stairs with her baby in her arms and Little Joan tightly clutching her skirt.

Captain Brown leapt to his feet in greeting, but she walked past him as if he weren't there, right out the front door with the girls.

I followed her down the street in my unlaced boots and shirtsleeves, slipping on the ice that was everywhere, casting pathetic, imploring words at her, trying to act as if I didn't know what she was doing, and why, when I knew perfectly well.

It did not matter to her that John Brown was about to change the course of History. It did not matter to her that my whole life had been mere preparation for this moment. The only thing that mattered to Joan Pinkerton was that I had promised her John Brown would never enter our house again. And he had. It is this kind of self-serving literalism that has made me despair over's Joan's ability ever to understand the actions I take for the greater good.

She reached the home of Mrs. Abigail McGill, the church choir mistress. A lamp was burning in the parlor, and the door swung open as Joan marched up the porch, as if some divine sign had alerted Mrs. McGill to Joan's need for sanctuary. Ushering my refugee family inside, the dour Scots bitch gave me a look of fierce disapproval as I stood shivering in the street.

WHEN I WALKED back into my house, Willie, bless him, had stoked the potbelly, gotten a fire going in the kitchen stove, and set the big coffeepot on top. At thirteen he already acted like a man, brooking no nonsense from his brother Robbie, who was still ridiculously childish, though only two years younger.

"Where's Ma?" was the first thing out of Robbie's mouth.

"Robbie," Willie commanded, "get some more stovewood. Ma's taken the girls to a neighbor's for safety. This is serious business, you hear me?"

The Captain was beaming, proud that I had a son who helped me in my cause the way his sons helped him.

After we fed the fugitives, attended to their wounds, and got them bedded down, I drew the boys aside and calmly told them that Willie was correct, this was serious business. I wanted both of them to maintain a careful watch until further notice. That meant no one entered without my say-so. I told Robbie to man his post on the second floor, listening for any signal from the fugitive slaves in the attic. I sent Willie to the parlor window as a forward observer, watching for anyone approaching the house.

When the boys left the kitchen, the Captain and I warmed our hands by the stove as he revealed to me his intended course of action. That is how I became the only man in America outside his closest circle who knew in advance of his plan to attack the federal arsenal at Harpers Ferry, Virginia, and seize its weapons to arm a slave revolt.

The uprising would be led by John Brown and Frederick Douglass. It would spread across the South, bringing Federal troops into armed confrontation with the southern militias. The conflict would not end until slavery was destroyed.

The first thing we had to do, though, was get these fugitive slaves safely across the border to Canada. That would not be easy, considering the fierce opposition in Chicago to John Brown. A lake steamer from the docks was too risky. We would have to transport them quickly, west to Wisconsin, where they could cross the border by land. That would take a good deal of money.

THE NEXT DAY I contacted my allies around the city without success. I considered my remaining options and chose the boldest. That evening there was a scheduled meeting of the Chicago Judiciary Convention, where I was sure I'd find every man of prominence and influence in the city. I marched into the meeting, and since I was well known to all, I was ushered to the podium. They figured I had something to say about the prospective nominees for the political plums of local judgeships.

Instead, I informed them that John Brown was in Chicago with men, women, and children who required substantial aid and assistance to escape to Canada, and that I did not intend to leave that meeting without the money to provide them with what they needed. Otherwise, I would bring Captain Brown himself to the hall and invite any U.S. marshal to try to lay a hand on him.

I brushed back my coat to reveal my loaded Colt. It was admittedly a dramatic gesture. But it was by no means *vainglorious,* which my detractors have called me so often you'd think that was the name my dear ma christened me.

After a moment of stunned silence, John Wilson, a politician on the rise but a young man with some spine, stood up. He walked down the aisle and took out his wallet. I doffed my hat, and he dropped two twenty-dollar bills in it. Within a few minutes I had six hundred in cash. I thanked them all politely and walked out.

I went straight to Colonel C. G. Hammond, General Superintendent of the Michigan Central. I had no idea what Hammond's politics were, but my Detective Agency was indispensable to his railroad. He told me I could have anything I needed and the less said the better.

At midnight, John Jones, the free Negro who had become my closest associate in the cause, pulled up at the back of the house with a small caravan of wagons he had requisitioned with the money I'd raised.

The fugitive slaves slipped out the back door and hid in the wagon beds. I lingered in the kitchen, alone with my two sons.

"Robbie, this is the most important assignment I've ever given you." He looked at me with suspicion. "I'm leaving you here to guard our house. Lock the door and don't let anyone in until I get back. Is that understood?"

"Even Ma?"

Now one might say that was a perfectly reasonable question from a child, but I cannot blot from my memory the countless occasions he's used that snotty tone, long after he became a man, to give me lip any time I told him to do anything.

Willie snorted in disgust. "Of course you let Ma in, you jerk." Then he looked at me expectantly. I went to the closet and took down my double barrel, cracked it and put in two shells, and gave it to Willie. He'd handled a pistol before, but this was a kind of ceremonial anointment. "You'll sit beside me on the buckboard and only use it by my instruction. Is that clear, William?"

"Yes, sir."

We went for the door.

"Da?"

"What the hell is it, Robbie?"

"I'll make sure no one gets in." He wasn't giving me sass. He was afraid. I ruffled his hair with my hand. He was trying, for once.

"You'll do fine. Come on, Willie. Lock up behind us, Robbie."

I DROVE THE lead wagon with Willie beside me riding shotgun, and Kagi drove the second wagon with Captain Brown next to him. We pulled up at a deserted siding where a railway boxcar loaded with provisions was waiting. After we got the exhausted slaves on the boxcar, Kagi and Stevens jumped aboard. The Captain wished them well and shut the door himself as an engine came backing slowly down the siding to hook up to the boxcar.

"Allan, would you do me the kindness of lending me this wagon, with the understanding that I might not be able to return it?" John Brown was radiant. He was not going to Canada with the others. He was going to incite the Apocalypse.

It was a bittersweet moment for me. Earlier, when I had rushed home after making the arrangements, I was ready to pack my traveling satchel and spare Colt to join the expedition, but Captain Brown said no. That was not my assignment.

I pleaded, one last time. "Let me drive the wagon for you, Captain."

He put a hand on my shoulder. "Allan, this is where you will do the most good. I know you'll make the right decisions." Captain Brown climbed up on the buckboard. He leaned down and gripped my hand. "Tell all you trust to lay in their tobacco, cotton, and sugar, because I intend to raise the prices."

I had to smile. As did he. Those were the last words we ever spoke. He whipped the team and headed off into the darkness. Willie and I were alone. I told Willie never to forget how he'd waved good-bye to the greatest man he would ever meet.

John Brown's body lies a-moldering in the grave,
But his truth is marching on.
Glory Glory Hallelujah,
Glory Glory Hallelujah,
His truth is marching on!

How many times did I choke back the tears when I heard our marching regiments sing his requiem as they went forth to take on the enemy?

Did he know that night he was riding to his death at Harpers Ferry? If Frederick Douglass had joined him as planned, it might have turned out differently, but Douglass did not, and there was no slave uprising. Douglass would never say whether he had actually agreed to join John Brown's rebellion. Years later, when my anger had abated, Douglass offered me his hand, and I shook it. He said simply, "We both loved Mr. Brown. And he succeeded in his mission, Mr. Pinkerton."

So perhaps I have to consider that Douglass knew exactly what he was doing when he failed to show up at the rendezvous at Harpers Ferry. I can even imagine the Captain was not surprised. On the morning of October 16, 1859, he attacked the arsenal with his small band. Several were killed in the initial assault. The rest, including John Brown, were hunted down and captured, some badly wounded.

Events moved quickly. By October 25, their trial convened in nearby Charlestown, Virginia. On November 2, John Brown was sentenced to die, the date of his execution set for December 2.

That meant I had thirty days to save his life.

I made no effort to conceal my activities on his behalf, contacting every person of influence I knew who might assist me. They in turn appealed directly to President Buchanan to pardon John Brown. When it became apparent that Buchanan would equivocate until the last moment and finally refuse, I took matters into my own hands. Only now I had to operate in utmost secrecy because all eyes were on me.

Adam Roche was assigned the task of *being Allan Pinkerton.* I purchased the rail tickets to New York, but he took the train and made the stops at public lodging houses as me. He carried identification and letters of credit and as a master forger could easily sign my name along the way. Thus my supposed whereabouts were well documented during those two crucial weeks.

In the meantime I headed south in disguise as J. H. Hutcherson, an affable commodities dealer from Memphis, a man always on the lookout for an angle and ready to buy drinks. When I reached Atlanta, I found a city in panic. John Brown's failed attack had succeeded in his greater purpose of setting the fire of fear burning across the South. Every slave was suddenly perceived as a threat to murder his master in his bed, incited by imaginary hordes of invading Abolitionists. Despite the highly charged atmosphere of suspicion, I easily passed for a loyal Son of the South with my perfect Dixie accent.

When I revealed that I had contacts in Springfield, Massachusetts, where most of the rifles and revolvers in America were manufactured, the bastards' eyes went wide. They wanted weapons. If they only knew that Springfield was where John Brown had long resided, and it was through him that we had obtained the guns Mrs. Warne smuggled into Kansas. Now I was using the names of those connections to insinuate myself among the enemy. That is how I gained one introduction after another, bolstering the credibility of my disguise as I made my way north until I finally stepped down from a train in Charlestown, Virginia.

I was greeted on the platform by one of the biggest planters in the region, who entertained me with a personal tour of the heavily guarded jail where John Brown was being held. I was even allowed to climb up on the newly constructed gallows. They were expecting a last-minute assault by his allies, and Federal troops on horseback patrolled the roads night and day. Though they wore the uniform of the United States of America, they were led by southern officers whose true allegiance was to Virginia and to slavery.

I seized the opportunity to memorize every square foot of the layout of the jail and every feature of the surrounding terrain.

My departure for the North aroused no suspicion, since Massachusetts was my supposed destination, but as soon as my train reached Philadelphia, I headed straight for Chicago. Upon my return, Timothy and I spent hours going over the maps I had drawn on the train ride back. I had determined that a coordinated group of six heavily armed men, weapons concealed beneath trench coats, could get close enough to plant explosive charges during the night and manage a raid just before dawn.

I told Webster this was my personal mission. He was free to decline to take part in it. Those would be the terms for everyone.

"I have no intention of declining," he replied, in a slightly wounded tone, as if I would even suggest such a thing.

"We have never discussed politics, Timothy."

"That is not the point, Mr. Pinkerton." He didn't care if we were crashing the gates of Hell. We were going to crash them together.

"REALISTICALLY, MR. PINKERTON, what do you think are your chances for success?" Mrs. Warne stared at me with barely concealed anger.

"I do not conceive plans that are doomed to failure."

"Do you believe that you have *any* chance of freeing John Brown and escaping alive?" Her voice actually quivered with fury.

I hesitated. For one damn second. One second too much, because I never hesitate in response to any challenge to my intentions. She seized the opportunity to leap like a mountain lioness trying to claw me to pieces.

"Of course you don't! This mission is not about freeing John Brown. It is about your wish to die for the cause. If that is what you are determined to do, go ahead. But you cannot take five others to their deaths with you!"

The woman was hysterical. I felt relieved. What if she had presented a reasonable argument to dissuade me? Instead, it was obvious that her female mind was not suited to the high stakes of danger in this enterprise, and she had jumped to catastrophic conclusions. I wanted her to take part in the mission, because a female among us could move more freely than the men without attracting suspicion, but I betrayed no anger or even disappointment when I told her, "Mrs. Warne, I fully respect your decision not to take part in this mission. There will be no repercussions in regard to your employment at the Agency."

"Because there will be no Agency! You and every man you drag with you will be dead!"

My mind went hollow with rage. "Mrs. Warne, your insolence is intolerable! You are terminated from my employ!"

"You can't fire me. I have already resigned."

She slipped from her pocket a neatly folded piece of stationery and handed me her letter of resignation. She had walked into my office with it. How the hell did she already know about the mission?

The very foundation of my Agency had been undermined. My operatives are under strict orders that if I give them an instruction prefaced by the words, "These are your instructions . . ." that means they are not to repeat those orders to anyone, even another operative.

"Who told you?" I demanded.

"Does it matter?"

"Did Timothy reveal the plan to you?"

She shook her head in disgust, as if my question was beside the point.

It was Webster. Goddammit. Webster!

But who was protecting whom? Had he told her to protect her from the risk? Or had she wormed it out of him to protect him by scuttling the entire mission as she was trying to do now?

It was intolerable! I could understand my wife's actions. A religious fanatic acts without a sense of right and wrong. But I had taken Mrs. Warne into my confidence because I believed she comprehended what I stood for. I had entrusted her with a vital role in my campaign. Our campaign!

"Mr. Pinkerton, how can you ignore what Captain Brown has made so clear?"

What was she talking about? "Mrs. Warne, you have resigned. Not just from this Agency but from the cause to which I mistakenly believed you were dedicated. It will serve no purpose to extend this conversation—"

"You are disobeying the orders of Captain John Brown!" she shouted. "Your pride has blinded you to the simple truth that *you are not John Brown.* This cause needs a martyr, and he is the one. That is his destiny, it is not yours. And no matter how highly you think of yourself, the one thing you cannot create is your own destiny. Only God does that. Believe it or not."

I had trained myself so well to search for the truth that when confronted by its starkness, it stripped me bare to the bone. It was a horrible feeling. Two women had now told me that I was utterly and dead wrong.

Except Mrs. Warne felt bad about it. Well, so did Joan. She felt quite bad and was surely planning her revenge for the misery I had caused her. Mrs. Warne, though, she felt bad for *me.* I could see it in her eyes. She was not afraid to look at me. As we sat in a deepening silence, there was no look of triumph on her face, only genuine sadness. I never wanted that from her, but right then it was a kind of cold comfort.

John Brown's body lies a-moldering in the grave
But his truth is marching on.
Glory Glory Hallelujah,
Glory Glory Hallelujah,
His truth is marching on!

On December 2, 1859, when John Brown's neck snapped at the end of a rope on the gallows at Charlestown, Virginia, something snapped in me. I lost my Captain and, much worse, my certainty. If, as Mrs. Warne said, I was not and never could be a man like John Brown, then who was I?

I had told myself that my cover as the great detective, the prominent citizen who rubbed shoulders easily with the powerful and wealthy, the dutiful husband and father—they were all just skillful means to my great ends.

The truth was it had all been nothing but vanity.

I fell into some dark place. My mind was screaming so loud I could not hear the words in my head, the beliefs that had always held me upright, and so I tumbled, with nothing within my grasp to slow my nightmarish fall. Below, no bottom awaited my plummeting being. There was no relief from the horrifying plunge.

Eight

For a while my condition was viewed as understandable. I was mourning the death of John Brown, as if I had lost my own father in the most tragic circumstances. I was spared having to explain my dark silence, my inattentiveness to the world around me, or the nights when I sat bolt upright in bed at three in the morning, frightening poor Joan with my hands around my own neck, wrestling with the hangman's rope that was strangling me.

When I absolutely had to, I donned a mask that became as much a part of my public apparel as my shirt and collar, the mask of Allan Pinkerton, The Eye That Never Sleeps. Thus masked, I could meet with my clients and operatives.

The effort was exhausting.

On February 27, 1860, not three months after they cut John Brown's body down from the gallows, Abraham Lincoln delivered a speech to a crowd of several thousand at the Cooper Union Hall in New York City. The speech was described in the newspaper I was reading as "a stirring address," in which Lincoln declared that he, as well as his supporters in the newly formed National Republican Party, unequivocally disassociated themselves from the rebellious acts of John Brown at Harpers Ferry.

Joan had dropped the newspaper in my lap as I sat in my wooden rocker by the parlor window staring out at the leafless trees, an activity I was recently able to devote my entire attention to for hours at a time. When she delivered the newspaper, it was accompanied by a grunt of satisfaction. "Here. See what your good friend Mr. Lincoln had to say about your good friend Mr. Brown."

Obviously, breaking my promise not to let John Brown enter our house again had not been forgiven. I felt this was an uncharitable attitude on the part of my wife. After all, the sanctimonious bitch had done worse than break a promise to me. She had committed an act of deceit so monstrous that it placed her beyond forgiveness.

But I forgave her. I did.

I DID NOT initially set out to reveal what I have kept to myself for over forty years, but having undertaken the arduous task of setting down the true facts of my life for posterity, it would be irresponsible to misrepresent myself as a worse character than I really am just to embellish my wife's good name. When I'm dead she can write her own fucking memoir.

Here, then, are the facts.

Joan and I fled Scotland in the middle of a night in 1842, when I was informed by trusted allies that a warrant had been sworn out for my arrest. This turned out to be true. I assumed, naturally, that the warrant was a result of my treasonous opposition to the tyrannical rule of the Crown.

This turned out to be false.

What I did not know at the time was that the warrant actually charged me with forging a marriage certificate and fornicating with a minor. Nor did I know that these crimes had been reported to the authorities by none other than Joan Carfrae, my young wife. I did not discover what she'd done until we arrived in America. Robbie Fergus had learned the truth by way of a letter he received from the lads back home, after Joan and I had already set sail from Glasgow to Canada.

When I confronted Joan, hoping desperately for a denial that I would have happily accepted, she defiantly declared she had nothing to apologize for. Instead, she said, I should thank her for saving my life, which I surely would have lost if I had kept up my nonsense back in Glasgow. *My nonsense!*

Even four decades later my hand trembles as I clutch the pen that set down those words. As I dip it back into the inkwell to proceed with this narrative, it looks like a bloody knife in my fingers.

Nevertheless, I forgave Joan for her deceitful sabotage of my life, because there is nothing more abhorrent to me than carrying a grudge. Once you hold a single one to your heart, your mind becomes preoccupied with your ugly burden, even as you grasp greedily for every new resentment within your reach to provide perverse comfort to your cause.

I forgave her, but she did not forgive me. Not ever.

THE FIRST REPUBLICAN National Convention was held right around the corner from my office in Chicago in May of 1860. I walked up the block to the Cow Palace and was welcomed by my old friends, men like George McClellan, president of the Illinois Central. The hall was hotter than hell, but they insisted I stick around for the balloting, which they promised would be quite amusing. The whole country was expecting Governor Seward of New York, a genuine statesman and committed Abolitionist, to be nominated as the presidential candidate of this new Republican Party which he helped found. Then, just before the voting began, huge amounts of cash changed hands quicker than a livestock auction. Seward's supporters were confounded when he wasn't nominated on the first ballot. They were outraged when Lincoln was nominated on the third.

The northern railroad men had suckered them. The entire country would come next.

Today no one even cares. The War of the Rebellion is long over, and the Transcontinental Railroad is nearly complete, the biggest boondoggle in history, the bankers having fleeced the public of untold millions.

In 1860, however, those millions were still only avaricious dreams in the minds of a handful of powerful men more divided over where to put the railroad tracks than they were over slavery. The northern railroad men had paid good money to survey the entire country back in 1849, when gold was struck in California. They plotted their dream of linking the major cities of the East Coast with the ports of the Pacific, creating centers of commerce and population along the way in the vast territory added to America by the Louisiana Purchase. Naturally, they intended to run their railroad through the free states north of Mason and Dixon's line.

Every year, though, their plan was blocked in Congress by Southerners dreaming of an empire of their own, a slave empire created by the transcontinental tracks crossing the Mississippi River at Memphis and snaking through Texas to the south of California.

Instead of going to war over it, the northern railroad men bought the presidential nomination for one of their own, Abraham

Lincoln. They were so confident of victory they began purchasing stock futures in the Crédit Mobilier, the financiers of the northern route, even before the election.

There would be no secession, because where's the profit in a transcontinental railroad if you cut our great continent in two? Instead, the South would be bought off. Lincoln promised a panicked nation that if elected he would preserve the Union, even if the price was the accommodation of slavery.

Cool heads would prevail and solve this vexing problem.

My mind became infected by the fear that John Brown had been wrong. There would be no conflagration, no war between Good and Evil that would destroy the abomination of slavery. John Brown had died in vain.

"MR. PINKERTON, WE are trying to prevent a goddamn civil war! There cannot be such a war! There will not be one!" That's what Samuel Morse Felton, president of the Pennsylvania Railroad, declared to me in his office in Philadelphia on an afternoon in January 1861, not long after Abraham Lincoln had been elected President of the United States without carrying a single southern state. I had last seen Felton in Chicago, puffing contentedly on a cigar as he applauded Lincoln's nomination, to which he had contributed considerable support.

Felton had requested my services to protect his line, which had its railhead in Philadelphia and its terminus in Baltimore, from the Secessionists in Maryland who were rumored to be plotting to destroy vulnerable sections of the railway.

Though I had no interest whatsoever in providing any service to Samuel Morse Felton, George Bangs had replied to him on my behalf and put me on a train to Philadelphia. Such was my state of mind at the time that, incredible as it may sound, I lacked the will to resist George's intolerable presumption.

Drinking for both of us, Mr. Felton declared that he knew the true feelings of the South. He'd spent considerable time in the cosmopolitan city of Baltimore and had close relationships with men of commerce from all over the region, "men who are exactly like us, Mr. Pinkerton, men who are interested in America for what it is and always has been—a land of unlimited opportunity for commercial enterprise!"

It cheered me not at all to admit that Felton was correct. The fortunes of America, South and North, floated on a vast deep sea of cotton. King Cotton fed the insatiable appetite of the same mills in Britain where my family had toiled, and the precious commodity was making not just the southern planters rich but the northern cotton brokers too, as well as the shipowners of Boston, Rhode Island, and New York who transported it across the Atlantic. The whole country was getting richer by the day, and the only threat to this prosperity, as Felton so colorfully put it, "are a motley bunch of hotheads and radicals in the South and the North!"

"You mean like John Brown?" I asked innocently.

"Of course I mean John Brown. If that lunatic hadn't—" He stopped and peered stonily at me, realizing I'd baited him. Child's play after his three whiskeys. Insulting the memory of John Brown to my face wasn't too smart.

"Look, Pinkerton, what's done is done. Lincoln is supposed to travel to Washington on my railroad in less than a month. What the hell do we do if they blow up a bridge? Haul him over the mountains to his inauguration?"

I was familiar with Lincoln's planned route for his triumphal procession. It would begin in Chicago and end in Washington, where he would be sworn in as our new President. Along the way he would stop in the major cities of the North that had been crucial to his election: Cincinnati, Buffalo, Pittsburgh, New York, Philadelphia, and Harrisburg, the capital of Pennsylvania, where he would commemorate the entrance into the Union of the Free State of Kansas.

Since his election, although a half dozen states in the South had declared their secession from the United States of America, the legislatures of Virginia and Maryland had not yet voted to join what was being called the Confederacy. Without them the rebellious movement was just a lot of toothless posturing.

"Pinkerton, Maryland and Virginia are inhabited by men of reason. The fire-eaters want to incite them, but we are going to prevent that. Lincoln will resolve this situation to everyone's satisfaction. We just have to get him to Washington."

"Is that why you've called on me, Mr. Felton?"

"Who else? General Scott can't send Federal troops to protect a private railway! It would just give the fire-eaters in Maryland more ammunition for secession."

I remained silent for a long time, hoping to convey to Mr. Samuel Morse Felton the erroneous impression that I gave a shit. I finally delivered a carefully crafted reply. "I will take the night train back to Chicago and discuss your situation with my staff. You will hear from me soon with a plan of action."

He smiled broadly, as men like him always do when they think they got their way.

ONCE I WAS out of there I had to sit down on a bench and take a few deep breaths. By coincidence I was in the center of the city, right beside that stupid cracked Liberty Bell. I almost wet my pants laughing, because that was where the whole sham began back in 1776. The Virginia Gentlemen, those plantation-owning, slave-holding Founding Fuckers, had pulled a fast one by coming to Philadelphia to draw up the rules and regulations for this United States of America in a Quaker City with all its free Negroes wandering about and not a slave in sight.

While that addled inventor Ben Franklin and his Yankee friends were going on about tea taxes, Washington and Jefferson and Madison were hiding in some back room of Independence Hall, giggling like girls over the scam they were pulling up here in Philadelphia—founding a Republic guaranteeing life, liberty, and the pursuit of happiness to an aristocracy that answered to no one except the lucky few who got here first and turned a wilderness into a kingdom by working human beings to death!

Meanwhile, those sanctimonious northern pricks really couldn't wring their hands too hard over the immorality of slavery, since it was slaves who'd drug every rock out of their wretched New England soil to pile up those neat stone walls around the pretty little farms they'd built for their Puritan massas. When there was no work left for the slaves to do, they freed them because the real money up north wasn't in owning slaves anymore but in transporting them. In 1776, slave trading was the biggest industry in New England, run by the Hancocks and Winthrops and Welds and the rest of those high-toned Yankees. They sailed their fleets out of Boston and Newport in that money-dripping triangle—sugar and rum from the Islands to New England, over to Africa to fill their holds with captive blacks, and then back across the Atlantic to the slave markets of Charleston and New Orleans. That's why they all signed on to a Constitution whose tortured logic counted a slave as *three-fifths* of a human being, a wretched compromise between morality and commerce.

Now here I was, sitting in the very same square in Philadelphia where they had gathered less than a hundred years before, wondering what the hell I'd been thinking since I got to this country. Tear this thing down? No one wanted that.

John Brown was dead.

Henry Ward Beecher could rant till the cows came home, but where would his friends who owned the ships—not to mention the mills of Lowell, Massachusetts—get their cotton from if the South told the North to fuck off and created another country?

All Samuel Morse Felton and Lincoln and the rest of them wanted was to keep the machinery up and running and the cost of doing business down.

Well, they could manage without me, thanks. It would be easy enough to catch a train to New York instead of Chicago and book passage on a ship back to Glasgow. This was not my home. It was Bedlam, the inmates raving on about imaginary spirits like Freedom and Liberty.

I hadn't chosen to come here. I had tried to change the place but I could not; no one could. But I couldn't escape either, because once you entered, they locked the doors behind you, and you went as mad as the rest of the lunatics.

Nine

A week later Mrs. Warne walked into my office and seated herself with a look of determination. She was holding several lengthy telegrams from Mr. Samuel Morse Felton requesting with increasing impatience the details of my plan *as promised* for protecting his precious railroad. I had read the telegrams when they arrived and tossed them into the trash receptacle beside my desk. Mrs. Warne had somehow retrieved them and smoothed out the crumpled balls. I wondered if she had used a heated iron, although I detected no scorch marks on the thin telegraphic paper.

"Mrs. Warne, I would have you refrain from examining the contents of my wastebasket, since what goes in there, in my professional opinion, is of as much value as what I deposit in my chamber pot." I was in no mood for debate. "Do we have any other business to discuss?"

"We are not yet finished with this business. Please explain why we can protect the entire Illinois Central Railroad and not Mr. Felton's line, which is less than a quarter of the length."

I rose from my chair and went over to the fine oak map cabinet I had constructed myself. I enjoyed on occasion putting my professional skills with wood and tools to use. I have found in the course of my career that the display of unexpected talents keeps both allies and opponents off guard, which is always a good thing. This cabinet was three feet deep and contained many pigeonholes, in which were stored long thin wooden cylinders containing the finest maps available of every region of the continent, in various scales of detail. I selected the map that I had in fact perused not two days before and spread it on my desk. Its size and the tightly wrapped curl of the paper made it difficult to lay out. I reached for the inkpot at the edge of my desk.

"Mrs. Warne, could you be of assistance?"

She came around to my side of the desk and placed the inkpot on one corner of the map and my appointment book on another. She held down the corner closest to her with her hand, while I did the same with my corner. We were now side by side, examining the line of the Pennsylvania Central Railway, depicted as a red snake connecting Philadelphia and Baltimore, as it passed through the states of Pennsylvania, Delaware, and Maryland.

I placed my finger on a spot halfway across the desk. We both had to lean over to see what I was pointing to, and her arm pressed against mine, below my shoulder and above my elbow.

It was not the first time we had touched. In several years of traveling in carriages, railway cars, and wagons, or entering cramped quarters to search for clues, our bodies had often brushed against each other. After the first or second time, by unspoken agreement, we did not react with exaggerated propriety. At any rate, leaning over the map, as she leaned against me, I leaned against her. She did not lean away. She held her ground, establishing herself as a pillar against which I could rest my weary being.

"Do you see, Mrs. Warne?" I asked, almost dreamily. "Mr. Felton's railway crosses the Susquehanna River here. The tracks disappear. That is because the cars and locomotives must be ferried across the river. That is only the most obvious point of vulnerability along the line. Notice"—I moved my finger farther down—"there is another river here, with a bridge, and many smaller bridges over creeks, and this tunnel here. How many Pinkerton guards do you think it would take to protect every vulnerable point from armed men bent on destruction? Sixty? Six hundred?"

"I don't know. It is not my job to plan the Agency's operations."

"True. That is my job. Rest assured I have thoroughly examined the situation and determined that I can do nothing to give Mr. Felton the peace of mind he seeks. It would be a fool's errand." She stepped away from me. The intent of her gesture was unmistakable, even in my clouded state. "If you disagree, speak up, Mrs. Warne. You had no trouble expressing your opinion on the matter of rescuing John Brown. If I recall, you threatened to resign unless I pursued your strategy over mine."

"So now it is your turn to resign, Mr. Pinkerton?"

"Resign?" I tried to laugh but managed only a tepid cough. "I am engaged in more cases than I can keep up with."

She squinted as if I had suddenly shrunk and she was having trouble locating me. "Mr. Pinkerton, do not insult my intelligence." With that she turned and walked out of the office.

Insult her intelligence? The woman had just *pissed* all over mine—as well as my judgment, my character, and my manhood! Instead of flying into a justifiable homicidal rage, however, I felt a panicked urge, brought on by the bitter tone of disappointment in her voice, to prove her wrong.

You see, I disappointed Joan by refusing to acquiesce to her wishes, thereby proving that I was, in fact, exactly the man she thought I was. Mrs. Warne, however, was deeply disappointed because my actions indicated that I was *not* the man she thought I was.

But she was mistaken.

I was! Of course I was.

"SIX MEN?" MR. SAMUEL Morse Felton of the Pennsylvania Central Railroad looked at me incredulously.

"Six *operatives*. Four males and two females, to be precise."

"Women are going to protect my rail line from these fire-eating Secessionists? Pinkerton, we are one week closer to a civil war than the last time we met, and you bring me a force of six?"

"Mr. Felton, assuming there is a genuine threat to your railroad other than a lot of hot air emanating from the mouths of these so-called fire-eaters, the most expeditious course of action is to un-cover the identities and plans of the plotters *before* they act."

"With six men?"

"Men and women, as I previously stated. We will be disguised as Southerners, returning to Baltimore from various business in the North. We will make our Secessionist views known from the mo-ment we board the train and mingle with our fellow Southerners. Once in Baltimore, we shall follow my Agency's standard proce-dure of insinuating ourselves into the company of our quarry—namely, those in the city who are most likely to have knowledge of or direct connection to any persons intending to damage your rail-road. Once we discover these persons and their plans, you will be informed."

He was not particularly encouraged, but he had no choice. "All right. I will trust your judgment, Mr. Pinkerton."

"Good. Mr. Bangs will draw up the contract. The rate for these services will be considerably higher than usual."

ON THE MORNING of January 30, 1861, we appeared in our disguises on the platform of the Pennsylvania Central in Philadelphia to journey to Baltimore. To all appearances we had no prior relationship to one another, except that we were all Southerners.

Mrs. Warne stood at the far end, surrounded by a virtual mountain of traveling trunks that had been the subject of a heated discussion between us earlier that morning. Without my prior authorization she had spent the previous day in the finest shops in the city, acquiring a fortune's worth of brand-new costumes.

She claimed this was exactly what southern ladies of means did when they came north at this time of year. Therefore, she argued, her day's efforts had served the dual purpose of acquiring the perfect disguise for her cover as a wealthy southern widow and acquainting her with the very latest trends in high style so as to be knowledgeable in her conversation with her compatriots as they returned home from their annual shopping sprees.

Mrs. Warne's explanation did not dispel my suspicion that she was taking advantage of my recent resolve to prove her estimation of me wrong and was shamelessly indulging herself at my expense.

Even when she hissed at me to lower my voice lest I blow our cover, because we were standing in a corner of the hotel lobby and beginning to draw curious stares, I didn't give a shit, because in truth I felt an overwhelming sense of futility toward this entire misconceived mission and no longer cared what she thought of me.

When she finally revealed, rather haughtily, that she had gotten George to write a generous allowance for "supplies and materials" into Felton's contract, and that her entire wardrobe would not cost me a cent, I decided it wasn't worth the effort to call the whole thing off. She was certainly elegantly dressed that morning. If she was correct in her assumptions, it would place her in high regard among the other belles of the South.

At Mrs. Warne's side was Hattie Lawton, her first hire in the Female Detective Bureau of the Pinkerton Detective Agency. Hattie was twenty-three. She had been an actress, and perhaps more, but Mrs. Warne and I were both impressed not only by her enormous charm and skills of impersonation but by her steely nerve as well.

I was once more J. H. Hutcherson of Memphis, the commodities broker with secret connections to northern arms dealers. As Timothy strolled by, finely attired in a rakish outfit favored by southern gentlemen of a certain type, we made casual conversation that if overheard would indicate we were simply fellow travelers.

I had chosen two other operatives for the mission. One was Pryce Lewis, a British émigré who was a master at exploiting the peculiar American weakness for all things English that Southerners in particular are susceptible to. Lewis's cover was that of a bored baronet, sympathetic to the southern cause and quick with a pistol.

John Scully, the last member of our group, couldn't have been more different from Pryce. When Scully first applied for a job, he refused to answer most of my questions about his personal life. The only reason I didn't dismiss him on the spot was that he revealed such a detailed and cunning knowledge of Chicago's criminal underworld that I was sure Scully was in fact a professional thief who had decided to use his expertise in a new and presumably less dangerous career.

He was disguised as a boatwright from Charleston, South Carolina, who had recently been employed in the yards of New York City, until he got sick of his Yankee bosses and was now on his way to Baltimore to work in a good southern shipyard.

We boarded the train along with the rest of the passengers, composed about equally of Northerners and Southerners. There wasn't the slightest hint of a divided nation, aside from the pronounced regional accents. Our fellow Southerners seemed as affable and unconcerned with politics as Felton had claimed. As our train moved south, they mingled easily with their northern compatriots, sharing drinks and then lunch in the dining car, conversing amiably on diverse topics.

At about three in the afternoon, we crossed that invisible line drawn by Mason and Dixon, leaving the free state of Delaware for the slave state of Maryland. When we pulled into the railway depot at Perrymansville, the Southerners in our car rose as one with looks of grim determination and made their way down the aisle to exit the train. I quickly joined them.

The platform and terminal were patrolled by armed men wearing irregular military uniforms. They approached any passenger whose accent identified them as Yankees and demanded to know their destination and purpose for traveling south. The Northerners were ordered to wait on board the train during the two-hour layover. In my disguise I was swept into the station saloon with my fellow Southerners.

Before we had crossed into their homeland, I overheard them on the train amiably explaining to their northern acquaintances the true civilizing nature of the institution of slavery, which benefited white man and colored man alike. They didn't believe a word of what they were saying. Only the idiotic Yankees did. That drawling, charming accent was just a disguise to hide from the enemy their malevolent hatred of all humans of a darker hue. Now, as we entered the saloon in Perrymansville, they cast off their masks of civility with a vengeance, as if having to wear them for the hated Yankees had been an affront to their honor.

The men in that saloon longed for a violent resolution to the vexation that not only they but their fathers and grandfathers before them had suffered at the hands of the Yankees. They longed for the hated Yankees to finally let them go. Yes, let my people go!

They had the same wretched fixation of persecution as those Old Testament Jews, and they were just as certain that their God would bring down plagues on their oppressors, part the waters, and lead them to the promised land of Dixie, while drowning any infidel Yankees who might block their exodus.

Incredible? Nothing surprises me anymore. These slave masters were convinced that *they* were the slaves, chafing under the yoke of the North's moral opprobrium.

Oh, how I wished Samuel Morse Felton and even Abraham Lincoln himself could have been there with me, mingling with these gentlemen of the commercial and aristocratic classes of the South who hardly fit Felton's description of *hotheads* or *fire-eaters*. What would their reaction have been, witnessing, as I did, how these genteel folk took their fury out on every black in sight?

There were perhaps a dozen local Negroes in the saloon. Some were slaves attending their masters but others were legally free. Maryland had the largest population of free blacks in the country, but that status afforded no protection to the children who swept the floors or the old colored men who served the drinks in the saloon. They were cursed, intimidated, humiliated, and shoved violently if they so much as stuttered a wrong word. I've seen liquor-crazed crowds bait animals to tear each other to death. The white men in the saloon were baiting these people to overstep any one of the innumerable rigid boundaries between the races so the bloodbath could begin.

After all, isn't that what slavery is really about? Blood. The white man's hands are unfettered by law, morality, or even social disapproval from taking blood as he pleases, a man's or a woman's, as long as it is colored.

As for the southern belles who'd cooed over their light-skinned house servants like sisters back on the train, they now slapped the girls' faces hard to make sure they knew they were back home. Their fury was also about blood; after all, these colored women might well be their *real* sisters, since what flowed through their mulatto veins probably came from their mistresses' own fathers, brothers, or even husbands. That's what slavery had done to white people. It made them all blood crazy.

Cold water had been thrown in my face, and it woke me up.

I could hear murmurs beneath the shouting in the saloon. There was indeed a plot, but it was much more far-reaching than Felton could possibly have dreamed. The aim was not to blow up a bridge to disrupt his precious railroad. The intention was to assassinate Lincoln in Baltimore before he reached Washington!

Was this just saloon talk? Or the prelude to their so-called liberation?

I did not know. All I knew was that Lincoln would arrive in Baltimore in two weeks, and I had to find out before then if the threat to him was real. If it was, I had to identify the assassins and thwart their plot before they could carry it out.

I made my way out of the saloon and stood on the platform smoking a cheroot, contemplating the task now facing me. Timothy approached casually. To any onlooker we were merely two southern gentlemen discussing the weather or the price of cotton. We spoke in practiced whispers as he delivered his report.

While I had been inside, Timothy was following the scent of three men who had kept to themselves on the train for the entire journey. Perrymansville was their final destination, and they got down with their traveling bags. Timothy tailed them as they walked through the station and were met on the street outside by two men in semimilitary attire who had good horses waiting. They all mounted up and rode out of town.

As Timothy moved about Perrymansville and struck up conversations with the likeliest sources of information—livery stable owners and gunsmiths—he learned that a well-armed militia was secretly encamped in the nearby countryside. I decided on the spot that he should remain here and attempt to enlist in this militia to uncover their plans.

Timothy eagerly accepted the charge. He retrieved his traveling case from the train, and we made a great show of bidding each other well in our various enterprises with exclamations of support for the Cause—southern liberty.

As I watched him walk off through the train station into Perrymansville, I was elated. For the first time since John Brown's death I remembered what feeling alive feels like. You want to kill someone, and you have a damn good reason to do it!

Neither John Brown's death nor my descent into darkness had been for naught, and now the light was shining again. The coal smoke of the locomotive boiler mixed with the scent of the first buds of southern magnolia trees made me dizzy with joy. The shout of the stationmaster to reboard the southbound train was like a call to arms.

Mrs. Warne stared at me from the far end of the platform, and I had the unmistakable sensation that she knew exactly what was on my mind, because she was smiling in approval.

Ten

On the afternoon of February 6, 1861, I sat in the lobby of Barnum's Hotel, located in the center of the commercial district of Baltimore, appearing to any passerby to be engrossed in reading *The Baltimore Sun*, whose front page, as usual, was devoted to lurid denunciations of Lincoln in words and pictures. In that day's edition he was depicted as a naked baboon with uncontrollable sexual urges he wished satisfied by a flower of southern maidenhood.

We had only been in the city for a few days, but I had already concluded that if Abraham Lincoln set foot in Baltimore he would leave in a casket. My certainty, however, would not make it any easier to convince him to alter his plans.

Lincoln had to believe, worse than children have to believe in Saint Nicholas or my wife has to believe in God, that not only did the good people of Maryland wish him well but that for the preservation of the

Union he had to come to Baltimore en route to his inauguration to make a stirring speech to his southern friends.

The fact that the details of the heinous plot against his life which I had so far discovered strained all credulity would not make convincing him to change his mind any easier. How could I get Lincoln to accept that scores of Baltimore's most prominent citizens were following the machinations of a *barber*? An ex-barber to be precise. A Southerner, but from the south of Italy whence he had emigrated, retaining a thick accent and the extravagant gesticulations of his native land. He used one name as a dashing signature. First or last, to this day I do not know.

Fernandina.

His name was whispered in awe around Barnum's Hotel, where until recently he had pursued his tonsorial activities. Now he had no need to cut hair. He was engaged full time in the enterprise of assassinating the President-elect. Every day he swept into the hotel saloon, gathering place of the city's Secessionist stalwarts, accompanied by a bodyguard of local toughs, and they would retire to a private room in the back where Fernandina met with his followers.

J. H. Hutcherson's connection to the arms manufacturers of Springfield, Massachusetts, was an even more powerful calling card for me than it had been a year before, when I had journeyed through the South in my attempt to rescue John Brown. With the promise of Springfield rifles I easily gained an audience with Fernandina.

Up close the Sicilian barber seemed at first merely ridiculous with his maniacal threats to kill Lincoln, kill Lincoln, kill Lincoln! I challenged him as to whether it was possible, expecting a man of his temperament to immediately reveal his brilliant plan.

Instead, he clammed up and eyed me suspiciously, and his men closed ranks around their leader. Each wore a pin on their lapel in the shape of a gilded leaf. "The Palmetto Guards," Fernandina pronounced smugly, as he caught me eyeing the pins. "What they call here in America a *secret society*. I am like Orsini in Italy. He taught me everything, Mr. . . . Hutcherson." He downed the rest of his drink dramatically and stood up. "We will kill Lincoln. How can I be so sure? Because when men are willing to die for a cause, anything can be accomplished. And we have many such men."

He led his entourage out of the room, and I was left alone. Now, so many years later, I realize that a seemingly ridiculous Italian had explained to me why the War of the Rebellion would last four years and take a million casualties even though the North vastly outnumbered and outgunned the South. As Fernandina understood so well, they had a *cause* and we had none. They had men who were willing to die for that cause, while all we had were men with no choice except to die.

As Lincoln's train moved east on its collision course, the temperature of war fever in Baltimore continued to rise. Only the night before, a boisterous group of Bloods burst into the saloon. These young men affected a dashing theatrical style of long pomaded hair, twirled mustaches, flowing silken trousers stuffed into knee-high patent-leather boots, and ornate swords hanging from their waists. They were from some of the most prominent families in the city, second sons in this feudal society with its laws of primogeniture, landless young lords who could not inherit honor but were determined to earn it in blood. Like their brethren across the South, they had taken up the banner of the Cause with a fanatic fervor that was incomprehensible to any Northerner. There were no sons like these in the families of the Adamses, Winthrops, and Vanderbilts.

Leaping onto the bar, the Bloods unfurled a banner, and the crowd roared as they danced back and forth, waving their flag, which I had never seen before but would of course see too many times until this very day.

It was the flag of rebellion, the stars and bars of the Confederate States of America, a country Abraham Lincoln had no idea even existed but which was a nation more real and inspiring to these young men than Lincoln's precious Union.

I LOWERED MY newspaper and forgot about Lincoln entirely, my attention captivated by Mrs. Warne performing in the hotel lobby in her role as Mrs. Amanda Baker of Montgomery, Alabama, a widow of considerable means from a fine old southern family. She was here in Baltimore to settle some financial matters of her recently deceased husband.

She was surrounded by a group of southern ladies, two of whom I recognized from the train. They were Mrs. Warne's—or, rather, Mrs. Baker's—entrée to this circle. The entire group was imbibing sherry with a gusto rarely seen in the North in a gathering of respectable women at this afternoon hour. While Mrs. Warne fully agreed with my personal judgment that a clear head could out-think a liquor-befuddled one, she possessed an inhuman ability to consume alcohol in outrageous quantities and maintain a perfect clarity of mind while reducing others to blithering drunks. Her companions' liquor-soaked voices carried clear across the room, proclaiming their traitorous sentiments. If any of these drunken cows really feared some buck slave, or even homely Lincoln himself, wanted to sneak into their beds to fuck them, it was strictly wishful thinking.

One of them rose unsteadily to her feet and pinned a small brooch in the shape of a tricolored cockade upon the breast of Mrs. Baker's fashionable afternoon dress.

Mrs. Warne's southern charm quickly gained her an invitation to a gala at a mansion on a hill overlooking Chesapeake Bay, attended by the cream of cosmopolitan Maryland society. Their roots ran deep to the very founding of the colony and the original plantation grants.

Mrs. Warne reported to me that Fernandina himself was in attendance at this gathering, as were the same young Bloods who had pranced atop the bar at Barnum's waving the Confederate flag. She proudly recounted how, even though she was ten years their senior, they were all mesmerized by the low cut of her gown, but Mrs. Amanda Baker waved them off with her fan. She had bigger prey to hunt, such as Mrs. Josephine Hill, whose acquaintance she had first made on the train and whose husband, Lieutenant Bradford Hill, was deeply involved in the conspiracy.

Mrs. Baker quickly gained Mrs. Hill's confidence, and the desperate woman confided that her husband, Lieutenant Hill, was in torment, drinking himself into oblivion. He had served in the Federal Army and should have made a career of it, but instead he had resigned his commission and drifted into Secessionist politics in his home state.

This was only the first secret Mrs. Baker wormed out of Mrs. Hill. She learned how Lieutenant Hill had taken a blood oath at a candlelit ceremony of the Palmetto Guards administered by Fernandina himself to the select group of patriots who would commit the murder of Abraham Lincoln, but he was now overcome by indecision and remorse, weeping openly to his wife that the best thing he could do for everyone was to shoot himself.

Mrs. Baker soothed the hysterical Mrs. Hill, counseling that her husband needed a trusted confidant who could safely guide him through this thicket of intrigue: a believer in the Cause, her dear friend, the English baronet Pryce Lewis.

That is how my operative became Hill's constant companion. In a bout of drunkenness, the Lieutenant revealed the outlines of the plot. He swore he could not go through with it but would instead put a bullet into his own head that very night. This would not serve our purpose, so Pryce Lewis convinced Hill to buck up, do the deed, and cover himself with glory, nobly offering his assistance: "Sir, you must lean on me."

He did. Lieutenant Hill brought Pryce Lewis into the inner sanctum, where he, too, took the blood oath before Fernandina and was sworn to secrecy. In attendance was none other than Chief Marshall Kane, head of the Baltimore police department.

Pryce now learned the specific details of the plot.

Once Lincoln's train from Harrisburg, Pennsylvania, reached the Baltimore terminus, Lincoln would exit the train to cross the city by carriage to the Relay Station, where the only train from Baltimore to Washington originated. Lincoln expected cheering crowds along his route and a large crowd assembled at the Relay Station for his address, but he would never reach the station. His carriage had to first descend several times to pass beneath the main thoroughfares. Fernandina's assassins would be at both ends of the first underpass. Once the carriage entered, they would block the exit and Lincoln would be trapped, surrounded by his killers.

The night before Lincoln's arrival, a ceremony would take place to draw lots for the man who would discharge the fatal pistol. In this way the identity of the actual murderer would remain a secret, even from his companions, until the last moment. If that man lost his nerve or was somehow thwarted, the others would be armed with knives to make sure the deed was accomplished. Meanwhile Kane's police would keep any bystanders clear of the scene.

Fernandina modeled the whole thing on the murder of Caesar in the forum by Brutus and the other so-called defenders of the Republic of Rome.

Was he insane?

Was John Wilkes Booth?

Or the millions of other southern patriots who came within one hill at Gettysburg of winning the War?

LATE ON THE night of February 17, 1861, I secretly assembled my operatives for the first time since we left Philadelphia. J. H. Hutcherson had rented an office for his commercial activities on a side street near the center of the city. We arrived separately—myself, Pryce, Mrs. Warne, and John Scully, who had been in place among the lower echelons of the city, frequenting the cheap saloons of workingmen and the criminal element. Scully reported that Fernandina had sent agents provocateurs among these men, whipping up hatreds and fears of an imaginary armed black rebellion planned for the day of Lincoln's inauguration. Hundreds of these men would be in the audience waiting for Lincoln to make his speech, and if Fernandina's assassins had not already killed Lincoln, this mob surely would.

Earlier, I had sent Hattie Lawton back to Perrymansville to pose as Timothy Webster's fiancée, enabling her to smuggle brief dispatches to me on the situation there. She had returned to Baltimore that day on the pretext of visiting relatives in order to be present at this important meeting.

Timothy was the last to arrive, dressed in a dashing outfit that Southerners were to favor for the entire War. He snapped off a martial salute. "Lieutenant Timothy Webster, formerly of Montgomery and Bristol, England, currently serving with the Confederate Militia of Northern Maryland."

Now at last we had a chance to hear Timothy Webster's full story, which I can recall almost word for word.

"Hands in the air. And dismount that horse, slowly, sir."

I cursed myself for my carelessness. Up until then I had been scrupulously careful, obtaining a fine mount, a brace of pistols, and directions to the militia camp north of the town. I should have anticipated the armed sentry who appeared suddenly, blocking my path. The young man was wielding a musket, and the damn thing was primed and cocked. I dismounted and politely answered the sentry's questions about my identity, background, and political affiliations, making clear my intention to join the militia.

The sentry had been ordered to turn back any man without a written pass, so great was the fear of Federal spies. I launched into a ferocious denunciation of Lincoln, local Unionists, and cowards who would not pick up a weapon to defend their honor. I told him if his superiors learned that Timothy Webster of Montgomery, whose exploits as a British officer in the Crimea earned him the Victoria Cross, had been rebuffed in his attempt to add his considerable military skills and financial resources to the Cause, they might question the loyalty of this young man—Sandler is it?

Reluctantly, Sandler led me on a twisting trail through the woods that finally emerged in a meadow on the far side of a hill. There were numerous tents in the encampment, and men were engaged in orderly drilling. At the far end of the camp was a small farmhouse, where I tethered my horse and was led inside.

I had never met a man like Major Thaddeus Longwood, commander of the Confederate Militia of Northern Maryland. Longwood flew into a rage at Sandler for disobeying his orders and allowing a potential Federal spy to enter the camp. He dismissed Sandler and placed his sidearm on a small field desk. When I told him that my loyalty was beyond reproach, he spat on the floor.

"Mr. Webster, Baltimore is full of men like yourself, full of blustery support for the Cause, men of considerable breeding and

even financial resources, none of which qualifies them to serve under my command. Have you ever killed a man, Mr. Webster?"

"When they were removed from the field of combat, the grievousness of their wounds indicated to me that they would expire, but some were still breathing."

"Were these duels of honor?"

"They were men who had forfeited their right to live. As has Mr. Lincoln."

He appreciated my response. The man is an utter fanatic. He is a West Pointer and former U.S. Army officer with experience in cavalry combat in the Mexican War, but after the election of President Abraham Lincoln, the former United States of America, as he put it, no longer commands his loyalty. His allegiance is now to the Confederate States of America, and he intends to see that the state of Maryland becomes part of that nation. When I asked him how he would achieve his ends, he eyed me narrowly.

"You will find out when you need to know. Until then, I grant you the provisional rank of lieutenant. You will not leave camp without permission. Is that clear?"

Now Timothy implored me to convince Lincoln that he could not pass through Baltimore. That very day Timothy had finally learned Longwood's role in the plot. The Major was in direct contact with Fernandina. Once Lincoln was killed in Baltimore, the militia would blow up the railway bridges, cutting Maryland off from the North. They would then enter the city and force the legislature to pass a bill of Secession joining Maryland to the Confederacy.

Timothy's news merely bolstered my own conviction. "There is only one among us capable of convincing Mr. Lincoln of anything," I announced. "That is Mrs. Warne."

She was as astonished as the others. I had deliberately caught them off guard. The Master of Stratagem had returned to his helm. "Mrs. Warne, what do you think?"

She was beaming. "I am certain I can convince Mr. Lincoln with the evidence we have amassed."

"We will do it together. We leave for New York in the morning. Lincoln is scheduled to arrive there in the afternoon with his entourage. When we present him with our case, he will be amenable to riding a mule over the Blue Ridge Mountains with a burlap sack over his head rather than take the train through Baltimore."

Laughter filled the room. How good it felt! We had not laughed in a long time. I gave them their instructions. "Until Mr. Lincoln reaches Washington safely, the conspirators cannot suspect he changed his plans, or they will change theirs and intercept him on his altered route.

"Mr. Scully, return immediately to your friends as if all is well. Pryce, knock on Lieutenant Hill's door first thing in the morning and do not leave his side until our mission is completed." Pryce nodded enthusiastically. "Timothy, you have little time to lose returning to your regiment."

"I'll slip back into camp before dawn." He gave me a wry salute and headed for the door.

"Miss Lawton, you will remain in Baltimore with the loyal ladies, Mrs. Hill in particular, and allay their suspicions by informing them of your daily communications with Mrs. Amanda Baker, who has been called to Montgomery on urgent family business but will return several days hence."

"Yessir, Mr. Pinkerton!" Ah, Hattie, what a good soldier.

"J. H. Hutcherson," I continued, referring as I often did to my alias in the third person, "will announce that he has received an urgent communication from his friends in Springfield, Massachusetts, that a consignment of weapons can be procured if he arrives there by tomorrow evening. That will be his cover for his sudden departure. Mrs. Warne, I will work out a plan for you to leave simultaneously yet unnoticed. I will inform you as soon as I have made the arrangements."

There was an air of excitement in the room. The Pinkerton Detective Agency was fully mobilized once more.

Eleven

We dispersed as cautiously as we had arrived. I stood sentry from the second-floor window, with the curtain parted just an inch, making certain that each of my operatives left the building undetected. Then I locked the office door and slipped out into the narrow street behind the building. I was halfway to the corner of the main street when I heard the unmistakable snuffling and pawing of a horse in the alleyway just ahead. I drew my pistol and slid silently against the brick wall in the shadows until I reached the edge of the building that abutted the alley. I took a deep breath and peered around the corner.

Timothy was standing beside his horse, holding the reins with his back to me. I exhaled and lowered the hammer on my pistol. What could be the cause of his delay? Before I could whistle to gain his attention, Mrs. Warne, hidden from my view until that moment, stepped out of the shadows. I ducked back quickly before she could see me. What was this all about?

I leaned forward again and peered down the alley until my eyes focused in the darkness and I could see what I was not meant to see.

They were kissing.

I barely stepped back in time as they broke from their embrace. I gathered my resolve to confront them, but the next moment I heard his horse galloping away. When I leapt out, he was gone and so was she.

What in hell was going on?

I could not spare a single precious moment to find out, when the fate of the Nation weighed so heavily on my shoulders. I had to maintain at all costs my composure under fire and not allow myself to be distracted from the most important mission of my life by the silly romantic byplay of my two operatives.

Even if I had mistakenly trusted them and they had repaid my trust by stabbing me in the back!

THE NEXT DAY I made meticulous arrangements for myself and Mrs. Warne to sneak out of the city without arousing any suspicion that might tip off our purpose.

J. H. Hutcherson's Secessionist comrades wished him well on his rendezvous with the arms dealers in Massachusetts. Mrs. Amanda Baker's departure from the city was more problematic. She could not be observed going north, so I purchased for Mrs. Baker a south-bound train ticket via Annapolis. When the train left at midday, Mrs. Baker was seen off at the station by her close friends, including Mrs. Hill.

At Annapolis, Mrs. Baker abandoned her disguise, and Mrs. Kate Warne, a nondescript Yankee widow, crossed the platform and took a train back to Baltimore, arriving just in time to board the same Philadelphia-bound train that I was on. She would remain in her compartment until a prearranged hour, when she would slip the bolt on her door so I could enter to convey the details of the plan I had developed to intercept Lincoln and alter his route.

By the time our train pulled out of the Baltimore station, I had successfully compressed all extraneous thoughts of Webster and Mrs. Warne into a tiny mental ball, which I stuffed into a niche in the back of my brain. Three hours later, when we passed into Delaware, I made my way down the passageway of her car and slipped into her unlocked compartment precisely on schedule.

She looked up with an innocent smile, and the little ball in my brain exploded.

"What exactly is going on between yourself and Timothy, Mrs. Warne?" How could the first thing out of my mouth at this critical moment be an inane question about her and Webster?

"What exactly do you mean by *going on,* Mr. Pinkerton?"

She was comfortably ensconced on the leather banquette, as I swayed dangerously on my feet in her train compartment. "I observed the two of you, immediately following our secret meeting, when you were ordered to disperse without further contact, engaged in the act—"

"Of kissing." It was even worse when she said it than when I thought it.

"Exactly."

"You were spying on us."

"Mrs. Warne, do not turn my inquiry into the appropriateness of your actions into a judgment of mine."

"I was merely suggesting that you improve your technique. Timothy and I were well aware that you were spying on us."

"I was not spying."

"Whatever you wish to call it, then."

"I wish you to answer my question."

She squinted as if trying to make out my expression more clearly in the dimly lit train compartment. "What was the question again?"

"What is going on between you and Webster?" I attempted to look rational, to assure her that my inquiry was grounded in some strategic purpose and not the result of another malfunction of my mind.

The train lurched, and I just managed to put my hands out to prevent myself from falling on her. Holding myself against the wall above her head, our faces were so close I could smell the alcohol on her breath. She had been drinking!

"Shouldn't you sit down, Mr. Pinkerton?"

I took a seat on the banquette beside her and regained my composure. She stared out the window until she announced a bit wearily, as if she would have preferred not to discuss it, "Timothy and I are engaged to be married."

"Engaged. To be married." I hate assholes who repeat what you have just told them in plain English.

"That is what I said, Mr. Pinkerton."

"For how long?"

"Well, till death do us part, I suppose. That is the intention of marriage."

"How long have you been *engaged,* Mrs. Warne?"

"Since last night. That is what our kiss signified."

"In the midst of our desperate attempt to save Lincoln's life, Timothy asked you to marry him?"

"He asked me several times before, but I always demurred. Last night, however, I felt it was the appropriate time to satisfy his wishes."

"Satisfy—" I stopped myself. I would not go on repeating her statements. Instead I kept blurting out stupid questions. "Why?"

She snorted a laugh. "Why would he want to marry me?"

"That much I can ascertain."

"Why, thank you, sir." Her coquettish smile completely un-nerved me.

"Why the hell did you tell him you would marry him last night? That is what I wish to know because"—I had to think fast—"because it directly impinges on our operation."

"My thought precisely. I felt that, of all of us, Timothy is under-taking the most dangerous mission, and I wished to fortify his resolve. Give him something to fight for, as it were."

"Meaning yourself?"

"That is not exactly what I mean." She shook her head as if our interchange was genuinely trying her patience. I pressed on, trying to focus on the facts. Wasn't I entitled to the facts?

"And when will the happy couple be united in holy matri-mony?"

"We did not discuss a date."

"Are you trifling with Timothy? Do you really intend to marry him?"

"I said I did."

"Then certainly you must envision a time for this to occur?"

"When all of this is over."

"All of what?"

Her voice seemed like some Cassandra prophesying. "You have finally gotten your war, Mr. Pinkerton. And from what we have learned in the past days, how can we even pretend to know who among us will survive, much less triumph?"

I pondered that as she reached into her traveling case and pulled out a finely wrought silver flask. "Would you care for a drink?"

I shook my head irritably. She knew full well that I was a teeto-taler and had been since eighteen. Not for inane religious reasons, only practical ones. As I have noted previously, I believe a mind uninfluenced by spirits always has an edge on one polluted by alcohol. Nonetheless, I did not impose my personal beliefs on my operatives.

She shrugged as if it were my loss, removed the cap from the flask, and took a sip. "This bourbon from Kentucky is quite fine. We don't know how long we shall have access to it. Kentucky might join the other side."

"You're drinking bourbon?" I winced at the sound of my prissy disapproval. I thought she limited her intake to sherry.

I rose to go.

"Oh, for God's sake, Mr. Pinkerton, just this once have a drink with me. If only to celebrate the occasion?"

She was as good as challenging me to a duel. Anyway, we had not gone over our plan of action, so if I walked out then, I was going to reveal myself as a bigger horse's ass than I already had. She held up her silver flask, and with remarkable skill, given the movement of the train, she filled the cap.

"I have only one thimble cup."

I reached for it. Our hands touched. I sipped it. It was indeed excellent. I had tasted whiskey before. I am not a prig. When I gave it back to her, she refilled the little cup and handed it back to me. "There is no need for concern on your part regarding Timothy and myself." I had no idea what to say to that. "Really, it will all work out."

"Yes, I suppose so."

"Right now, Mr. Pinkerton, your spirits should be quite high. We have finally embarked on your crusade." She raised her flask toward me. I realized she was proposing a toast. I touched my cup to the flask. There was a *clink* of silver in the near darkness of the train compartment. She took a long swallow, and I was transfixed by her neck stretched back. I swallowed my drink, slowly this time, savoring the liquor, the taste, the sight of her.

"It is good, isn't it?" She smiled slyly.

"Very."

She filled my little cup again. "We are spies now. There will be things you will not be able to tell anyone else." She inhaled deeply and her nostrils flared. "I will never betray your confidence. All I want from you, Mr. Pinkerton, is your belief in me."

"I've never doubted you."

"Of course you have. You doubt me right now."

She fixed me with her eyes. The bourbon felt warm and good. She reached for my hand with the cup in it and held it steady. She poured more bourbon and let go of my hand, and it rose like a balloon to my lips and I inhaled the smell of her hand and the bourbon and swallowed it all.

I tried to say it right, the way it felt. "Never trusted myself with liquor in me with anyone, so maybe I don't doubt you after all, Mrs. Warne."

I knew that made her happy. So was I. We discussed our plan for approaching Lincoln, how we would tell him of the plot and arrange for his safe passage to Washington. Then we talked of other things. Things we had never talked about before.

She asked me about Scotland. She asked about my mother. She just wanted me to talk. People had asked about my past before, but I've never believed anyone's interest in any person except themselves. I myself am a unique observer of others. While my interest is professional, when I ask someone about themselves, I actually listen to what they have to say.

Most people don't. Or can't. They are so consumed by their memories, opinions, and fears that they can't hear a word about anyone else without thinking of their own foolish predicament. They can only take your words and stick them in the pigeonholes of their own minds encrusted with a lifetime of hardened bird shit.

Mrs. Warne's mind was spotlessly clean. No one could listen the way she could. On that night in the railway car speeding north, she got me to talk of things I had not thought about for a very long time.

I was nineteen years old and had been on the tramp in the Scots countryside for a year. I had my legs solid under me by then, travelling light, with only some well-sharpened cooper's tools, a bedroll, and a few spare clothes in my rucksack.

I told her of a certain morning when I awoke shivering in the hayloft of a farmer's barn. I had paid a shilling to stay there because I was what I considered flush, having worked two full weeks in the village distillery. My shilling would get me a hot breakfast too. I stood outside the barn on a little rise and gazed through the thick mist at a pasture where sheep were grazing. The budding hedges had a purple tinge on that chill April morning. I made my way carefully down the dew-slick slope to the water pump. The trough was full, but a thin layer of ice covered the water like a pane of glass. I shattered it with my fist and made a vessel of my hands and dug into the cold water and threw it all over my face and hair, then dug in for more and sucked it up, first spitting some out to clean my mouth, then swallowing handful after handful of the cold clean water.

I looked around at the plume of smoke rising from the chimney of the thatched-roof farmhouse. My breakfast would be ready soon, but I didn't need food. I needed nothing.

I was a free man. That day I would hoist my rucksack on my back and walk down a country road to any destination I chose because no man had a hold on me, no man could command me. My life was my own. I was not full of plans or desires. I was content just to be free.

As I described all of this to her more than twenty years later, she leaned close to catch each word, taking the pictures from my mind and placing them in hers. Her listening gave the tale its meaning, because someone has to hear you to make your life real.

I finished my story, describing how the sun was coming up as I walked out of the village. "It was as fine a moment as I've ever lived, Mrs. Warne."

In that train compartment, speeding north, I was free again. I had found what had been lost. This time, though, it was even sweeter, the water more precious because, after all these years, the well was almost dry. There was not all the time in the world left to me, but I had finally caught up with that young man walking down the road, and now I had a purpose for my remaining days.

"I thought it had passed me by."

"It is just beginning."

"Aye."

I stared into her luminous brown eyes. When I finally stood up I was steady on my feet. I said good night and left her compartment. Then, in the hallway of the car, I collapsed against the window and had to hold on tight, because something had exploded in my chest.

I was hopelessly in love with her.

Twelve

S ince my Agency's inception I have required each operative to maintain detailed accounts of their activities while engaged in official business. They present their logbooks to me at regular intervals for inspection. The old logbooks are stored in the Agency's archives, in the event that a dispute arises regarding an operative's actions. When the Great Fire broke out in Chicago in 1871, I led my sons in the middle of the night into our burning offices, and we risked our lives trying to save what we could of our most important records.

I was intent on preserving Mrs. Warne's logbooks.

I succeeded, although no one knew that until now.

These then are her words, verbatim.

I arrived at the Astor House in New York City at noon on the nineteenth of February, after we had parted at the train depot in Philadelphia, where you remained to put into motion your plan for the secret conveyance of Mr. Lincoln to Washington.

When I approached the clerk at the desk, he treated me with the customary courtesy expected by any guest of this prestigious hotel. However, I was still a woman traveling alone, and I did not want to be confused with the legion of high-priced whores who filled the lobby.

The place had the air of a convention. Even though New York City is a Democratic Party stronghold, the state had gone for Lincoln, and now men of power and influence awaited an audience with the President-elect to establish their claim to Federal appointments and contracts.

In such a gathering, where favors are dispensed, whores play an indispensable part.

Since my employment with the Pinkerton Detective Agency, I have spent much time in the company of whores from all rungs of the ladder of their profession. I probably have a greater understanding of the hierarchy than anyone else in America.

As I have told you on several occasions, Mr. Pinkerton, the mind of a female is impenetrable to a male. You are, I freely admit, as much of an expert as any man I have known in matters relating to the actions and intentions of females, but still you know almost nothing.

Quite simply, a successful woman of any social class is able to discern clearly the desires of the most powerful, influential, and capable men within her purview and create the impression that she can fulfill those desires. The impression is everything.

A cheap whore's eyes promise desperately to please. The great whores promise no such thing. The women in the lobby of the Astor were the crème de la crème of their profession. What they promise is that there is no price a man can pay that will make them submit to his will. Oh, certainly they will perform any sexual act you can describe, and better than any female you have ever known. But that is not what a certain kind of man wants after he has looked into her eyes. He wants her soul, which she will never give him, which actually gives him intense pleasure, since men like that can get anything else in the world they want.

All this is mere background to the immediate problem I was facing. It was crucial to our mission that I establish to the desk clerk that even though I had arrived at the hotel alone, I was not to be confused with a woman for sale. Once I had the clerk's absolute understanding on this point, I proceeded to hand him the envelope you had given to me, addressed to *Mr. Norman Judd Esq. of Chicago*. I explained to the clerk that if he checked his reservations he would find Mr. Judd among the arriving party accompanying the President-elect.

"Mr. Drew"—I inflected my words with the most educated upper-class accent of Boston—"I assure you that Mr. Judd anxiously expects the delivery of the envelope I have just entrusted to you, and his failure to receive it would gravely disappoint both himself and President-elect Lincoln. In that case, I am afraid, I would have no choice but to hold you personally responsible."

Men loathe such treatment at the hands of a woman, since that is the way they treat each other. I stared him straight in the eye. This is the key to the power of those rare whores, because that is not what an ordinary woman does. My stare, however, had nothing whatsoever to do with sex, and therefore was even more unnerving to the poor man. Mr. Drew gave me a dignified nod of assent and quickly summoned a bellboy to carry my bag, and I was soon settled in a small suite on the third floor.

Two hours later I heard the commotion outside as the presidential party arrived. My room faced the street, so I got a clear view of Lincoln as he stepped down from the carriage with his entourage.

It was not until ten o'clock that night, however, that a knock on my door announced the appearance of Mr. Norman Judd, whom I recognized from your description. Seeing me, he was utterly flustered. He waved the envelope with your letter and apologized for disturbing me. "I must have gotten the wrong room."

"Come in. Quickly." I practically dragged him in and bolted the door. He looked panicked. "Mr. Judd, I am Mrs. Kate Warne of the Pinkerton Detective Agency. Mr. Pinkerton is in Philadelphia as we speak. He sent me to inform you that a dangerous plot exists in Baltimore to assassinate Mr. Lincoln upon his arrival in that city."

I don't think he heard a word I said. I ushered him to a chair, poured him a half tumbler of whiskey, and let him ramble on about how he had missed the train and only just arrived and received this letter, and he had been expecting to meet Pinkerton. I refilled his glass. It was helpful to know that, among Lincoln's entourage of friends, secretaries, advisers, and hangers-on, Judd is the man you hold in highest regard. Also that he likes his whiskey and it improves his demeanor.

I poured him another drink, which made it easier for him to engage in conversation with a female detective who was describing to him the plans of the good citizens of Baltimore to kill Abraham Lincoln.

When I finished recounting what we knew, Mr. Judd leapt to his feet and announced his intention to inform Lincoln immediately as well as Lincoln's closest advisers: namely, Ward Lamon, William Herndon, Major Hunter, and his secretary, John Nicolay. You had warned me of this possibility. I went to the door and pressed my back against it, barring his way.

I told him bluntly that saving Lincoln's life depended on not one word of our plans reaching the plotters in Baltimore. Secessionist spies were present in this very hotel—disloyal local politicians, professional agents, and possibly even members of Lincoln's own extensive entourage.

"Mrs. Warne, Lincoln will never agree to alter his plans without the agreement of the men he trusts."

"Does he trust your judgment, Mr. Judd?"

"I believe so."

"Then he will have to rely on your judgment alone, yours and Mr. Pinkerton's. You must arrange for an interview for Mr. Pinkerton and myself with Mr. Lincoln on the day after tomorrow upon Mr. Lincoln's arrival in Philadelphia. At that time we will present to him evidence of the threat along with our plan of action. You cannot reveal to him before then the information you now possess, only the urgent necessity of our meeting with Mr. Lincoln alone."

Mr. Judd had that helpless look you know I detest in men.

"Why isn't Pinkerton here?"

"Mr. Judd, tell Mr. Lincoln that Mrs. Kate Warne is here and that I look forward to seeing him again in Philadelphia, if, and only if, he is willing to meet confidentially with Mr. Pinkerton and myself. In the meantime do not say one word of this to anyone else."

Then I gave him a look that the most expensive whore in the lobby of the Astor House would greatly desire to have in her arsenal.

It still makes for fascinating reading, these many years later. Here is her account of our interview with Lincoln.

Mr. Pinkerton, your resolve to kill Mr. Ward Hill Lamon in order to save Mr. Lincoln was understandable, if utterly mad.

When we walked into Lincoln's private parlor on the third floor of the Continental Hotel in Philadelphia, Mr. Lamon blocked our way, insisting on searching your person for weapons, proclaiming that he was solely responsible for Mr. Lincoln's safety. I had met Lamon briefly in Chicago and made inquiries into his role in Mr. Lincoln's career, which no one quite understands, except that Mr. Lincoln considers him an old trustworthy friend, while most others consider him a leech. Unfortunately, Mr. Lincoln seems to genuinely enjoy the man's company and, worse, values his political advice. I understand entirely why you cannot refer to Mr. Lamon other than as the Moronic Fat Fuck.

He is indeed a buffoon, with his ridiculous baggy trousers, rough shirt, high boots, and habit of carrying upon his person at all times a pistol, Bowie knife, and brass knuckles. These references to his Cavalier Virginia origins would be merely amusing, except that the President-elect of the United States keeps this man at his side at all times, which undermines Mr. Lincoln's credibility anywhere east of Chicago.

Our interview with Mr. Lincoln got off badly when you

realized that Mr. Norman Judd had disobeyed your instructions and told Lincoln everything. Worse, Lincoln had informed Lamon of the sensitive facts and had even invited Lamon to this interview to serve as a judge of your credibility.

Lamon further enraged you by interrupting Mr. Lincoln's folksy, meandering greeting, demanding, "Tell us everything you claim to know about the danger to Mr. Lincoln's person, so that I may deal with this danger, if it actually exists."

Perhaps you were a bit terse in your presentation to Mr. Lincoln and should have allowed me to speak. I agree with you that the man lacks a certain kind of vital common sense. When he heard what we had learned firsthand in Baltimore, he simply refused to believe it. Nor did he contradict Lamon's characterization of our detective work as "mere speculation," maintaining that there was no good reason to alter his plans.

What you did not recognize was Mr. Lincoln's lack of self-confidence in this moment of crisis. He was terrified of appearing exactly as his enemies characterize him: namely, a bumpkin from the West. He feared being made a laughingstock if he followed your advice and abandoned his magisterial parade.

Then we got lucky. I know you hate to admit that luck plays its part, but how else can you explain the appearance of young Lieutenant Seward from Washington, literally barging into the room with a warning to Lincoln from General Winfield Scott? Young Seward made it clear he had absolutely no knowledge that we had been on this case, yet his description of what the Federal Army had learned matched the plot almost exactly as you described it.

Lincoln had no choice but to ask for your intervention. Although it pained him greatly, he finally accepted that greeting his southern admirers in Baltimore was not a prudent course of action.

He seemed fascinated by your arrangements for a special train that was awaiting him at that very moment at the Philadelphia depot not fifteen minutes from his hotel. Only Samuel Felton of the Pennsylvania Central knew of its existence. It would speed Lincoln directly to Baltimore without his entourage. He would arrive far in advance of his schedule and the gathering of his assassins and be met by a force of our armed operatives, who would spirit him across the city to another waiting train at the Relay Station, which would deliver him safely to Washington a mere nine hours hence.

"What could be more straightforward?" As you would repeat ad nauseam over the next two days.

Even I was embarrassed by the way Mr. Lincoln started prevaricating, declaring how vitally important it was that he not miss his scheduled engagement in Harrisburg, the state capital, the next day. Pennsylvania's staunch support for his election could not be slighted! Then he looked at you with that hound-dog face as if expecting you to satisfy his ridiculous request.

Lamon declared that Mr. Lincoln would go to Harrisburg, then return to Philadelphia, where the special train would still be waiting to hasten him to Baltimore. Of course, we both knew this was impossible.

I was encouraged by the patient tone you maintained in response to this idea, as if you were speaking to children, as you explained that their plan added twenty-four additional hours of delay, would remove the special train from our control, and burden us with the immensely difficult task of spiriting Lincoln out of Harrisburg in complete secrecy.

This alteration of your plan would almost certainly eliminate its most important element—stealth.

If anyone in his entourage found out what he was doing, they would eagerly share the news with the press. Worse, if it were surreptitiously discovered by one of the many ardent Secessionist agents dogging the presidential procession, the information would immediately be telegraphed to the Baltimore assassins, who would change their plans, and Lincoln's life would be in danger no matter what means we attempted to use to get him through Baltimore.

When you calmly pointed this out, Lamon belittled your skills and declared he would personally guarantee Lincoln's safety and not leave his side.

Fortunately, you agreed to my suggestion that we two confer alone for a brief period in order to present an alternative plan to Mr. Lincoln. Otherwise you surely would have killed Lamon, who had no idea how close he came to his life's end when he shouted at us as we left the room, "We're going to Harrisburg, Pinkerton, and that is that!"

When we returned an hour later with a revised plan that satisfied Mr. Lincoln, he finally agreed to place himself entirely under your protection.

Of course, your plan worked brilliantly, Mr. Pinkerton. It is part of history.

Her written words are as compelling as her spoken ones could be, and as likely to stray from the truth.

Perhaps it was an attempt on her part to apologize for hiding her involvement with Webster that she gave the credit to me for devising the new plan to save Lincoln. The truth is that the plan was hers, and she skillfully managed to get me to go along with it.

Thirteen

When we walked out of Lincoln's suite to confer alone as Mrs. Warne suggested, I was so enraged that all I wanted to do was march back in, coldcock the Fat Fuck, toss Lincoln over my shoulder, and deliver him to our waiting train.

In my blind fury I didn't realize she was leading me through the crowds in the hallway to her own room in the hotel three floors down. As she opened the door, she briskly explained that while we had to formulate a new plan to present to Lincoln as quickly as possible, we could hardly sit in the lobby discussing it. She was right, of course. I had thus far taken great pains not to be recognized, lest the legion of spies surrounding Lincoln discover that Pinkerton was on the case. I was lodged at a cheap hotel across the city.

Her room was not large. My operatives are on a strict budget. In the close confines I was barraged by visual and olfactory impressions, particularly Mrs. Warne's unmade bed, which had not yet been changed at that hour of the morning by the chambermaid, revealing to me the indentations of her form on the sheets atop the mattress where she had slept and upon the pillowcase where her face had pressed. I inhaled the lingering humid fragrance of her morning bath, the salts mixed with her perfume—a modest scent, of course, but magnified in the small room, a bedroom for rent. . . .

I made a strategic retreat to the armless chair in the corner to collect my thoughts. Then I declared that if saving Lincoln's life required the United States Army, I didn't give a damn about political repercussions. That was Lincoln's problem. I told Mrs. Warne I intended to telegraph General Scott immediately.

She got up and went to her traveling case; I had no idea what she was doing. The next thing I knew she was pointing a gun at me. A pearl-handled five-shot revolver of a caliber that can do genuine damage. I must have looked alarmed because she quickly reassured me. "Timothy can vouch for my expertise."

"Timothy?" I practically squeaked. How quickly I had forgotten him.

"He assisted me in its purchase and trained me in its use." I did recall that. "He showed me various techniques to hide a weapon upon my person."

"I see." And wished I couldn't.

"I would have you take this into account in your alternative scenario for protecting Mr. Lincoln."

My alternative scenario. That was the beginning of how Mrs. Warne's harebrained and exceedingly dangerous scheme became *my* plan.

We would accede to Lincoln's whining demand to go to Harrisburg. However, instead of proceeding on by train from Harrisburg to Baltimore, as publicly scheduled, Lincoln would secretly leave his entourage behind the night before and take a train back to

Philadelphia. I would go to Harrisburg as well, to arrange for Lincoln's clandestine return from the state capital. Since he could no longer travel via our special private train to Baltimore as we had originally planned, he would have to journey south in disguise aboard a secure coach on a regularly scheduled train. Mrs. Warne would remain in Philadelphia to make the arrangements. It was much riskier, but if his presence remained undetected, we could still arrive in Baltimore well ahead of his published schedule and catch the assassins napping.

I would have to remain in Harrisburg for a time after Lincoln's departure to cover his tracks and maintain the veil of secrecy before following him back to Philadelphia as quickly as possible to catch the same train to Baltimore. To board that train, he would have to cross the city by carriage from the smaller Harrisburg depot to the main terminal of the Pennsylvania Railroad. Until I arrived, the responsibility for Lincoln's physical safety in the crowded, chaotic station would rest solely on Mrs. Warne's shoulders.

"Mr. Pinkerton," she declared, "I assure you that I would not hesitate for an instant to use my weapon to stop any person attempting to harm the President."

It now seems impossible to avoid the conclusion that Mrs. Warne took full advantage of the fact that I had recently fallen in love with her to seduce me into going along with a plan that cast her in a leading role in this drama.

While I had said nothing of my newly realized feelings toward her, obviously she knew. Women can intuit this sort of thing, even in a man like myself, so practiced in the art of dissimulation.

Still, I might have withstood her wiles had she not at that moment begun preparing for her departure by going to the bureau and removing her undergarments, which she held in her hands as she walked past me to place them carefully in her traveling case. They were not merely of fine quality, they were frankly intoxicating. I imagined how they looked on her person.

She then retrieved her pearl-handled pistol. I watched, hypnotized, as she checked the action and inserted five bullets into the chambers.

Dainties and a gun. Oh, she was irresistible!

THAT AFTERNOON, A dour middle-aged widow of considerable means reserved the entire rear portion of a sleeping car departing the following evening from Philadelphia to Baltimore to accommodate herself and her invalid brother. The flinty widow dispensed gratuities to the stationmaster, the ticket agent, and the porters to ensure that her private section in the last car of the train would be curtained off. Since her brother's poor condition did not permit him to be exposed to drafts, she made arrangements for his carriage to be allowed to enter the yard so he could board the train without having to pass through the station or tarry on the cold and windy platform.

Meanwhile, I traveled to Harrisburg shadowing Lincoln's party. No one suspected that Pinkerton was in the vicinity.

The next day I blended into the assembled crowd as he gave his usual vague speech from the statehouse steps in which he put forward the obviously contradictory sentiments that the Union would be preserved, the Constitution upheld, and all would be right with the world.

That night Lincoln dined with his flunkies, who innocently expected to accompany him the next morning from Harrisburg to Baltimore. When Lincoln retired to his room, he changed from his formal evening clothes to a traveling suit per my instructions. Then, accompanied by Lamon, whom I had no choice but to allow to come along, he made his way unseen down the back stairs of the hotel to the street, where I had a carriage ready.

I drove them quickly to the depot and saw them off on a special train back to Philadelphia that Samuel Felton had provided.

Then I raced to the main office of the American Telegraph Company in Harrisburg. Henry Stanford, the head of the company, was a man I could trust. He agreed to allow me effectively to cut Harrisburg off from the rest of the world. He assigned me an eager young linesman, a Scots kid, Andy Carnegie, to whom I took an immediate liking. He's gone into the steel business lately. Together, Andy and I fixed the main telegraph lines with copper sheathing, blanketing the city in silence. If any spy sniffed out our plan, he could no longer communicate it to the Baltimore plotters.

I jumped back in my carriage. Driving the horses like hellhounds, I just caught the next regular Philadelphia-bound train as it was leaving the station.

Meanwhile, Mrs. Warne prepared for Lincoln's arrival at the main depot in Philadelphia. Directing porters to carry a virtual mountain of suitcases on board, she secured the rear compartments in the last car of the Baltimore-bound train. There was a nervous moment when a group of drunken southern Bloods entered the coach, having bribed a reservation agent to obtain a sleeping compartment for them on short notice.

Mrs. Warne stood her ground, hand on her gun, as she shouted anti-Secessionist oaths, bringing a crowd of patriotic gentlemen to her rescue. They surrounded the young southern interlopers and rudely ushered them back into the depot. Mrs. Warne then coolly dispersed the crowd, fearing someone might recognize Lincoln when he arrived.

Through some miscommunication, Lincoln's carriage was denied the direct access to the train that Mrs. Warne had been promised.

She raced out through the depot to find the carriage stuck in the crowded street in front of the station. That idiot Lamon was about to jump out and start shouting for all to make way for the President, but Mrs. Warne firmly dissuaded him.

Lincoln donned his disguise, which he later recounted proudly was of his own design. It consisted of a floppy knit tartan cap: Scots. That was typical of Lincoln's sense of humor. He also wrapped a heavy shawl around his shoulders. His final piece of subterfuge was to walk through the depot with knees bent so that he appeared to be of average height.

As Mrs. Warne guided him through the crowd with one hand on his arm and the other clutching the revolver under her shawl, the drunken Bloods appeared once more and spotted her. They began shouting rude epithets against Yankees and their leader, Nigger Abe, not knowing he was standing right in front of them. Lincoln, of course, laughed out loud. Mrs. Warne kept him moving out onto the platform to the rear of the train, where they boarded the last car. She settled him in his compartment, locked it from the outside, and stood sentry in the passageway.

Lamon had remained with the carriage and now entered the station through the main entrance, wearing the disguise I had given him, a black bowler hat under which he tucked his flamboyant hair. He got on the train unnoticed and made his way to his own compartment and stayed put, following my orders for a change.

There was some grumbling among the passengers when the train did not leave the station on time. That was my doing. My train from Harrisburg was delayed, but I had taken this possibility into account. Samuel Felton himself had given the conductor of the Baltimore train explicit orders not to depart until a package was delivered to him, addressed to *E. J. Allen, Washington, D.C.*

A half hour after the scheduled departure time, the conductor was relieved when I showed up and handed him the packet. It was filled with newspaper scraps.

As the train began to roll, I swung up on the observation deck of the last car. This would be my post for the duration of the journey. I checked my watch. It was 10:30 P.M. The train was an express that would make few stops, and we would arrive in Baltimore at 3:30 A.M. Along the route, Pinkerton guards who had arrived in the past day from Chicago were stationed every five miles, dressed as railway workers. Their instructions were to wave a white lantern as the train passed to indicate that all was clear for the next five miles. If I saw a red lantern, I would immediately stop the train.

Mrs. Warne stayed with Lincoln in his compartment. I did not want to leave him unguarded. From my post outside I could hear him laughing uproariously as she told him jokes. "Mr. Lincoln, have you heard the one about the Swede just off the boat and the unscrupulous tailor?"

For the next three hours I concentrated on the all-clear signals, reviewing in my mind every step of the procedure we would employ to transport Lincoln in secrecy across Baltimore in the dead of night to the Washington depot.

"Perrymansville."

She scared the hell out of me. I hadn't heard her slip up behind me.

"Mr. Lincoln is asleep, and his compartment is locked. I thought it was safe to leave him."

In the darkness all I could see were her eyes and the outline of her swaying body as she held the railing with both hands.

"We're passing Perrymansville," she repeated. "Timothy is in the greatest danger of us all tonight." She turned from me, peering off to the west where the Northern Maryland Militia was encamped. He was preparing to blow the rails—or pretending to. "In the morning," Mrs. Warne went on, "once the plotters learn that Lincoln avoided the trap, they will turn on each other trying to unmask the one who betrayed them. We did not fix a plan for Timothy to disengage without arousing suspicion."

There was a grave look on her face. Was she accusing me of taking insufficient precautions for Webster's safety?

"Mrs. Warne, I assure you, Timothy is the most resourceful man I know."

Her face lit up in a smile. It was the smile I wanted to see for this night's exploits, but her smile was for Timothy Webster, not me.

I experienced a sudden sensation in my stomach as if I had been gut-shot. In a heartbeat the dizzy, loony dance of excitement, complete with vague fantasies concerning her person, collapsed like one of those hot-air balloons that explodes just as it rises above the crowd of awestruck onlookers.

She would never be mine.

At that moment I did not care if Lincoln crawled out the window of his compartment in a somnambulant blunder and was crushed on the tracks.

What did I care about anything?

She went back inside, and I noted a waving white lantern in the distance. All clear.

WE DID NOT see each other again for the next twenty-four hours. When the train pulled into Baltimore at 3 A.M., our car with its curtains drawn tight was uncoupled and drawn across the city to the Relay Station by teamsters with drayhorses. There it was attached to the Washington-bound train, a common practice that attracted no undue attention.

I sat beside Lincoln as we crossed the city of Baltimore, and I did not leave his side until we pulled into Washington, D.C. at six in the morning. I almost drew my revolver when a man shouted out as I was hustling Lincoln down the platform, but it was only Senator Washburn of Illinois, doing who-knows-what at that hour. I grabbed him. His breath stank of alcohol. I didn't want Lincoln's arrival announced yet, so I bundled him into the carriage that young Officer Seward had waiting for us outside the depot, and we all proceeded to Willard's Hotel.

A few hours later, the presidential party arrived by train on schedule in Baltimore from Harrisburg. A loud public announcement was made that Mr. Lincoln sent his regrets from Washington, D.C., where he had arrived the night before. This news incited angry mobs to gather in the street denouncing Lincoln.

Mrs. Warne had slipped out of our car when we arrived in Baltimore. There were few people in the station at that hour, and she had no trouble making her way unnoticed to a private room in the women's parlor, where Mrs. Amanda Baker reappeared. She waited until a train from the South pulled in, and then she melted into the crowd of arriving passengers.

When she entered the lobby of Barnum's at about noon, the place was in an uproar. Once she was settled in her room, she remained there to receive reports from our operatives still in place.

When I returned to Baltimore in the evening, J. H. Hutcherson entered Barnum's in a very public rage, announcing that he had hopped the first train south when he found out Lincoln had slithered like a coward into Washington under cover of night.

I tarried at the bar of the saloon before making my way stealthily up the service stairs to Mrs. Warne's floor and down the hall to her room. I rapped out our coded knock, and the door quickly opened. When I stepped inside, she closed the door behind me and threw her arms around my neck. She was so happy she grabbed my hands and made me dance in circles with her. Then she made me sit in a chair and drink bourbon to toast our remarkable feat in saving Lincoln and outwitting them all.

I grilled her on every detail she had received from our operatives. Then I began to berate her. I was particularly critical of how little she had learned from Webster. She had endangered Timothy by not obtaining a more complete report from Hattie Lawton as to his whereabouts. I stood up and put my drink down, shouting at her about the necessity for thoroughness in our operation and the dangers that still remained. I was baiting her. I didn't care! I had fallen in love with her and been rebuffed!

"Mr. Pinkerton."

"Yes, Mrs. Warne?"

"I cannot satisfy your wishes if you do not make them clearly known to me."

What was I supposed to say? *Mrs. Warne, I would like you to bend over that chair, raise your skirts, and lower your drawers?*

I said nothing. Just trembled.

"Ah," she said. She took my left hand in hers and twined our fingers while she placed her right hand on the back of my neck and drew our faces together into our first kiss.

I MUST STOP here. I have discovered in the process of writing this memoir that recounting one's own life does not have to be entirely excruciating. Every man has at least a few moments he actually wishes to recall. For these moments, you can dam up the river of reminiscence and loll about in its pool.

Our first kiss. I will recall that moment immediately prior to my final exhalation before I die.

I thought I knew something about kissing, as much as any man who's been married a long time. In this delicate revelation I wish to be entirely objective about the whole physical business between me and Joan. I once lusted after her mightily. Even after the terrible consequences of that lust were revealed to me, our activities in bed remained pleasurable for quite a while. Joan wasn't much of a kisser, though. She had a squirmy mouth, and there was a lot of bumping chins. Whenever I did get her square on the mouth, she'd start gasping for breath, as if she forgot what her nose was for, and she had no idea what to do with her tongue—much less mine—during the activity.

I might have instructed her, but I knew little more about the activity than she did, since you never kiss a whore.

Of course I had congress with whores! I make no apologies for it. I kept it a secret from Joan and caused her no distress.

Some nice ones, too. Damn these wretched moralistic days we must endure now. Twenty-five years ago I used to keep a little tin can in the bottom right-hand drawer of my office desk: personal funds, even though whores were expected to engage in sex with coppers as a kind of gratuity. It surprised them to get paid, but I wanted to keep matters on a businesslike footing.

Anyway, that's beside the point. You don't kiss whores. They won't let you. I never inquired why. I learned about other sexual matters from them but nothing about kissing that I could use to improve Joan's technique.

Mrs. Warne, though, was an expert. I don't know if it was from practice or was a native gift. I didn't consider the question in her room in Barnum's Hotel that night. I wasn't thinking about anything. Her kiss stopped my mind cold.

Our mouths came together exactly as they should so that our lips met perfectly. Then she opened her lips wider, opening mine with hers, creating a cavern inside which her tongue beckoned mine to her embrace. I swear my tongue felt like my cock inside her mouth, and then our hands, still twined at our sides, squeezed hard, and she pressed her body against mine, but still our mouths were open, and as I breathed in it felt like I was inhaling her, and when I breathed out she seemed to inhale me as well.

I had some sense of what infinity might be like.

I opened my eyes. I was not even aware I had closed them.

Her face was only inches from mine. There was only the smallest smile on her face, just enough to let me know that all was well. She let go of my neck, and let go of my hand, but did not step away.

"Is that what you wanted?"

I nodded.

She let out a long thoughtful sigh. "I thought it was, but it took you so long to ask that I was not entirely sure."

She started to unbutton her blouse. It was a fine silk blouse with tiny midnight-blue mother-of-pearl buttons. I stared intently at her breasts pressed against the silk as her chest rose and fell with the quickening of her breath. She removed the blouse and folded it carefully on her bed. Her back was to me as she undid the fastenings on her skirt, which she also folded and placed on the bed. Her upper corset was cut low, and her torso was covered by loose-fitting fine cotton knickers. Oh, memory is good for something.

She walked over and kissed me again. When this kiss was over she sighed with a theatrical look on her face that I knew was for my pleasure. Her eyes were wide, liquid brown like melted chocolate, sparkling in the haze of light from the gas lamp turned low.

"Mr. Pinkerton," she murmured. "I am removing my clothes because I see no sense in our wrestling breathlessly and ripping at each other's garments. Unless that sort of thing amuses you."

I must have been grinning like a fool. "No, Mrs. Warne, I'm not much for it myself."

She was satisfied with my reply and turned so that I could assist her with the crisscross laces and tiny hooks of her bustier. As it fell open I leaned forward and placed my lips against her bare shoulder and slid them up the side of her neck as my hands reached around and held her breasts, pulling her against me. I have always until now had to describe her in a way that gave no hint of my true feelings, so I called her a *handsome* woman.

She was beautiful.

To me. That's all that matters. She was not an obvious beauty, but that was merely her disguise. There were many moles and birthmarks on her body, but her skin was very soft. A softness that makes me weep when I recall how she felt in my arms.

I let her go, and she walked back to the bed, removing her upper garment and folding it next to her other clothes on the bed. It seemed odd that she was covering the entire bed with her clothes, but I did not pursue the thought because I was transfixed by the sight of her bottom as she pulled off her drawers and stood there completely naked, with her back to me, as she slowly folded them and placed them upon the bed.

I am no expert, but I do not believe that women, by and large, parade easily before a man without a stitch of clothes to offer a bit of modesty or hide a flaw, or just to accentuate their sexuality by concealment.

Mrs. Warne walked across the room as if she were strolling through a park.

She sat down on the edge of the divan. It had a camel back and a single rolled arm. She lowered the flame of the gas lamp beside her so that we were in the dimmest light. Then she swung her legs up and lay on her side, facing me, pressed up against the back of the divan, her head resting on the arm, her knees drawn up halfway to her chest. I sat down in the chair all the way across the room from her, but our eyes did not break contact as I removed my boots and socks, my coat and tie and shirt, my trousers, and my undershirt and drawers.

I crossed the room in a trance. The divan was wide enough for me to lie beside her on my side. We were face-to-face, so that we had to hold each other tight to keep from falling off. She lifted her left leg over my hip and reached down for my cock as our eyes remained wide open. Then I was inside her.

While I liked it very much the way every inch of us was pressed against each other, lying there on our sides, it didn't seem like proper fucking. I tried to get both my arms around her so I could raise myself up and slide her under me and have a good go at it. She easily resisted my efforts, since the maneuver required her cooperation. Instead, she pressed herself harder against me and then she moaned.

Oh, shit. I can hear it in my head right now. How can you *hear* memories?

We kept trying to drive our bodies deeper into each other until we exploded.

We said nothing for the longest time, holding each other in some kind of disbelief. Finally, I broke the silence. "Mrs. Warne, are you engaged in a sexual relationship with Timothy?"

"Mr. Pinkerton, is that what is foremost on your mind after we have made love for the first time?"

"Will you please answer my question?"

"About Timothy?"

"Yes."

"No."

"You're not?" I was delirious with joy.

"No, I will not answer your question."

"Mrs. Warne . . ."

"If you are so intent on obtaining a reply, ask Timothy, because I will never answer it."

Instead, she kissed me again. And bit my tongue.

Fourteen

I firmly resolved never to engage in sexual relations with her again. What in the world had I been thinking? Let me not be too harsh on myself. The blunder was perfectly understandable. We were swept away on the tide of historic events! Understandable or not, I had suffered a monumental lapse of judgment by engaging in sex with the fiancée of my dearest friend, Timothy Webster. To my credit I did not turn my wrath for this indiscretion upon her. Instead, I accepted full responsibility.

After saving Lincoln's life, we took great pains in departing Baltimore to maintain our identities as southern patriots. I foresaw that Maryland would be an important battleground in the coming conflict and knew it would be of great value to leave the traitors we had uncovered in place, still believing my operatives were their staunch allies.

I left first and was back in Chicago several days after my regrettable indiscretion with Mrs. Warne. The others left individually and met up in Philadelphia to return together to Chicago. On a chilly morning in early March, I was waiting on the platform as they stepped down from the train: Pryce Lewis, John Scully, Hattie Lawton, Timothy Webster, and, of course, Mrs. Warne.

I couldn't help it. In my mind I traced the route of the train, calculating its location (somewhere west of Buffalo) when, in the middle of the night, Timothy had almost certainly made his way to her compartment on some prearranged signal, and they had—

"Mr. Pinkerton, how good it is to see you, sir!"

Timothy threw his arms around me in greeting. It startled me. I am a man for whom a handshake will usually suffice, but I returned his embrace. Over his shoulder I saw Mrs. Warne smiling.

I wanted to hear all the details from Timothy about what transpired in the militia camp since the night I left to travel north with Mrs. Warne. I gripped his arm, and we walked ahead on the platform, leaving the others behind. As we walked, I wasn't allowing Timothy to say a word, though I asked him many questions. I was going on in a most uncharacteristic way, and I couldn't look him in the eye, even though I told myself there was no way in the world she would have revealed to him what had happened between us.

We proceeded directly to the office. After all, I still had a detective agency to run and many diverse clients to serve. I had to get Pryce and Scully back on two major cases. Mrs. Warne disappeared into her office with Hattie Lawton in tow.

George and I met for a good two hours, and then I must have lost track of time, because it was dark when Mrs. Warne knocked on my half-opened door and entered briskly, carrying a pile of folders. She seated herself, and as we briefly discussed each case she made quick, precise notes, all the while not giving me one look in the eye.

I felt like the kind of man I have always despised in my encounters with criminals and lowlifes—a user of women. I had been intimate with Mrs. Warne, my trusted employee, and now I was acting as if nothing had happened.

Then it dawned on me. This was *exactly* what she wanted!

That raised my spirits, and I engaged more avidly in the discussion at hand, praising her thoroughness. Lincoln had sent his regards, which I now conveyed to her. She was pleased.

I was pleased! And greatly relieved. I had clearly conveyed to her, without the embarrassment of an awkward conversation, my assurance that the unmentioned event had been a spur-of-the-moment adventure that would in no way impact on our work or our friendship.

When our business was concluded, she rose and gave me a look that was not in the least bit intimate, yet full of goodwill toward my person. We had skillfully reestablished our former relationship, and all was well.

Why then, when she walked out, did I experience the same sick feeling in the pit of my stomach that I felt on that train to Baltimore, when I mistakenly concluded that I was never going to see her naked body?

THAT NIGHT I was determined to alleviate my physical distress by having sexual relations with my wife, Joan, even though it was a Wednesday. She surprised me and was receptive in her way.

Unfortunately, her way was not the way of another, whose way I much preferred. Fucking your wife while thinking of another woman is not a good thing. It was causing me to lose my ardor. I desperately threw myself into the activity, not with the woman who was beneath me but rather with the one lodged in my head like a goddamn bullet.

I once more pressed Mrs. Warne against the back of the divan in Barnum's Hotel until I exploded. I was horrified. I was about to leap out of our bed, but Joan stunned me, touching me on the back, speaking in a tone I had never heard before.

"You did a fine thing, Allan."

I nearly toppled to the floor. What a double cad! She was not, however, referring to my attempts at physical affection.

"You saved Mr. Lincoln's life."

"How do you know about that, Joan?" I had not yet said anything to her about it.

"Willie told me the story, just the way you told him."

"He's a fine boy."

"He is, Allan."

He really was. On the night of my return from Baltimore I sat him down, and his eyes were wide with a kind of soldier's respect as I recounted every detail of our adventure in saving Lincoln. The other children wandered in to hear the story. Robbie asked silly questions, for which his elder brother cuffed him around the head. Young Joan, displaying her serious nature, hung on my every word, while the baby, Belle, cooed to her dolly in imitation of her father's voice. Willie had told his ma because he was proud of me. They were my children and I was their father.

I had a family once, and they thought highly of me.

WITHIN A FEW days the high spirits at the Agency evaporated. Scully went on a two-day drunk, Pryce Lewis came down with some ailment and stayed home in his rooms, and I was stunned to hear Timothy and Mrs. Warne arguing, shouting at each other in her office. He walked out and slammed her door and was down the stairs before I could stop him. Mrs. Warne gave me a look that warned me not to even ask.

I had been so preoccupied that I had not noticed. Timothy Webster had changed.

IT IS A sad thing that people change. There are so many sad things in this wretched world, but I find this one of the hardest to bear.

You're drawn to people for who they are when you first encounter them, and that impression burns deep, fixed in your mind forever. Then they are altered by their life's experiences. What they once wanted is changed by what they attain and how they attained it. Or they simply grow up! After all, Joan was only fourteen years old when I first laid eyes on her.

They change, but you can't erase their initial portrait from your mind and meet them anew each day. Instead, you don't recognize them. They shouldn't be talking the nonsense that comes out of their mouths. The very ones closest to you now enrage you most, because while they resemble the person you once knew, they are not the same. Not really. In the end you find yourself wandering helplessly across a blasted landscape inhabited by ghosts.

Timothy had changed at Perrymansville, serving as our spy among the Northern Maryland Militia. On that breathless night when we all met and decided the threat to Lincoln was real, I saw a fire in his eyes and heard a passion in his voice that pleased me greatly, because I misunderstood him.

I had always felt the greatest fondness for Timothy Webster because, unlike myself, he was not what you'd call an inquisitive man and abstractions meant little to him. He simply loved the adventure of the hunt, and never made any judgment of his quarry. Even when Timothy pursued the most reprehensible men, he bore them no ill will. They were simply mice he fed upon.

Now he had changed. There was blood in his eye and a hatred in his breast for those whose ranks he had infiltrated, the *traitors* as he now called them. It was not an impersonal hatred of slavery, like mine. His animus was much darker, and it was personal.

The day after his argument with Mrs. Warne, Timothy entered my office, closed the door behind him, and stood before my desk as if at attention. "Mr. Pinkerton, when war commences, as we surely know it will, what exactly will we do?"

"I have not yet given it my consideration."

"I have." His tone was chilling. "Since they drove the British off the continent, the South has been a military society and proud of it. A man achieves honor by shedding blood. The code duello has long been outlawed in the North, but it is a way of life in the South to this very day. Their militias are well prepared for war."

"I am quite aware of that, Timothy. I was in Baltimore too." Why the hell was he lecturing me?

"With all due respect, you did not encounter trained soldiers eager to kill their hated enemy—*us,* Mr. Pinkerton—not because we oppose slavery but because we have insulted their honor, and the insult must be repaid in blood."

I tried to make light of his fury. "No wonder you easily infiltrated those fire-eaters. You imitate their sentiments perfectly."

He did not even smile. "After the news of Lincoln's safe arrival in Washington reached our camp, Major Longwood ordered the regiment to disband quickly before the Federals discovered us. I approached a man named Johnson, a slacker who was already suspected of disloyalty. I told Johnson he was under suspicion for revealing our plans to northern spies and that he might be summarily executed. I urged him to speak directly to the Major and deny the charge. I then went to Major Longwood and told him that I feared the traitor Johnson intended to kill him. Longwood said that, indeed, Johnson had requested an interview. I volunteered to be present in hiding when Johnson appeared, and if the man threatened violence, I would shoot him on the spot.

"My intention was to kill the Major first, and then Johnson, and report that I had killed Longwood's assassin."

I was stunned. "You killed—"

"I was not able to execute my plan. The coward Johnson fled rather than face the interview, and the next day the militia disbanded. Before I could act, Longwood was gone."

"Otherwise you would have committed cold-blooded murder."

"They would have killed Lincoln in cold blood. If they had discovered my identity they would have killed me in cold blood. There will be much cold-blooded killing to come."

Timothy had been transformed, as millions would be in the next four years. For my fair knight the world had already become a killing field. He announced his intention to enlist immediately in the Illinois Militia, First District, of Chicago.

"And leave the Agency?" I could not believe it.

"Mr. Pinkerton, won't we all?"

The militia would be commanded by politicians, maybe even by the Copperhead mayor himself. That was happening all across the North. I couldn't see myself taking orders from a horse's ass.

Then Fort Sumter fell on April 12. Still Lincoln promised peace, trying to organize a conference in Washington with the government of Virginia, which had not yet seceded. Meanwhile, as a precaution, he called upon the northern states to send men to defend the Capital.

On April 19 a train carrying the Massachusetts Militia led by Benjamin Butler passed through Baltimore, and murderous mobs set upon it, killing and wounding scores of Union soldiers. The War of the Rebellion had begun.

"MRS. WARNE, YOUR fiancé is abandoning my Agency with little remorse, yet you have made no attempt to get him to consider the consequences of his actions."

"Timothy relies much less on my advice than do you."

At least she had compared me favorably to Webster.

"Then what do you suggest we do, Mrs. Warne?"

"Form our own military organization and keep Timothy within its ranks, along with the others."

"The Pinkerton Militia?"

"I think it will have to be something less well advertised."

"What exactly do you have in mind?"

"It is a secret."

"Do not play games with me."

"Hardly."

And so, with Mrs. Warne's assistance, I composed the following communication addressed to *His Excellency A. Lincoln, Pres. of the U.S.*

I told her he was not excellent at anything, but she insisted that he was not immune to flattery, and we wished our plan to succeed.

When I saw you last I said that if the time should ever come that I could be of service to you I was ready. If that time has come, I am on hand. I have in my force from sixteen to eighteen persons on whose courage, skill, and devotion to their country I can rely. If they with myself at the head can be of service in the way of obtaining information of the movements of traitors, or safely conveying your letters or dispatches, on that class of Secret Service which is the most dangerous, I am at your command.

In the present disturbed state of affairs, I dare not trust this to the mail, so send by one of my force who was with me at Baltimore. You may safely trust him with any message for me, written or verbal. I fully guarantee his fidelity. He will act as you direct and return here with your answer.

Secrecy is the great lever I propose to operate with. Hence the necessity to keep this movement (if you contemplate it) strictly private. Should you desire another interview with the Bearer, you should so arrange it that he will not be noticed.

My force comprises both sexes—all of good character and well skilled in their business.

The Bearer, of course, would be Timothy Webster.

THE SECESSIONISTS OF Maryland still had not succeeded in getting the legislature to pass a bill joining that State to the Confederacy, but they followed up their assault on Butler's Massachusetts Militia with the destruction of poor Mr. Felton's Pennsylvania Central rail line and the telegraph lines as well, cutting off Washington from the North. It would take weeks for Federal troops to capture the port of Annapolis and secure the railway from that city to the Capital. Until then the only way to deliver my message to the President was to have it carried by one disguised as a Secessionist traveling on horseback through Maryland to Baltimore, and from there to Washington.

Webster carried not only my letter but other important communications as well, from Lincoln's political allies in Chicago and other cities in the North. If Timothy had been caught in Maryland with

these papers on his person, who could say that he would not have suffered the same fate as the men of the Massachusetts Militia who were
hacked to pieces in Baltimore? Instead, he performed his mission
flawlessly. When Lincoln's secretary ushered him into the President's
office, Timothy removed his coat, took out his folding knife, and slit
the lining, revealing the important missives he was delivering. He
gave Lincoln a telegraphic cipher page to reply to my letter. For once,
Lincoln didn't hesitate. He scribbled his request for me to come to
Washington.

Timothy crumpled it in a ball, unscrewed the top of his hollow
cane, and stuffed the cipher inside. A few days later, having made
his way back up through Maryland to Philadelphia, he telegraphed
the message to me.

I left the next morning for Washington.

Fifteen

O ur nation's Capital was a god-awful sinkhole. Chicago back in the 1840s had better sewage than Washington did in the spring of 1861, a problem only aggravated by the arrival of seventy-five thousand northern troops who had poured into the city once we secured the railhead at Annapolis. Our so-called army was almost wholly composed of overnight soldiers from the various state militias. Unlike their southern counterparts, these organizations were primarily social clubs, whose members brought little in the way of functioning weapons or the skill to use them. They clumped down throughout the city in rude encampments, many sleeping in the government mint and other official buildings. They spent their days in disorganized drilling on the vast empty public spaces, saving their energies for drinking and whoring at night in the numerous saloons and bawdy houses that had always been a major commercial enterprise of this city but had now exploded into its leading industry.

The Capital was laid out on such a grand scale that there was no way to secure the perimeter, surrounded as it was on all sides by hostile forces. The most dangerous enemy, however, was its own citizens. They would be firing at the backs of the Federals as they faced the Rebels charging across the bridge over the Potomac.

Washington was a southern city and always had been. Prominent locals brazenly strolled the streets accompanied by their slaves, confident that the Rebels would easily overwhelm the Union forces. The dome of the new Capitol building at the far end of Pennsylvania Avenue was still enmeshed in scaffolding, only half complete, but the local laborers continued to work enthusiastically to get it ready for its new occupants, the Confederate States of America.

Lincoln had gathered all the military might the Union could muster in the one place they could not possibly defend. The man was a fucking genius.

"MR. PRESIDENT, SINCE you have asked my opinion as to what should be done, I will be forthright. You must immediately organize an orderly disciplined evacuation from Washington of yourself, your Cabinet, and all loyal government officials in order to establish a temporary capital of the Union in a secure northern city, from which base a swift war can be successfully waged against the traitors who not only surround but inhabit this city."

There was an uproar in the room. I had expected to meet with Lincoln alone, since my message to him via Webster had emphasized secrecy. Instead, I was ushered into a meeting of his entire Cabinet to present my views. Lincoln didn't take a shit for the next four years without consulting his menagerie. Imagine the pitiful results I would have achieved if personal weakness had hobbled me into running my Detective Agency in this embarrassing manner.

Each of his cabinet members thought they should have been president instead of him. William Seward was a good man, but he meddled in everything. Simon Cameron was the best of the lot, but that evil fuck Edwin Stanton soon got him sacked. When Stanton took over as Secretary of War, he acted as if he were commander in chief. Henry Blair simply ignored Lincoln and considered himself King. What a collection they were.

Lincoln once told me that he considered his so-called subordinates a pack of untrustworthy, malicious rascals. "See, Mr. Pinkerton, I sleep better each night knowing I have my worst enemies gathered around me, where at least I can keep track of their shenanigans."

That was his idea of running a government.

Even though the Dishonorable Secretaries knew I was right, they ridiculed my assessment of the situation because none of them had the guts to admit the blunder they had committed. Luckily I had left my sidearm in my room. The one I would have shot, though, was Lincoln. He's sitting at the head of the table, laughing at their barbs aimed at me, and he's winking, as if to say, *See what I have to put up with?*

I HAVE BEEN contemplating for several days now whether to include in this memoir my honest assessment of Abraham Lincoln, which until now I have publicly kept to myself. I finally decided that since I have mustered the courage to include in my memoir all the facts about myself, no matter how unflattering, it is only fair that I do the same concerning him.

First of all, I will never subscribe to the accepted opinion that Lincoln *won* the War or that incompetent generals prevented him from doing so earlier. Even though we had an overwhelming superiority of manpower, armaments, and supplies, the War was finally won, and just barely, with the gruesome surplus of a single commodity: blood. We traded blood for blood until we bled them dry. If you actually believe this was the only way to achieve victory, Lincoln was a genius. Otherwise he was a fool.

Lincoln's lack of imagination was staggering to me. In its place all I could ever detect were his cherished beliefs. As Moses cherished the Word of the Lord, Lincoln dragged around some imaginary stone tablets inscribed with obscure, legalistic bullshit that he made up while moping about in his early manhood. It never added up to twaddle, because he had no feel whatsoever for human nature.

What set him apart from other morons I've encountered, however, was his obsession to please everyone around him, no matter how absurd or contradictory their aims and ideas. That's pitiful, and it hurts me to say it because I liked him.

If the War had to be won by blood, it should have been *theirs*, and not ours, by half again as much. Every man, woman, and child in the South should have been screaming for mercy. Instead, Lincoln didn't want anyone to be angry with him, so he wouldn't touch their slaves, much less burn their plantations to the ground. After it was over, he wouldn't even consider hanging Jeff Davis or Lee or any of them. They repaid his magnanimity by singing "Dixie" all night long after they had gunned his moronic ass down.

And what about the four million blacks he supposedly set free? They're worse off now in 1883 than they were as slaves, because they still work on massa's plantation and massa can still inflict any punishment he wishes upon them with impunity, but now massa doesn't even have to feed or clothe them. These so-called freed men will bear the animus for the fallen fathers and sons of Dixie until the end of time.

As much as I blame Lincoln for all of it, I still felt sorry for him. Even today I can't blot out the image of him tiptoeing up to his room in that big white house and closing the door because he couldn't stand it anymore. The poor bastard should never have come out.

WE ALMOST LOST the whole thing in the first battle on that steamy morning of July 18, 1861. Washington's most eminent officials, journalists, and excitement seekers set out in their finest carriages, carrying food and beverage as if they were on a Sunday picnic. They crossed the Long Bridge over the Potomac into Virginia, following the Union troops, who intended to crush the Rebellion at Manassas Junction, where the Rebels were encamped under the command of General Beauregard.

Or so the Union Army believed. General Beauregard had actually snuck off during the night.

On July 10, a spy disguised as a farmer, a woman no less, had crossed that same bridge to rendezvous with the Rebel Major Thomas Jordan and reveal the intentions of the Union Army.

Major Thomas Jordan had only recently traded his blue uniform for a gray, leaving behind a network of Rebel spies in Washington who passed him precise information on the strengths and plans of the Federal forces, which he forwarded directly to his commander, General Beauregard. The report of July 10 was followed by daily briefings, right up until July 17. The next day when the Union Army charged Manassas they found empty tents and piles of wooden poles that from a distance had looked like a major encampment. Not comprehending the trap they'd blundered into, they started celebrating their victory that sent the Rebels fleeing to

Richmond. At a meandering creek known as Bull Run, Beauregard's troops fell upon them and cut them to pieces. The spectators who'd trailed along nearly got themselves killed as well.

If Beauregard hadn't been in a snit over the rank Jeff Davis had given him, he could have charged straight over the Long Bridge and that would have been the end of it. Instead, it was the last gift of dumb luck the Union would receive for quite a while.

Sooner or later Beauregard would get over his tantrum. He would attack from the west, and the Maryland Militias would rise up and join the battle from the east.

No matter how many troops Lincoln could muster, the Capital was a poorly fortified, blind bunker, infested by Rebel spies, who provided the enemy with details of the city's defenses faster than the Union Army could build them.

I HAD ONLY sixteen operatives to root out the enemy's secret legions in both Washington and Baltimore. To neutralize the well organized Maryland Secessionists, I sent Timothy back to Baltimore with six operatives to infiltrate the seditious network there, using his prior cover as Lieutenant Webster from Longwood's militia. Hattie Lawton went with him, now posing as his wife.

Meanwhile, the worst-kept secret in Washington was that Major Jordan's ring of spies was led by that infamous figure of popular imagination, Mrs. Rose Greenhow, the "Wild Rose of the Confederacy."

That was the reason I decided Mrs. Warne should remain in Washington. She was the Agency's most potent weapon for apprehending female lawbreakers, as she had proven so many times.

It all made perfect strategic sense. I am not going to waste the reader's time debating the question of whether I had some ulterior motive in sending Timothy Webster to Baltimore with Hattie Lawton while I remained in Washington with Mrs. Warne. I was trying to win a war! The idea that I set it all up just to have access to Mrs. Warne is preposterous.

WE DIDN'T HANG out a big sign, PINKERTON DETECTIVE AGENCY, WASHINGTON, D.C., BUREAU. On the contrary, we took great precautions to keep our presence unknown to the traitors we were hunting. Operatives entered our headquarters through a secret passage connected to an innocuous commercial building around the corner. When Mrs. Warne pointed out that if she lived on the premises she could serve as a round-the-clock guard against burglars or spies, I thought it was an excellent idea.

On a hot night in August I entered headquarters sometime after midnight and shouted up the stairs to announce my arrival because I had seen a lamplight in her room on the top floor from the street, and I did not want her to shoot me as an intruder. She called down a muffled acknowledgment, and I went into my office. I had just come from General McClellan's house, where he had furnished me with a roster of the officers on his staff he'd inherited from General McDowell. I intended to review the reports that my operatives had compiled in their clandestine observations of Rose Greenhow to determine if any of McClellan's officers were in contact with the ring of spies.

The reports were not in the file cabinets. I was tired, had not slept the night before, and found this extremely irritating. Mrs. Warne had organized the files.

I climbed the stairs. On the second floor was a cleverly concealed secret room of my own design. No door was visible. Instead, a part of the wall slid away when hidden bolts were loosened. Inside, the windows had been removed and plastered over so the room was invisible from the street.

I stood at the bottom of the stairway to the third floor where Mrs. Warne's personal quarters were located. Her door was closed on the landing above. I called out in a manner I hoped would not alarm her.

"Mrs. Warne?"

"Yes, Mr. Pinkerton?"

"I require certain files, which I cannot locate."

"Please, come up." Her door swung open halfway, so I trudged up the narrow stairway and walked into her room. She pointed to a pile of files on her small desk. "What you want is probably there. I apologize. I often take them up here at night to work on them."

"That's quite all right."

"Apparently not. It is inconvenient if you do not have what you require immediately accessible to you."

Our conversation was absurdly formal, but I was standing in the middle of her bedroom. It was good-sized and had several dormer windows. Her bed had a brass frame with a canopy over it. The room was furnished with an excellent Oriental carpet, a folding screen of intricately carved wood, and an impressive bureau. With a war going on, there was all kinds of trading in family furniture, but I had no idea Mrs. Warne would put such effort into decorating her quarters.

She handed me the relevant files from her desk.

She was wearing a chaste robe that buttoned to the neck and reached to the floor. I considered what lay beneath the robe, but it was a fleeting and perfectly natural thought. My imagination penetrated no further than her nightgown.

To be completely objective, however, I must record that I did—the accurate word would be—*linger.*

She looked at me questioningly.

I did not say anything. I had in my hands what I had come for, yet I was not moving.

"Is there something else, Mr. Pinkerton?"

I nodded dumbly.

She did not hurry as she doused the lights in the room. In the darkness I felt her hands removing my clothes. I unbuttoned her robe, knelt at her feet, took the hem of her nightgown in my fingers, and raised it over her head as she lifted her arms.

I have very much enjoyed writing those words.

LATER, LYING ON my back, I stared at her as she lay on her side facing me with her head propped on one hand. She placed the index finger of her other hand lightly on my sweat-slicked brow, and then, staring into my eyes in the dim light before the dawn, she slid her finger down my body at a pace so slow I was not sure if it was moving or not. Her fingertip magically made its journey over my nose and lips and chin and leapt to the top of my chest, like a delicate stiletto etching a line across my heart, and then across my belly, drawn in, not daring to breathe lest the finger lose its balance and fall off its path, until at last it arrived in the wet wilderness, soaked with my sweat and semen and the juice of her cunt. There her finger danced until it touched the tip of my quivering cock, making it jerk in crazy spasms as she smiled, as if she were playing with a puppy trying to bite her finger. Then, with an indulgent sigh, she grabbed it with her fist and held it tight.

Then she kissed me.

That's when I thought what a better place this world of horrors would be if only the divided population of males and females could devise a system superior to the one that now exists for assigning compatible partners from each group to engage in the type of activity we were engaged in.

The thought actually made me consider God. That miserable, lonely, horny bastard up there would never allow this plan to take hold on earth.

I COULD SEE the sun rising through the drawn curtains. In my arms she was no more asleep than I. While I knew that anything I said might sound foolish, I'd be damned if I was going to leave that room without getting things clear. I am a man who always makes his position clear.

"Mrs. Warne."

"Yes, Mr. Pinkerton."

"I came up to your room to get those files. I want to establish that I had no intention whatsoever—"

She started laughing.

"What the hell are you laughing at? I'm absolutely serious."

"Oh, that's obvious."

"It's true!" I roared.

"*Shhh!*" she whispered, and put her finger to my lips. I grabbed her wrist.

"Mrs. Warne, there has not been the slightest hint in your demeanor since that first time in Baltimore . . . that you wished for this to occur again."

"You made it perfectly clear that *you* did not wish it to occur again."

I frowned. It was true.

"And you believed me?"

She shrugged. Her face was just inches from mine. At that proximity you can only look from one eye to the other, so she leaned back to find the right distance between us, until we were locked in each other's gaze. She had the bravest eyes I have ever peered into. "I have no choice except to believe what you tell me."

I realized that I had hurt her in some way.

"I am sorry, Mrs. Warne. It is not a simple matter."

"Mr. Pinkerton?" she whispered in my ear, pressing her whole body against mine.

"Yes, Mrs. Warne?"

"When we are together in these circumstances, instead of calling me *Mrs. Warne,* could you call me *Kate?*" I nodded. "Then say it, please."

"Kate." The name came out of me as if squeezed from my gut, where I had buried it until then. Where it is buried again now.

She pulled me on top of her, led me inside her again, and I heard something like a deep purr of satisfaction. As soon as I uttered her name, I knew what I had done.

I didn't care.

She kissed me as she dug her fingernails into the back of my neck. I bit her shoulder. She made some wonderful sound—"*Tsoooo*—" half pain and total pleasure. I started to bite harder but she pulled away. Then she whispered in my ear, "We can't leave any marks upon each other."

What finer, nobler sentiment could a man and a woman ever agree upon?

We can't leave any marks upon each other.

If only it were possible.

She bit my earlobe, and I could feel her holding back, her jaw clenched as if she wanted to bite my ear off. But she would not leave any marks.

"Kate," I whispered.

"Yes, Mr. Pinkerton. Mrs. Warne isn't here. But whenever we leave this room, whether we are alone or not, Kate does not exist. Only Mrs. Warne."

It made perfect sense. We had managed to find some sanity in a world gone utterly mad all around us.

Sixteen

I'm afraid we have no other choice, Mr. Pinkerton, except to adhere to the law of the land." That single sentence uttered by the President of the United States of America perfectly illustrates the second-rate nature of Abraham Lincoln's intellect better than any commentary I have to offer.

On a steamy summer afternoon in 1861 in the course of our discussion, he claimed he could do nothing to prevent his government from being undermined by an infestation of enemy spies who were devouring the foundation timbers of the Union like termites.

I had just revealed to Lincoln that Mrs. Rose Greenhow was in direct communication with the highest echelon of the Rebellion in Richmond. My operatives had maintained round-the-clock surveillance on her mansion on 16th Street for the past two weeks, recording in their logbooks the procession of visitors. She had entertained many of the most prominent military men and politicians in Washington, several members of Lincoln's Cabinet among them.

I brought my operatives' logbooks to our meeting and waited patiently as Lincoln read them in his infuriatingly deliberate manner.

When he displayed great interest in the detailed account of Mrs. Greenhow's recent visit to a gala at this very house, I mistakenly thought he finally understood the situation.

"Remarkable!" Lincoln exclaimed. "Your detective managed to gain entrance disguised as a food purveyor! He even describes Mrs. Greenhow's gown right down to the brooch she wore. Mrs. Lincoln couldn't stop talking about that gown. Mrs. Greenhow has placed her dressmaker at Mary's service. She insists on helping my wife master the subtleties of Washington society, which would take a load off me."

"Mr. President, whatever Mrs. Lincoln tells Rose Greenhow will be repeated within twenty-four hours to Jefferson Davis."

"I'm sure Jeff Davis isn't interested in Mrs. Lincoln's gowns."

"And I'm sure Rose Greenhow won't have Mrs. Lincoln talking about dresses."

"Aren't you exaggerating a tad?"

"Read the report of Mrs. Greenhow's intimate conversation with Congressman Wilson of Massachusetts. Isn't he Chairman of the War Committee?"

"Mrs. Greenhow is undeniably charming."

"Yes, Mr. President, and so was that big bad wolf dressed as Granny, when Little Red Riding Hood went knocking on her door." When you are dealing with a childlike mind, it is always good to have a fairy tale close at hand to make a point.

Lincoln roared with laughter; I heard the joke repeated around Washington for months. I handed him another logbook, recording how Rose Greenhow had passed to Major Jordan blueprints of the new defensive fortifications of Washington, Forts Ellsworth and Cochran. I showed him copies of dispatches we had intercepted detailing her plan to lead an insurrection in the city coordinated with a Rebel attack. She and her followers intended to spike the cannon ringing the city and assassinate General McClellan in his home, before entering the residence of President Lincoln and personally (she insisted on this) murdering the nigger-loving traitor in his bed.

Lincoln leaned back in his chair, folded his hands across his belly, and closed his eyes. "And what exactly is it you would like me to do, Mr. Pinkerton?"

"Authorize me to arrest the bitch, charge her with treason, and haul her into a federal court with a sitting judge who is not a southern sympathizer."

Lincoln sighed. "The evidence you have furnished to me would be considered in a criminal court—according to the precedents of English Common Law, the prior decisions of our country's own courts, and the laws of the land—to be merely circumstantial. Now let me tell you why."

Then he started lecturing me about the law. He couldn't do anything just because it was right. It had to have some abstruse legal basis. The law was sacred to him, at least then. In another year things would be going so badly he would suspend the most basic law of all, the writ of habeas corpus.

He recited to me the particulars of a case he had once pled in southern Illinois, a boundary dispute that involved deeds, wills, and old land surveys as evidence. "Real evidence, Mr. Pinkerton. Hard evidence, as we call it."

"Mr. President, we are not considering on which side of the fence a cow can drop dung without trespassing. We are concerned with Mrs. Greenhow's aiding and abetting the enemy during wartime!"

That's when he uttered his remarkable judgment. "I'm afraid we have no other choice, Mr. Pinkerton, except to adhere to the law of the land."

I got up to leave.

He didn't want me to walk off angry at his sorry ass. "Imagine," he said, "if we were, just for argument's sake, to arrest this person and charge her with treason and bring her to trial. Imagine, given this person's influence, the status of the attorney this person would retain for her defense, and the likely composition of a jury of her peers. Imagine the implications if this person we had charged with treason were acquitted."

"IMAGINE, IMAGINE, IMAGINE. All he can do is imagine because it is so much easier than doing a damn thing." I had just recounted my conversation with Lincoln to Mrs. Warne, who proceeded to contradict my observations in their entirety.

"Mr. Lincoln is attempting to survive the onslaughts of his allies, who pose a greater threat to him than does the enemy. The Union is as deeply divided within as without. You must take Mr. Lincoln's predicament into account." I knew she liked the ugly bugger, but I expected more support than I was receiving.

"Maybe it would help poor Mr. Lincoln if we just packed up and returned to Chicago."

"Return to Chicago?" She looked at me with a wicked smile, dangling my words in front of me. Had I really suggested *returning to Chicago?* Mrs. Warne and I could certainly do that, but Kate wasn't coming with us.

"You are absolutely correct, Mrs. Warne. We must stop Rose Greenhow without Lincoln's prior knowledge or consent."

"Exactly, Mr. Pinkerton. For the twenty-five years since Andrew Jackson, with whom I believe she had an affair, was president, she has built her social connections into a ring of fortifications around herself that is, to make a wretched pun, nearly impregnable. We must breach this fortress and burn it to the ground!"

Though I had stared into those brown eyes and luxuriated in the depths of her desire, I was taken aback by the sudden blaze of an altogether different lust.

I BROKE INTO Rose Greenhow's mansion at night like a common burglar, without a warrant or official authorization. After watching her depart for the evening dressed in a ball gown, Pryce Lewis and I waited until we observed her resident household servant, a free black woman, leave the mansion carrying a small bag, which indicated from our prior surveillance that she would not return until morning.

Then I picked the front door lock. Once inside we worked in near darkness, rationing an occasional match, not wanting to leave a sulfurous trail, as we searched for incriminating evidence. If we were caught, McClellan himself would not have been able to save us. But we didn't find a damn thing except her appointment book. What secrets could it contain? She made no attempt to conceal her comings and goings. Fortunately, Pryce methodically perused it until he found among the familiar names of the cream of Washington society an appointment two nights hence here at her mansion with an unknown *Captain Ellison*.

We returned to headquarters, and Mrs. Warne pulled out the daguerreotypes I had requested from General McClellan of every officer on his staff. We found a likeness and description of Captain Ellison. He was twenty-seven, a West Point graduate with a degree in engineering. He was attached to the regiment that was building the fortifications for the defense of the city. Captain Ellison would certainly be a useful source of information to the Rebels.

I disguised myself as a Union officer and snuck into Ellison's regimental quarters while he was on duty. I found highly sensitive documents that he had carefully hidden, but I did not remove them. I did not want the Captain to know we were on to him.

On the night he was to meet Mrs. Greenhow, I stationed myself across the street with Pryce Lewis and Sam Bridgeman. It was nearly ten when a figure appeared out of the dark. Even with the collar of his cape turned up and his military hat pulled low, we recognized him. When he entered her house, we snuck around the back. I pulled off my boots so Sam and Pryce could hoist me on their shoulders. Through the parlor window I could see Captain Ellison and Rose Greenhow, faces flushed from the sherry they drained from their glasses. I had never seen Rose Greenhow up close before. The woman was in her late forties, but now I apprehended how her pure sensuality had attracted men for almost thirty years and continued to do so, even though she was old enough to be Ellison's mother. The blueprints to Fort Ellsworth, the major defense of Washington, were spread out on the table in front of them.

Then it began to rain torrential sheets. The images of Rose Greenhow and Captain Ellison shimmered through the water dripping across the windowpane like one of those funny mirrors in Barnum's Circus, until I was looking at the reflection of my own face contorted in rage, superimposed upon the two of them, arm in arm, leaving the room and disappearing up the stairs.

I leapt off the shoulders of my companions, who barely held their footing on the wet ground. I snatched up my boots, and in the downpour we took refuge under the eaves of St. John's Church across the street.

As we were planning our assault on the house to catch them together with the documents, the front door opened without warning, and Captain Ellison exited with remarkable speed, hastening down the street before disappearing into an alleyway.

I took off in pursuit. Unfortunately, I had left my boots off to dry under the eaves, and there was no time to put them back on. In mufti, soaked and unshod like some lunatic street predator, I raced after an officer of the Union Army who was undoubtedly armed.

At the guardhouse to his camp, two sentries grabbed me, and I was tossed into the regimental jail. Fortunately, I require my operatives to secrete large denomination bills on their person for emergencies such as this. I was able to slip my jailer a twenty-dollar greenback to deliver a note, and the promise of twenty more if he returned with a reply.

The recipient was Secretary of War Simon Cameron, whom I knew personally as a good man but a weak one. My only hope was that he would carry out the instructions in my note and not reveal its contents to anyone.

He did what I asked. I was released without my identity being made known so as to keep Ellison unaware that I was on to him and Mrs. Greenhow. I met with Cameron in the middle of the night at his home, made my report, and obtained two warrants, one to arrest Ellison, the other to search the premises of Mrs. Rose Greenhow for documents and articles whose possession by Mrs. Greenhow constituted a threat to the United States of America.

I didn't get back to headquarters until seven in the morning. Cameron had been kind enough to give me coffee and a spare pair of shoes, which completed my ridiculous outfit since my clothes were still soaked and mud-spattered. Pryce and Sam Bridgeman greeted me like Christ arisen, but Mrs. Warne merely yawned. I handed her the warrant to search Mrs. Greenhow's house. She frowned as she read it. "You do realize, Mr. Pinkerton, that Cameron is no fool. The wording clearly places the burden on you. If you fail to produce tangible proof of Rose Greenhow's treachery, your head will roll, not hers or Mr. Cameron's."

"Then let's get on with it, Mrs. Warne," I replied testily, "since any delay might alert her and give her time to hide what we must find."

MRS. GREENHOW'S HOUSE servant answered our insistent knocking at the door. We did not wait to be invited in. Myself, Sam, Pryce, and Mrs. Warne stood in the hallway until Mrs. Greenhow descended the staircase halfway and loomed imperiously above us.

"You're that German Jew detective from Chicago everyone is talking about, aren't you? Snooping about the respectable homes of this city. Leave immediately or I will send for the marshal and have you arrested and jailed."

She revealed much in those few words. First, through her connections in high places, she knew the closely kept secret that Pinkerton was operating in the city, and I was that man. The German Jew part was perplexing, but I assumed, given the sentiments of most Southerners, that she was merely cursing me without recourse to actual profanity.

She pointed at Mrs. Warne. "You must be one of the whores he brought from Chicago to have sexual relations with government officials to obtain your dirty secrets."

Mrs. Warne maintained a dignified silence, which I considered ominous.

I held up Cameron's warrant. "Mrs. Greenhow, this is a warrant signed by the Secretary of War to search these premises for documents and articles that may accidentally have come into your possession in the course of your extensive social life. We will retain said items to keep them from falling into unfriendly hands."

"If you so much as chip a teacup you will reimburse me for the damage."

That was not a good sign. Mrs. Greenhow was supremely confident we would find nothing.

For nearly half an hour we did not. During that time, Mrs. Greenhow managed to hand a note to her woman servant, who snuck out the front door, obviously to summon some powerful ally to thwart us.

I feared we would leave empty-handed. Mrs. Warne finally approached me. "We must search her boudoir, but you cannot risk her charging that an uncouth Yankee detective violated the sanctity of a southern gentlewoman's bedroom, no matter what you find. I will have to conduct the search with Mrs. Greenhow present." The proposal was sensible. The look in Mrs. Warne's eye was not. "I assure you it will take fifteen minutes or less for me to uncover what we are looking for."

"Mrs. Warne, are you armed?"

"I am following our standard procedures for a field operation."

"Give me your pistol."

"I am not about to enter her private quarters unarmed. You are naïve to think she does not have one or more weapons up there. After all, that is her battlefield."

"Then be careful."

"I will be fine."

"With *her*, Mrs. Warne. For chrissakes don't shoot her."

She dismissed my injunction with a shrug. "Do not, under any circumstances, come upstairs before fifteen minutes from this very moment. Are we in agreement?" We were not, but I looked at my pocket watch and nodded. She fetched Mrs. Greenhow and the two marched up the stairs. I detest it when situations escape my control.

I WAS NOT present in that upstairs room. However, Mrs. Warne later recounted what transpired in her official logbook. If anything, she probably left a few things out.

As they entered Rose Greenhow's boudoir, Mrs. Warne informed her prisoner that our operatives had abducted her beloved young daughter, also named Rose, age eight, from her tutor's house. The child was en route to a ship in Annapolis Harbor, bound for New York City, where she would be legally adopted by a prominent Abolitionist family unless Mrs. Greenhow handed over her cache of seditious documents. A well constructed, if slightly fabulous tale.

Sam Bridgeman, Pryce, and myself were seated in the first-floor parlor when we heard loud, anguished screams from Mrs. Greenhow above us, followed by a torrent of curses.

Then came the gunshot.

As Pryce and Sam leapt to their feet, I shouted, "Stop!" and ordered them to sit down. They babbled protests, but I was implacable. I had promised Mrs. Warne fifteen minutes.

I knew it wasn't her pistol that had been discharged. It was a derringer. It produces a different sound. Had Mrs. Warne secretly carried it on her person and fired it as a warning? Or had she not even warned Mrs. Greenhow, and was standing over her, offering to stop the bleeding in return for the evidence? There was even the terrible possibility that it was Mrs. Warne lying on the floor, shot by Rose Greenhow's derringer, while Rose Greenhow was now making her escape from some upstairs window.

What really happened?

Mrs. Warne later reported that Mrs. Greenhow entirely disbelieved the fabricated account of her daughter's abduction, whereupon Mrs. Warne did produce a hidden derringer, and from a distance of no more than eight feet pointed it at Mrs. Greenhow, informing her that she had ten seconds to produce the goods or her child would become an orphan.

Rose Greenhow snorted and told Mrs. Warne that if she shot

her, she would not gain the information she sought, without which Mrs. Warne would be charged with murder.

Whereupon Mrs. Warne discharged the derringer. She later assured me that she had no intention of killing or even injuring Rose Greenhow. Nevertheless, a derringer is a notoriously inaccurate firearm, even at a distance of eight feet. When the lamp beside her head shattered, so did Mrs. Greenhow's nerves. She undoubtedly had never been shot at before.

Mrs. Warne tossed the derringer aside, drew her pistol, and placed the barrel against Mrs. Greenhow's temple, whispering, "Mrs. Greenhow, after I kill you I will not be charged with murder. When your body slumps to the floor I will place the smoking derringer in your hand, the gun *you* drew and fired at *me,* causing me to kill you in self-defense. Before the authorities arrive, I will rip this perfidious nest of treachery to pieces and find the evidence to convince all of Washington of your treason. And you will no longer be alive to defend yourself against the charges."

"*No-o-o!*"

I checked my watch. Ten minutes had passed. The escaped servant had by now summoned help that was on the way.

At precisely fourteen minutes and twenty seconds after leading Mrs. Greenhow up the stairs, Mrs. Warne rudely directed her down with a gun to her head. Mrs. Greenhow nearly stumbled into our waiting arms, her hands bound behind her back by a cord fashioned out of some intimate apparel, a nice touch. Mrs. Warne carried a thick pile of notes, diaries, purloined government documents, and several leather-bound journals containing damning information beyond our wildest expectations.

Rose Greenhow had recorded in minute detail how she'd fucked a staggering number of men of consequence in the city of Washington. Lincoln's predecessor in the White House, the amiable bachelor

President James Buchanan, was among the prominent names on the list, along with William Smithson, the most important financier of the Union cause, as well as the staunch Abolitionist Henry Wilson of Massachusetts, Chairman of the Congressional War Committee. Mrs. Greenhow had saved Wilson's insanely smitten love letters and wrapped them in a pink ribbon. As I was perusing these documents, the door burst open, and the Mayor of Washington, James Barrett, entered, waving a pistol and accompanied by four unimpressive district cops. Mrs. Greenhow wailed to Barrett about the indignities she had suffered, but when Barrett ordered his men to place me under arrest, I showed him the diary entries in Rose Greenhow's hand that described *his* visits to this house. Mrs. Greenhow shrieked curses as he beat a hasty retreat out the back door.

WHEN WE RETURNED to headquarters, Mrs. Warne and I lost no time examining the captured booty to prepare a concise report that would be delivered to Cameron, Lincoln, Seward, and several gentlemen who had been fucking Rose Greenhow.

I finally asked her, "Mrs. Warne, were you really prepared to shoot Mrs. Greenhow if she did not reveal her secret hiding place?"

"More than prepared. It took great effort to restrain myself."

In the course of examining the documents, Mrs. Warne burst out laughing several times and insisted I listen as she read from the diaries, verbatim, in a rich southern accent, mimicking Rose Greenhow's voice. The passages she chose, by no small coincidence, happened to be the most graphic descriptions of Rose Greenhow's sexual encounters. The finest pornographers of the day would have been proud to publish them.

I sat, rooted to my chair by my rock-hard cock straining against my trousers, as the words tripped off Mrs. Warne's lips.

Our eyes did not meet. Mr. Pinkerton and Mrs. Warne were having sexual intercourse. She must have believed this reward was our due for the risks we had taken.

I INTERROGATED CAPTAIN Ellison after he was arrested and confined to his quarters. I was tired and planned to return the next day to question him in detail about his activities with Rose Green-how, hoping to learn the identities of other spies in her network, but there was an urgent question I needed him to answer that night.

"Captain Ellison, you are not an innocent boy. You are twenty-seven years old, is that correct?" He nodded insolently. "Answer me according to military protocol, or further charges will be lodged against you."

"Yes, sir, I am twenty-seven." The flatness of his voice chilled me.

"Captain Ellison, you have now lost your career, your future, and, most importantly, your reputation. Certainly you were aware that the woman you risked everything for was, simultaneous to yourself, intimately engaged with other men."

"Is that a question, sir?"

"No. It is an observation. My question is, what did this woman promise you in return for what you gave her?"

"Mrs. Greenhow made no promises. There was no quid pro quo. I will not testify otherwise. Sir."

"I see. It was all about the pussy, then?" His jaw tightened as if to take my blows and not break.

"Was it worth it, Captain? The pussy, I mean." I was torturing the man. He was my prisoner and I was torturing him. I wished I could stop, but I couldn't. I was leaning close, our faces only inches apart. Did he realize he was staring into a mirror?

He could not hide his disdain when he finally answered me. "I do not expect a man such as yourself to understand these matters. Sir."

Oh, but I did. That is why I was torturing him. Because I understood completely.

THAT NIGHT CAPTAIN Ellison hanged himself in his cell, while I was back at headquarters, upstairs in Kate's bed.

Seventeen

A fter the disaster at Bull Run, Lincoln gave full charge of the Army of the Potomac to General George B. McClellan, a man we both knew well from his days as president of the Illinois Central. In the fall of '61, McClellan began training and provisioning his troops at Fortress Monroe on the Union-held southern peninsula of Virginia between the James and York rivers, in preparation to drive north and capture the Rebel capital of Richmond.

On one of my visits to his elegant headquarters in Washington, I presented Little Mac with a proposal. The Pinkerton Detective Agency would establish the first U.S. Army Secret Service in order to provide him with reliable field intelligence that we would obtain from Confederate deserters, Union sympathizers behind enemy lines, and the flood of escaped slaves now fleeing to freedom.

McClellan took me up on my offer, and I was commissioned under his command as Major E. J. Allen, my nom de guerre.

My hands were now full chasing spies, supervising my growing number of agents in the field, compiling intelligence reports for McClellan, and fulfilling Stanton's latest request for my services: to investigate private contractors from the North who were providing shoddy goods to the U.S. Army at outrageous prices and half the quality the contracts demanded.

In the meantime, just because there was a war on, crime had not taken a holiday, and clients were still clamoring for my detective services. It soon become apparent, however, that I could not return to Chicago on a regular basis, and so I delegated to George Bangs authority to oversee the day-to-day operation of the Pinkerton Detective Agency in my absence.

As busy as I was in Washington, I still found time to compose a lengthy telegram to George each day containing detailed instructions on how he should proceed with our cases, and, naturally, I insisted that he reply with similarly detailed progress reports for my review. Unfortunately, the quality of his reports did not meet my standards.

It is not my intention in these pages to denigrate the abilities of George Bangs—or anyone else for that matter—but only to present the reader with a coherent narrative of my actions. George was simply not equipped to fill my shoes, but then, who possibly could? Assigning him the task of running the Pinkerton Detective Agency was a blunder, but I take full responsibility for it. That is why, as soon as I realized my tactical error, I summoned George to Washington, where he could best contribute to the war effort by serving closely at my side under my constant supervision, the way we always worked so well together.

While all of this was going on, my son Willie had been writing me that he was going to enlist soon, even though he had not yet turned sixteen. I decided the best thing would be for him to serve directly under my command, and I instructed George to bring Willie along with him.

Mrs. Warne thought it was a marvelous idea, and she accompanied me to the Relay Station to greet them on their arrival from Chicago.

As they stepped down from the train, Mrs. Warne saluted Willie. "Corporal Pinkerton, welcome to the War of the Rebellion."

Willie beamed and saluted her back.

"Chrissakes, Willie, she's having one on you. You don't salute civilians."

"Yessir, Da."

Mrs. Warne hugged Willie, and a feeling arose in my breast that even now is hard to describe. I mean no disrespect to Joan, who is the boy's ma and has always been a good one, but Mrs. Warne had great affection for him, and he for her. She was like his aunt. Back when I told him about Mrs. Warne running guns to John Brown, he'd sneak into her office and beg her to tell him stories about her adventures in Kansas with the Captain.

As we gathered up their bags, Willie handed me an envelope on scented stationery. "It's from Ma. She thinks maybe you don't get her letters, since she hasn't heard much from you in reply."

I was aware of George's bemused expression at my distress. Mrs. Warne did not seem to notice, or pretended not to. I quickly tucked Joan's letter inside my jacket.

"George?"

"Yes, Allan?" He smiled innocently, as if he didn't have the slightest idea what I was inquiring about, which the jackass most surely did, only wishing to increase my discomfort by making me say it aloud!

Although my inclusion of this anecdote might appear to cast me in a dim light as a neglectful husband, the fact is that I had been in constant contact with Joan. Via George. I had specifically instructed him to pass on to her the brief summaries of my activities in Washington that I appended to my daily telegraphic dispatches. So what the hell was Joan referring to when she'd told Willie *she hadn't heard much from me in reply?*

I certainly wasn't going to discuss it with him in front of the boy. Or Mrs. Warne. "We'll speak of it later, George."

We sure as hell did. After I gave him a dressing-down for his laxness in following my instructions, George blandly informed me that Joan had requested that he cease delivering communications to her that were *clearly meant for you, Mr. Bangs.*

"What choice did I have, Allan, except to respect Mrs. Pinkerton's wishes?"

"You could have informed me earlier."

"I assumed you were simultaneously communicating with Mrs. Pinkerton via more personal channels, and that she had informed you."

"Your assumptions were inaccurate as usual, George."

"Apparently. And I heartily apologize, as usual." And, *as usual,* George apologized with something less than genuine sincerity. "Allan, would you like me to telegraph Mrs. Pinkerton immediately and inform her that the misunderstanding was entirely my fault?"

"I would prefer that you go fuck yourself and then get to work, which is why I brought you to Washington, and I will write Mrs. Pinkerton myself."

As I have previously noted, George can be insufferable at times.

I DESIGNED MY field camp for the Secret Service of the Army of the Potomac with the same meticulous care I apply to everything I build. I have kept a daguerreotype taken by Mathew Brady. In it

I am leaning against the solid center post of the mess tent with a jaunty and confident look on my face, holding a lit cheroot, flanked by twenty of my best operatives. Willie is among them.

Willie and I spent our finest days together in that camp. I'd trained him since he was born to be a soldier, and he made me proud. My unit dressed in field clothes of our own choosing instead of Union Army uniforms, so Mrs. Warne found him a slouch hat and a striped tunic that drew whistles of approval from my men. He carried a pistol and before long he grew a credible mustache on his lip.

He did not play up that he was my son. He volunteered for the dangerous task of carrying dispatches on horseback between sentry posts, across ground infiltrated by enemy snipers. But nothing gained Willie more respect than taking to the air over enemy lines in a gas balloon.

As a former railroad man, McClellan was always interested in new inventions that might improve his battlefield advantage. When I was called to Fortress Monroe to observe Professor Thaddeus Lowe demonstrate his contraption, I took Willie along with me. Professor Lowe had hung a wicker basket beneath a much smaller helium balloon than had ever been used before. The special stove of his own invention, he explained, could lift the balloon above the range of hostile fire, affording the passenger a safe perch from which to view the enemy's position through a mounted telescope.

When Little Mac put a volunteer in the basket, though, the thing didn't rise more than two feet off the ground.

"I could do it, Da."

"What are you talking about?" I said, knowing perfectly well.

"The balloon would lift me." In later life Willie has thickened quite a bit around the middle, but at that age he was as slim as his mother had once been. I was terrified imagining Joan's reaction if

I let her eldest child disappear into the clouds or get his head blown off by a Rebel sniper.

I clapped Willie on the shoulder and laughed, as if that should be reward enough for his brave offer. He stared at me with a fierce look almost identical to the one I behold each morning in the mirror.

Unfortunately, Gus Thiel, one of my best operatives, was standing near us and overheard the interchange. I was now in the difficult position of having to humiliate my son or risk his life.

"Willie." I leaned close and lowered my voice. "Get the professor to show you every trick he's got to maneuver that thing. And here's your orders. You listening?" His head bobbed, unable to contain his excitement. "Get your ass back down *alive!*"

He hopped into the basket, and as it lifted off I had to restrain myself from chasing it and grabbing the trailing ropes. The balloon rose so fast I was sure it would explode. Then somehow it stopped rising and floated high above us, higher than any minié ball could reach. Willie leaned out and waved, and a roar went up from the crowd.

A few days later, Willie made his first *aerial reconnaissance,* as Professor Lowe called it, over the lines. He came down with reports that all agreed were of great value.

As he climbed out of the basket, I deliberately hung back from the crowd of soldiers gathered to greet him. They paraded Willie on their shoulders, tossing him around like a sack of flour, proclaiming that the Brave Young Flying Soldier would never touch ground again!

What a proud father I was then.

GEORGE WAS WITH me in my field tent when a coded dispatch arrived from Mrs. Warne informing me that Timothy Webster was on his way to Washington from Baltimore on a most urgent matter and requested a meeting with me in secrecy.

Out of necessity I had not seen Timothy for months. He had so thoroughly insinuated himself into the highest levels of the Secessionist faction in Baltimore, providing us with invaluable intelligence on their activities, that when he traveled to Washington it was as a known Rebel sympathizer, and he stayed clear of our operation to maintain his cover.

I set out immediately from camp on horseback, arriving at headquarters at eight the next morning in my mud-stained field clothes. Pryce Lewis greeted me, informing me that Timothy was upstairs with Mrs. Warne.

I could hear their laughter as I let myself into the secret room with the hidden levers. Timothy rose out of his chair, grabbed my hand, and clapped me on the back. The sight of him after such a long absence filled me with affection. He looked the perfect southern gentleman, his hair grown out in the back, his beard neatly trimmed. He was wearing a smartly cut coat, and his high leather boots shone with fresh polish. He held a lit cigar in his hand.

"Would you like some coffee, Mr. Pinkerton?" Mrs. Warne asked, the perfect hostess to this reunion. "I believe it is still warm." The remains of their breakfast lay scattered on the table.

"No, I'm fine." I wasn't fine. "When did you arrive?"

"Late last night."

"And you stayed . . . ?"

"At Willard's, of course. I was warmly welcomed by the desk clerk, a known Rebel symp."

Mrs. Warne watched our interchange impassively, as if I were merely conducting my usual interview of an operative to make sure every detail of his actions had been performed to my standards, except she knew, while Timothy did not, that the detail I was most interested in was Timothy's whereabouts in regard to Mrs. Warne.

Or did he know that too?

I couldn't look Mrs. Warne straight in the eye, but I would have to, or I was going to come off as some embarrassed schoolboy who has expelled gas and hopes no one identifies him as the source of the stink. A weakling. As opposed to the lad who farts mightily and laughs heartily.

"Mrs. Warne," I declared, "on second thought, I would very much like some coffee. Unlike our fine southern friend, I journeyed on horseback, haven't had a wink of sleep, and won't even take a bath until I hear Timothy's news."

There. That righted the ship.

"THE MARYLAND SECESSIONISTS have maintained their well-armed secret militias as far north as Perrymansville and to the south of Annapolis. The Federal troops in Baltimore barely control the city and have no idea of the whereabouts of these militias. The same men we left in place who led the plot to kill Lincoln are still the leaders of the Rebellion: Fernandina himself and that fellow Merrill, the gun dealer. They are in close contact with General Beauregard's spymaster in Richmond, Major Jordan." Timothy puffed on his cigar and I on mine as he brought me up to date on the situation in Baltimore. "They have organized an undercover society to coordinate their traitorous activities. With the information you secretly provided me, I was able to warn several of my *comrades* that they were in danger of arrest and assist them in fleeing Baltimore, an act of patriotism that has earned me entrance into the Order of the Sons of Liberty."

"Excellent work, Timothy!" Mrs. Warne exclaimed.

"Thank you, Kate." Timothy gave her a frankly charming smile. He was a charming fellow.

She reached across the table and patted his hand affectionately. No harm in that.

"Mr. Pinkerton," he continued, "I came in haste because orders are expected any day from Richmond for the Sons of Liberty to co-ordinate an uprising. The militias will attack the Federal garrisons, seize control of the Maryland Legislature, and force them to finally pass a bill of secession."

I pondered this. "We must neutralize the Sons of Liberty to cut off the head of the snake. When do they meet next?"

"Two nights from now."

"I will travel to Baltimore to organize a squad of Federal troops to invade the meeting and arrest the traitors. Timothy, you must devise an elaborate excuse to be absent to avoid capture."

Mrs. Warne shook her head in disagreement. "If Timothy is not at that meeting, it as good as announces that he was the spy who brought the Federals down upon the conspirators."

"I obviously considered that. However, it would attract even more suspicion if he were the only one subsequently released from custody. Timothy cannot be arrested."

"Mr. Pinkerton, Kate is correct. I must attend the meeting to maintain my cover. But you are also correct. I cannot be arrested."

"I see no way of accomplishing both ends."

He leaned back and struck another match to relight his cigar, taking a few good puffs to get it going. "When you lead the Federals into the house, I'll be there, but I'll flee without giving the impression that you let me go."

Mrs. Warne's interest seemed piqued. "And how will you manage that?"

He smiled. "Mr. Pinkerton will assist by firing his pistol at me as I attempt to get away. After I fire at him to make my escape."

I looked at Mrs. Warne, but she placed her gaze in the space between myself and Timothy. "It's a harebrained idea!" I barked. Timothy was startled. I'd never spoken to him that way before.

I quickly adopted a more reasonable tone. "Bullets ricochet in close quarters. One of us could easily get killed."

He shrugged. "Frankly, I don't think it would be *that* easy."

"Mrs. Warne, surely you see the danger!"

She raised her eyebrows, indicating that she had no opinion on the matter, which was ludicrous, because she always had an opinion on every matter.

Suddenly, it was clear to me. I was being lured by these two masters of deception into a fatal plot whose intended victim was myself! Timothy Webster and Mrs. Warne, affianced to be married, were plotting the murder of Allan Pinkerton, to restore their relationship to its pristine state, prior to my defiling it, and take control of my Agency!

"Of course there is some risk." Timothy spoke in an almost soothing tone. "Though not much greater than the risks we take every day." Then he chuckled. "After all, we're both crack shots. I'm sure we can miss our mark if we try."

His blue eyes gleamed with innocent enthusiasm, awakening me from my nightmare. What had I been dreaming? It was a grand scheme!

"Mr. Webster, I'm sure that missing you with a pistol shot is easier to accomplish than putting a bullet in your elusive self."

"And even if I'm not as accurate as you, I doubt if one round can do much damage to Allan Pinkerton."

That was for certain! We both laughed out loud, infected by the excitement that always arises in anticipation of a caper.

Mrs. Warne was not even smiling.

I ARRIVED IN Baltimore by train late that same afternoon and went directly to the provost marshal's office, presenting myself as

Major E. J. Allen with orders from McClellan. A certain Captain Forrest was placed under my command. He had experience in rooting out traitors and escorting them to the lockup at Fort McHenry. I gave him only the minimal details of my mission he needed to know, omitting Timothy Webster's identity and role in this operation. I trusted no one, not even Captain Forrest. I told him to have a squadron of troops ready to move the minute I learned the exact time and location of the meeting. Since our purpose was to capture the traitors for interrogation, I made clear to Forrest that I would not hesitate to shoot any of his men if they fired a weapon without my order.

Late the next day, Webster sent me a coded message. He had managed to insinuate two more of our operatives into the Loyal Sons. They would take a turn as guards on the night of the meeting and wave our raiding party in. These two would then escape to Washington. They would not be able to return as undercover agents in Baltimore but would be identified as the Union spies who called in the troops, thereby strengthening Timothy's cover.

Near midnight I hid across from a modest mansion situated on the edge of the respectable part of the city. I observed a dozen men whispering passwords to the guards as they entered. The Sons of Liberty. Timothy Webster was among them.

IT WAS ONE of the strangest moments in my life. In the dimly lit parlor of that mansion in Baltimore, as I led my squad of soldiers through the door, ordering the enraged traitors to their knees and pistol-whipping those slow to surrender, I looked across the room at Timothy Webster pointing a gun at my head.

Time froze. I swear I saw him smile. Well, that would be natural.

This must have seemed to him like more fun than he'd ever had. The look of horror on my face, however, was real. I ducked just as his big Navy Colt went off. What was he doing with that monster sidearm? It sounded like a cannon had been discharged in the small room. The damn chandelier came crashing to the floor beside me.

He was halfway out the back door when I fired at him.

I missed.

I hope, on the faint chance there is a God, that He knows I was not trying to kill my dearest friend. Unfortunately, I was brassed that he had tried to kill me, so, I must admit, I shot at him.

Fortunately, Timothy is quite skilled at his profession. He dove out the door, rolled to the side, and was on his feet and already running down a welter of dark alleys when I raced out of the house and gave chase. This wasn't part of the plan, but it was a good thing that I did, because the troops outside would have shot him had I not appeared, shouting, "Don't shoot!" even though I was firing at Timothy in the dark.

I am positive that by then I was aiming well above his head.

At the end of the alley he gave me a cocky wave and disappeared into the night.

THE NEXT DAY I interrogated the prisoners. From their conflicting stories and transparent lies I obtained a trove of valuable information on the Secessionists' plans in Baltimore. Our raid put the Sons of Liberty out of business.

That evening I boarded the train at the Relay Station to return to Washington. I hadn't slept in two days. The master cooper was having a hard time keeping the little barrels he had constructed in his mind from splitting apart.

Timothy Webster, Mrs. Warne, my son Willie, George Bangs, and of course Joan each occupied their own tightly sealed cask, whose contents had to be kept separate lest they flood my brain.

As I fought off sleep, my head bouncing against the window of the train, I tried to recall exactly when Mrs. Warne explained to me that she and Timothy agreed it would be best if they did not announce their engagement. Was it before or after we had begun our betrayal of Timothy?

Timothy knew. I was sure of it now.

Had she told him? Or had he confronted her?

That was a warning shot he had fired at me. Leave her alone, Mr. Pinkerton.

Of course I should leave her alone.

What had possessed me to take this mad risk?

THE TRAIN GOT into the Washington Station at 2 A.M. Half an hour later I approached headquarters, out of breath, soaked in sweat. I had run all the way.

Mrs. Warne was downstairs in the dimly lit building, waiting for me. When I walked in, she stared at me as if I were a ghost.

"It went off all right, Mrs. Warne."

She seemed to exhale a breath she'd been holding since I left. She did not ask for further details but moved past me and climbed the stairs.

When I entered her room a short time later, after washing my face in the basin in my office, she was already in her bed. I silently removed my clothes in the dark. As I approached, Kate threw back the covers and reached up to embrace me.

We made love as if the few hours remaining before dawn were our last on earth before our sunrise execution. She bit my tongue and drew blood. As I came inside her I started to cry out, and she pulled my mouth to her shoulder to silence me. I bit her hard. I left a mark. She did not care.

Later, as the light of dawn crept into the room, I felt her waiting for me to leap up and slip away, as I always had to do, because the time we could seize for ourselves alone together was brief. Instead, I held her tight.

"Kate, does Timothy know?"

"Of course not."

"How can you be sure?"

"How could I not?" There was a look of fear in her eyes I'd never seen before.

"I am sure that George suspects. It was a mistake bringing him here."

She was silent for a long time. She finally spoke in a low voice I did not quite recognize. "George may or may not suspect, but he is a detective and will not make an accusation without proof. Where will he get that? We take sufficient precautions. Unless you wish to suggest further measures."

"No precautions are perfect. As detectives we know that." Now it was my own voice I could not recognize.

"We are not detectives in this room, Mr. Pinkerton, we are criminals. Like all members of this fraternity either we believe we'll never get caught, or we must cease committing our crimes."

"So you believe we're committing a crime?"

"Not at all, but suddenly it seems that you do."

"No," I answered. "I do not." It was the truth. I did not believe I was committing any transgression. But that did not mean there would be no punishment.

I was finally standing on the battlefield I had dreamt of all my life, at the command of my troops, about to affect the course of

History, and I was just a whisper away from a scandal that would wreck everything.

I had to quit her.

As if she heard the thought in my mind, she broke the silence before I could speak. "If we are ever discovered, Mr. Pinkerton, I will disappear." Her words snapped across my face like a whip. She went on, almost dispassionately. "First, I will tearfully take the blame for filling you with bourbon, and perhaps even laudanum—yes, that would be a good touch—and luring you to my room on the pretense of discussing important matters of an investigative nature, whereupon one time, just that one time, using all my wiles and the drugs, I overcame your resistance and got you to submit to my salacious advances. Mrs. Warne will then resign from the Pinkerton Detective Agency."

"Where would you go?" I could not believe I was asking that question.

She was silent for a long time, and I thought she had realized how absurd her idea was.

"California," she declared decisively. "Yes, that is where I would go."

She must have felt me shudder because she drew me close to her, and we held each other tightly. My voice was thick. "I don't think I could stand that."

What was I going to do? How do you quit your own life?

I had not lost my reason, only the ability to obey my reason. Something stronger had taken hold of me, something which to this day I still cannot find words to describe. And if I know anything, I know this: People must have words to explain their actions to themselves or a black panic crawls over them and they are lost.

I was lost.

My only hope was that, as I stumbled blindly, she would guide us, because I could not leave her.

Her eyes were moist as she held my head in her hands. "Don't worry, Mr. Pinkerton. Everything will be fine. Isn't it wonderful that there is such a place as California? It is there for escaping. The late Mr. Warne and myself were on just such a journey." I was silent.

"You could come with me if you wanted to," she whispered in my ear. I did not know what she meant. Not then.

Eighteen

Willie came running up to me at my small wooden field desk, trembling with a righteous indignation which I proudly recognized. I could barely make out the words scrawled with a piece of charcoal on the scrap of paper he handed me.

Help me Marse William Pinkerton. I em in gaol in Washintown an will die here.

Yrs, Jonas Cain

"Jonas must have bribed a guard to deliver it to an army officer who knows you. Mrs. Warne sent it to me in today's pouch."

I frowned, wishing that she hadn't.

"Da." Willie went on, sensing my hesitation. "Jonas ain't no criminal. What's he doing in jail?"

I had only too good an idea. "Willie, this is a difficult situation. Be patient."

"He's gonna *die.* Jonas don't take shit off no man, white or colored. That's how come his back is like knotted ropes from all the whippings he got. Da, he risked his life helping us. We told him he'd be a free man, didn't we?"

We had. Willie had picked Jonas out of the scores of escaped slaves who flooded into Fortress Monroe once a secure Union presence was established on the Virginia peninsula.

I immediately recognized their potential as a valuable source of information concerning the local terrain, the secret Union loyalties of those Virginians who opposed the Rebellion, and, most importantly, the whereabouts and strengths of Rebel troop locations they had recently observed firsthand.

Unfortunately, it would never be General McClellan's intention to free a single slave. I bit my tongue at McClellan's outspoken remarks that a Negro's intelligence was limited to thinking up schemes to shirk labor, but I insisted that he allow me to interrogate all "contraband" before the Army took possession of them.

When it came to interviewing escaped slaves, there were few white men who had the kind of experience with Negroes that Willie had. His calm, reassuring manner put these frightened refugees at ease.

My earlier dealings with men like John Jones in Chicago's Underground Railroad had convinced me that colored men had at least as much ability and bravery to fight for their own freedom as the white men who took up their cause. Out of the crowds of bedraggled refugees, I picked out not just men but women who were willing to cross back over enemy lines disguised as slaves once more, accompanied by one of my operatives who played the role of master. The spying party would stop at local inns and towns and gain valuable intelligence.

The most outstanding of these volunteers was a twenty-five-year-old former slave named James Scobill. His name should be remembered forever as America's first black detective. I officially designated him an operative in the United States Secret Service and put him on my payroll. Scobill was as fearless as Webster and as cool under fire. One time he was chased down on foot by two mounted Rebel pickets who pursued him into a swamp, guns blazing. Scobill slipped behind a tree and shot them out of their saddles, an unimaginable act for a black man in Virginia. He then crossed back over the lines and returned to camp with important information on Rebel sniper positions.

Still, McClellan and his soldiers refused to allow black men in their ranks. With the exception of Willie and George, even my own men in the field would not fully accept them as equals. They had to sleep outside our tents and eat apart from the rest, even Scobill.

Willie refused to go along with it. When he found Jonas, he set up his own little tent which he shared with "my operative, Mr. Cain." We sent Jonas on many dangerous missions, and the young man acquitted himself well each time. Only two weeks before his desperate note arrived, Willie had shaken his hand as he put him on an army wagon headed for Washington, carrying a letter of commission signed by myself. Now my son was standing in front of me in righteous indignation. "Da, where is he?"

I knew exactly where Jonas Cain was.

THE VALIANT SLAVES who escaped their traitorous masters and risked their lives crossing Union lines assumed they no longer had to flee to Canada for their freedom. They were wrong. They were treated exactly as before the War, as stolen property. While Lincoln dithered over an Emancipation Proclamation, he did not even bother to repeal the odious Fugitive Slave Act. Any escaped Negro who reached Washington was led at gunpoint to the county jail, that vile place of incarceration known as the Blue Jug, commanded by Colonel Marshal Ward Hill Lamon.

Yes, the Fat Fuck himself who nearly got Lincoln killed in Baltimore. At the War's outset Lamon wangled a commission from the President as a colonel in the United States Army. He raised his own regiment in the Union-held portion of his native Virginia and set his troops to rounding up escaped slaves, returning them to their masters for the prewar bounty.

His activities were so outrageous that the genuine Abolitionists in Lincoln's Cabinet roasted His Excellency's ass in the northern press, particularly Greeley's *Tribune*. Lincoln couldn't understand what all the fuss was about, but he yanked his toady out of Virginia and appointed him Marshal of the District of Columbia, where, among other lucrative activities, he took command of the Blue Jug.

"MR. LAMON."

"It's Colonel Lamon, Pinkerton."

"Colonel, through some unfortunate misunderstanding an operative attached to the Secret Service of General McClellan has been incarcerated in the county jail."

Lamon snorted. "Not unless Little Mac is employing runaway niggers." Willie and I stood in front of the Fat Fuck's desk on which he'd propped his feet. He was wearing ridiculous boots that only some Confederate dandy would sport.

"The Secret Service is under my command, Colonel." I was not going to make a scene in front of Willie. I am perfectly capable of using diplomacy to achieve my ends. I handed Lamon the leather-bound secret commission from McClellan that identified the bearer as Major E. J. Allen, head of the Secret Service of the Army of the Potomac. "Colonel, I am employing Jonas Cain, who has been mistakenly incarcerated in your jail. I know that you are familiar with secret operations, and I have the utmost faith in your discretion."

He didn't look at the document, staring suspiciously at Willie instead. "Who is this?"

"My son William, attached to General McClellan's staff via my offices. William, please meet one of President Lincoln's oldest and most trusted advisers and confidants, Colonel Ward Hill Lamon."

Willie snapped off a smart salute. "Colonel Lamon, sir, it is an honor and great pleasure to meet you, sir." William can be effortlessly polite, unlike Lamon, who was incapable of displaying any manners except those of a feral swine. He sneered at my son.

What occurred next I would ordinarily have omitted from this memoir, since I have no desire to humiliate any man. However, after the War, Lamon decided to cash in on his parasitic relationship to Lincoln by writing one of the many so-called "authoritative biographies of the Late Great President by One Who Knew Him Well." In his piece of tripe, entitled *Recollections of Abraham Lincoln,* Lamon spuriously recounts my exploits in saving the President-elect from certain death in the Baltimore Plot as follows: *Lincoln was convinced afterwards that he had committed a grave mistake listening to the solicitations of a professional spy and of friends too easily alarmed.*

For over a decade now this vicious slander has enjoyed the status of accepted truth. After all, what ulterior motive could Ward Hill Lamon have to distort the facts of that crucial event in American history?

Well, the Fat Fuck had the basest motive in the world for denigrating me!

Revenge.

I will now substantiate this grave charge by continuing my

account of the incident which I would otherwise never have included in this memoir had Lamon not smeared me first.

"Pinkerton, I am afraid I cannot help you." He contemptuously tossed my commission on his desk and leaned farther back in his chair in pathetic imitation of a man securely protected by his own authority.

"I am not asking for your help, only for you to obey a proper military order."

"I'm a colonel, you're just a major, and barely a real one. Either way I outrank you." Those were his exact words, witnessed by my son William in Lamon's office at the Blue Jug. The man was mocking me.

I slowly made my way around his desk, giving him plenty of time to grab one of the ludicrous weapons that hung from his pendulous person. The coward didn't even unsheath his Bowie knife. I hauled the Fat Fuck out of his chair and held the barrel of my Navy Colt under his chin as I stood him up hard against the wall. He squealed like a stuck pig. "Lincoln will have you jailed for treason!"

I shut his mouth by pressing the revolver upward against his jaw and cocking it. He ceased to breathe, and his eyeballs bulged from his head as I spoke.

"Lamon, the President will have your ass in a sling when I march you over to Willard's Hotel, where every member of the press is gathered for lunch. They will surely be eager to interview the President's adviser, who now does his slave trading right here in the Capital!"

There you have it. The subsequent calumnies he hurled against me from the safe redoubt of his fabricated memoir were a blatant attempt to even the score for the humiliation I inflicted upon him that day in the Washington, D.C., jail.

Willie and I walked out an hour later with Jonas Cain waving cockily to the guards at the gate, as if he had promised them this outcome. My son was in equally high spirits, and I sent them both packing back to camp, instructing Willie to fix Jonas up with a permanent kit.

Yet I knew this was no solution to the problem.

Did Lincoln have any real interest in winning this war? Then why weren't we using the greatest weapon at our disposal, *four million imprisoned slaves?*

Ask him that and he'd start whining about Britain recognizing the Confederacy, the morale of the Union soldiers, and what his wife would say.

AFTER SENDING WILLIE and Jonas off I made my way to headquarters, and for once it wasn't Kate I was after. It was Mrs. Warne I needed to see.

I paced in the small confines of my office like some caged beast, practically bumping into her as I whirled around. She gripped my arm firmly above the elbow, guided me to a chair, and poured two glasses of water, sipping hers while I bolted mine down.

"Mrs. Warne, I do not see any possibility of achieving the only end I have sought for nearly a decade: namely, the abolition of slavery. The situation is hopeless."

"It is not hopeless," she stated, with her customary blunt conviction. "Every man of influence in this city is seeking his own ends. Everyone is fighting his own war."

"And meanwhile the Rebels are united in their single-minded pursuit of establishing a separate nation with slavery as its foundation. They will prevail, Mrs. Warne. I am not speaking in the voice of despair, simply giving you my cold assessment of the facts."

"How can you arrive at that conclusion, when our Army has not even launched its campaign?"

"Because the campaign will fail. McClellan cannot capture Richmond."

My pronouncement shocked her. "Why? What have you found out?"

"Nothing that isn't staring us in the face. Even though Lincoln and Stanton hound him to attack immediately, McClellan knows his troops are barely soldiers yet. What chance do you think they have of overcoming a battle-ready enemy willing to fight to the death to defend their way of life?"

She did not bother to debate the accuracy of my assessment. She was unwilling to admit defeat. Or, more precisely, allow me to accept defeat.

Is that why I put the matter to her this way, as I had every time I reached the limit of my own means? She had not allowed me to get myself killed rescuing John Brown. She had not allowed me to lie down and let Samuel Felton's railroad get blown up. I must have known she would not allow me to give up now.

But was the idea hers or mine? Or was it ours?

That is what I cannot clearly recall, even though I have been trying for days now, if not all these years since.

All I know is that before I left that room, my prediction of defeat had yielded to a calculation of victory. A victory not just for McClellan's Army of the Potomac but for the architect of that victory, the man who would throw off the disguise of Major E. J. Allen and triumphantly reveal himself to a grateful nation to be none other than Allan Pinkerton!

I would fulfill John Brown's prophetic injunction at last. I would tear the abomination of slavery from the ground, root and vine.

I would send an operative behind the enemy's lines to infiltrate Richmond. He would transmit reports to me on the city's defensive fortifications and the number and placement of Rebel troops within the city. Even more importantly, he would map the best route of attack for McClellan's forces to outflank the enemy and seize the Rebel capital.

To gain access to the highest echelons of the Rebellion, the operative needed impeccable credentials as a bold agent for the Cause. He would prove his dedication by risking his life crossing the lines to deliver secret dispatches from their spies in Washington and Baltimore.

The risk was real. His true identity could not be revealed even to the Federals. A single loose tongue could compromise his cover. He would be acting as a genuine southern agent attempting to cross the Potomac, trying to elude the heavily armed Federals who patrolled the shores and manned the gunboats along the river. They had recently sunk several enemy craft making just such an attempt.

The dangers only began there. Richmond was not Washington, where, as Rose Greenhow demonstrated, enemy sympathizers were welcome in respectable society. The citizens of Richmond had been sleeping with loaded guns beside their beds since Nat Turner's slave uprising. They could smell a Yankee a mile away. What would they do if they caught one in their city stealing secrets?

"Timothy can accomplish it," Mrs. Warne assured me, when we had enumerated the risks involved. Timothy Webster, her fiancé. "I am quite certain he can."

"RICHMOND!" TIMOTHY WAS as excited as a little boy on Christmas morning who receives a gift beyond his wildest expectations. "I know you're not a wagering man, Mr. Pinkerton, but I'll give odds of three to one that I can obtain an audience with Jefferson Davis himself."

"I won't take that bet because I am sure you will accomplish it."

His jaw tightened. "You know, when I sit down with Jeff Davis, I could seriously damage the Cause with one stroke of this!" With a speed that took me by surprise, he drew a ten-inch blade from the jaunty walking stick he carried. The gesture filled me with unease, and I chose my words carefully.

"If you so much as wound a Rebel private, you would wreck every carefully laid plan of this entire operation. You must exercise restraint at all times. Is that clear, Timothy?"

He made a mock bow of deference and gave Mrs. Warne a broad smile and a wink.

She may have smiled in return or not. I couldn't tell what she was thinking.

ON A COOL clear afternoon in late October of '61, a courier arrived with a coded message for me at my field camp. I leapt on my horse and rode across to General McClellan's tent with the news. Timothy Webster had crossed the Potomac and gained passage on a small steamer up the James River to Richmond, where he promptly checked into the Spottiswoode Hotel. Bearing superlative recommendations from the leading Secessionists of Baltimore, he had already obtained an interview with Judah P. Benjamin, Secretary of War for the Confederacy.

McClellan clapped me on the back. His hopes were as high as mine.

Our hopes bore fruit two weeks later, when Timothy smuggled out of Richmond thirty-seven pages of cramped script describing the defenses of the city in minute detail. The Rebel leaders had taken him on a tour of breastworks and forts, and he was even able to list the size and caliber of the cannon ringing the city. He gave us troop numbers and the price of staples like flour, butter, and sugar. He reported that the blockade was taking its toll. Inflation and shortages were rampant, and the troops were on short rations and beginning to suffer from disease.

He informed us that he would return to Baltimore in two weeks, carrying important dispatches from Judah P. Benjamin and other high Confederate officials to the Maryland Secessionists.

Nineteen

Mrs. Warne declared that Timothy deserved a celebration for his exploits in Richmond. Since Timothy's connection to our organization had to be kept secret now more than ever, the guest list was limited to the three of us.

When Timothy and I entered the secret room, we were astonished by Mrs. Warne's preparations. She had obtained fine oriental carpets, French furniture, English bone china, silverware, and crystal glasses.

"With the compliments of the city's most distinguished Madams, Tess Coburn and Elizabeth Daltry, proprietresses of the bawdy houses that bear their names."

Washington's best whorehouses were staffed by a veritable female army of Rebel sympathizers who pried sensitive information from Union officers frequenting the fancy bordellos to pass along to Richmond.

Mrs. Warne managed to turn a few of the Madams, and they were now on our payroll, helping us identify Rebel agents and Union officers whose political loyalties were suspect.

With the help of her new friends, Mrs. Warne presented us a groaning board laden with four types of Chesapeake Bay oysters, crabs with both hard and soft shells, river trout, a smoked Virginia ham, mutton chops, and bowls of southern vegetables that we had developed virtual addictions to: yams, collard greens, black-eyed peas, succotash, and rice cooked with pimentos. Our beverages included not only the anticipated Kentucky bourbon but several fine bottles of French claret, as Mrs. Warne called it, Webster and I knowing the stuff only as wine. She also displayed a dusty little flagon, which she promised would be one of the highlights of the evening.

Mrs. Warne was dressed in one of the costumes she had worn in disguise as Mrs. Amanda Baker back in Baltimore. Timothy peered admiringly down the front of her low-cut gown. She gave him a salacious look and squeezed my hand, which she had never done before in public.

We spent the night feasting, drinking, and celebrating. It was all a deception or, more precisely, a myriad of deceptions. None of us were who we were pretending to be, and each of us was pretending in different ways to the other two. Only the three greatest living detectives could have pulled it off.

Mrs. Warne wanted a full and entertaining account from Timothy of his exploits in Richmond. After all, her fiancé had just pulled off the most daring feat of the War.

Timothy is not a boastful man. He coolly recounted how he got Judah P. Benjamin, the Confederate Secretary of War, to reveal the plans for holding Richmond against the attacking Union Army.

Imitating his drawl, Timothy repeated Benjamin's prophecy that the Union's failure to capture Richmond would undermine its resolve and encourage Britain to ally with the South.

Then Timothy described his encounter with Jefferson Davis. The President of the Confederate States of America, a native of Mississippi, chose to reside throughout the War at the Spottiswoode Hotel, just two floors above Timothy's own room. One evening in the dining room, a party of prominent Richmonders who had befriended Timothy formally introduced him to the President. Davis commended Timothy for the risks he was taking for the Cause. If he'd only known how true it was.

Then Davis delivered an insane tirade, equating the creation of "our Nation" with the will of God. He prophesied that the War would not end until God's will had been fulfilled. Timothy heartily agreed, which pleased Davis immensely, allowing Timothy to prod Davis to reveal exactly how many regiments protected Richmond.

Mrs. Warne commented that lately Lincoln had also begun referring to God's Will, something we'd never heard from him before. "Perhaps," she remarked, in an exaggerated southern drawl, "those pagans are right after all, since different deities speak to each of these two great men. On the other hand, we must consider the possibility that our dear Lord simply says whatever anyone wants to hear, like He does at those séances that wicked woman Victoria Claflin conducts."

We all laughed until it hurt.

How could it not hurt?

I was staring at the most desirable woman in the world seated beside the man she intended to marry.

When all of this is over, Mr. Pinkerton.

"NOW THAT THE pipes have been laid, I can easily return to Richmond. This time I know I could determine McClellan's exact route of attack."

I was drunk as a lord, sprawled in a chair. Timothy was beside me, even drunker but more used to it than I was.

"What do you mean?"

"Exactly what I said, Mr. Pinkerton."

"And what exactly did you say, Timothy?"

He stared at me to see if I was having a joke on him and then burst into laughter, realizing my condition. I started laughing too.

Mrs. Warne heard us from across the room and called out, "What's so funny, gentlemen?"

"I have forgotten entirely," I replied.

"I see." She smirked as she approached us with small crystal glasses filled from the dusty bottle she'd displayed earlier. It was port. Rather than cast pearls before swine, she delivered an informative discourse on the history of Portugal, fortified wines, and the effects of aging in oak casks. She claimed this stuff was a hundred years old. Timothy and I would have believed her if she told us she'd made it herself the day before.

We clinked our glasses and drank. It was ambrosia. As she bent forward to refill our glasses, I stared down the front of her gown and indulged in memories of Kate. Timothy gave me a wink, and she theatrically rolled her eyes at us both.

"Time for cigars," she announced gaily, ordering us not to move, which was a superfluous caution because the port had solidified our position in our chairs. She brought out the humidor, and after we made our selections she prepared the cigars by licking the tips and nipping them with a pearl-handled cutter.

She chose a small panatela for herself and sat down in the third chair, putting her feet up on a small footrest with her ankles crossed. The hem of her dress rose to the top of her boots. We savored our cigars together.

Then she startled us out of our reverie, leaping to her feet. "No gala would be complete without live entertainment!" Timothy and I glanced at each other warily.

She unpacked a fiddle from its case and tuned it, as she explained that she'd received extensive training in classical violin as a girl but had confounded her father by insisting upon taking private lessons from a leading minstrel performer of the day to learn the songs of Stephen Foster. She commenced a stirring rendition of "Old Folks at Home," which brought tears streaming down our cheeks as Timothy and I wailed out the chorus.

I had been a regular habitué of the minstrel theaters back in Chicago. To my mind J. P. Christie's Minstrels were the finest practitioners of the art. Their performances of Foster's songs were the closest any white men came to capturing the gut-wrenching pathos of black song, which I'd heard on many occasions from fugitive slaves.

She played Foster's "Old Black Joe," informing us that back in the early 1850s there was a tradition of Election Day minstrel competitions on the town commons throughout New England. Free blacks competed for prizes along with white musicians. When the blacks kept winning, however, they were banned from the contests.

I announced that this injustice would be made right when we won the war.

Timothy raised his glass and called for a toast. "To Victory!"

"To Victory!" we proclaimed together.

Then she played on the fiddle, "I Dream of Jeannie with the Light Brown Hair."

That was the color of her hair.

When the song ended, Webster was sound asleep.

Timothy was a prodigious somnambulist. He could go for days without sleep, then leave this world to gather a week's rest, as he appeared to have done now. Mrs. Warne motioned for me to douse the lamps and candles, and we quietly removed ourselves to the dimly lit hallway outside the secret room.

"It was a grand gala, Mrs. Warne."

"Thank you very much, Mr. Pinkerton."

We could go downstairs and continue to enjoy each other's company in her office or mine. We could talk more of minstrel music. We were never at a loss for topics of conversation.

Or we could go upstairs.

"Timothy probably will not wake until noon," she declared, rather gaily. Her cheeks were flushed. I had never seen her so happy. She wanted to go upstairs, to take me to her bedroom, directly above the room where her fiancé lay in a deep and innocent slumber.

I wanted to very much, and my desire horrified me. Worse, it woke me from my own slumber. What had I been thinking all this time? That we were somehow *not* betraying Timothy? I looked at her, speechless. Surely she realized what we were doing?

Instead, she looked at me as if she did not understand what could be troubling me.

"Good night, Mrs. Warne. Thank you for the evening. All of it."

At least I didn't stumble and fall as I made my way down the stairs. Staggering through the streets, I was an easy mark in a city full of nocturnal predators, yet I was not accosted, probably because the self-hatred that rose in my throat like bile had transformed my face into a frightening mask that scared off any would-be attacker.

Somehow I found my room at Willard's Hotel. Unable even to remove my boots, I fell face down on the bed into the sleep of the dead, where I belonged.

THE NEXT MORNING I crossed the Chesapeake in a Union gun-boat and landed at Fortress Monroe on the Virginia peninsula. When I reported to McClellan, he informed me he was ready to bring his entire Army of the Potomac across the bay in April to launch a concerted lightning attack up the peninsula to capture Richmond.

The way he said it, though, he didn't sound like a man who liked his own chances.

Then I remembered what Timothy told me the night before.

I hesitated. I really don't know what calculations I made, but I reached a decision. "General McClellan, I believe I can improve your ability to conduct your campaign."

I told him I could send Timothy Webster back to Richmond, and that he would keep his reports flowing until McClellan marched into the city and dragged Jefferson Davis out in chains.

Little Mac's eyes lit up. He gripped my arm and said, "Major Allen, that would be a great service to me indeed."

This time Timothy would return with Hattie Lawton. She was by now well established as his wife in Baltimore and had been traveling under that cover throughout Virginia. She was trusted completely by the Rebels. Since women on both sides still easily obtained official passes, Hattie could safely cross back and forth from Richmond to Baltimore carrying Timothy's dispatches.

HIS EXCELLENCY PRESIDENT Lincoln chose the day after Christmas 1861 to make some obscure gesture to the Nation by coming all the way across the bay to inspect the troops. McClellan summoned me to deal with "Mr. Lincoln" in his stead. Little Mac was infuriated by the withering attacks on him from Lincoln's meddling Cabinet, which the Commander in Chief saw no reason to silence even if they were undermining the morale of the entire Army. On the other hand, McClellan was doing his cause no favor by portraying himself as Napoleon Bonaparte. They were no longer on speaking terms.

Nevertheless, Lincoln had brought Mathew Brady along with him, and he insisted that McClellan appear for a proper memorial of the occasion. I've got it in a frame. Lincoln wouldn't take off his stovepipe hat, and he looks about three feet taller than me and McClellan standing on either side of him. At least I look dignified. McClellan looks like he wants to kill Lincoln, probably because he knows His Excellency's hat makes him look even shorter. Lincoln has a thin smile on his face because he knows how brassed McClellan is.

That was when the dispatch arrived. As soon as Brady had his picture, I ripped it open and peered at Mrs. Warne's neat pen strokes of code. The birds had taken flight.

TIMOTHY STOPPED IN Baltimore to pick up dispatches and letters from the city's underground to deliver to Richmond. He and Hattie arrived separately in early January, 1862. He sent us a brief coded message alluding to a difficult journey. That was not good news. On his prior crossing of the Potomac on a cold autumn night, his small boat had overturned and he was forced to hide in a barn, spending a shivering night in a pile of hay. He contracted a fever and painful rheumatism, and though he recovered and was well enough when he left the second time, the illness was a worry because it is the type that recurs.

When he reached Richmond this time he checked into the Montgomery Hotel. Hattie Lawton arrived a few days later, bearing more dispatches, and for the next several weeks their activities bore abundant fruit. Timothy made such close contact with members of the Confederate War Department that he was given a

guided tour of the Tredegar Iron Works, the most important armaments manufacturing facility in the South. Every cannon in the
Rebel army came from Tredegar, where over a thousand workers,
whites and slaves, labored around the clock. Timothy smuggled
out a detailed report on the factory's stocks of armaments, produc-
tion capabilities, and, most importantly, precise descriptions of the
factory's defenses. If McClellan could penetrate the perimeter of
Richmond and destroy Tredegar, the Rebels' ability to continue the
War would be crippled.

Timothy even bragged how the war clerk, John P. Jones, was
clamping down on issuing passes to cross the lines, but Judah
P. Benjamin himself had interceded on Timothy's behalf so that
Timothy could practically travel at will.

Meanwhile, Hattie had taken a journey purportedly to visit family in Alabama. She compiled meticulous reports on Rebel troop
concentrations in the Carolinas, Georgia, and Eastern Tennessee.
Each report astonished and delighted McClellan.

Then the dispatches ceased. Three weeks passed and we had no
idea whether Timothy and Hattie were dead or alive.

"WHY HAVEN'T WE heard a single word from either of them?"
I demanded absurdly, as if Mrs. Warne knew the answer but was
keeping it from me.

"There are several possibilities," she replied, in a calm and reasonable tone. "The most obvious is that the situation in Richmond
has made it too dangerous to communicate with us right now."

"That's nonsense." I dismissed her suggestion with an impatient
wave of my hand.

"He could be ill. That is a distinct possibility. He was not fully
recovered from the fever he contracted on his last trip."

She was grasping at straws.

"He could *not* be dead or captured," she stated emphatically, unable to hide her growing irritation. "If he were dead, our agents in Baltimore would have heard it. If he has been captured, the Rebels would have trumpeted the news to raise their morale. Therefore, the only conclusion we can reach is that he is still alive. Once conditions permit, he will safely depart Richmond with Mr. Benjamin's blessings, carrying dispatches for southern agents in Baltimore and Washington."

Mrs. Warne waited for my response. When I did not say a word, she spoke again with an unmistakable sense of urgency.

"Any attempt on our part to contact Timothy will place him in a situation of jeopardy that does not currently exist." She was pleading with me.

I shook my head doggedly. I would not be led astray. "I cannot sit idly by when the life of my operative is in danger."

"Mr. Pinkerton, I understand . . . it is Timothy." I must have cringed when she spoke his name, but she went on. "That is why it is even more important not to allow your feelings to overcome your reason. You must trust me."

But it was too late. I no longer trusted her.

"Mrs. Warne, even if Timothy is merely ill, he must get out of Richmond. We will send our most skilled operative to arrange for Timothy and Hattie to pass back across the lines."

"No one can accomplish that."

"You can, Mrs. Warne." When I spoke the words, my panic receded. My reason had at last prevailed over my emotions. It had been a horribly close call.

"No."

I looked at her as if I had misheard what she just said.

"I will not undertake a mission that jeopardizes not just Timothy and Hattie but our entire purpose in this war!"

"You would let Timothy die instead?"

"I told you—" Then she stopped and shook her head in despair. "I am not going to Richmond. If you insist on sending someone, I will give my assistance, but I will not be that person."

Mrs. Warne remained true to her word, and later that day she stood silently behind me as Pryce Lewis tried to talk me out of the very same order that she would not carry out. Pryce argued that every agent in the field was laying low because the recent Rebel defeat at Fort Donaldson had created panic in Richmond. General Winder, the head of the Confederate Secret Service, had unleashed his detectives to round up anyone even suspected of Union sympathies.

Pryce turned to Mrs. Warne to confirm his judgment, but she was impassive.

For all his devil-may-care attitude, Pryce Lewis would not abandon his comrade Timothy Webster. That is the equation I presented to him.

"Then I will go, sir," he finally announced.

I looked at Mrs. Warne pointedly. Pryce's assent proved her utterly wrong. I felt a huge sense of relief that my mind was at last free from her grasp.

Pryce Lewis made another feeble attempt to resist me when I decided to send John Scully along with him. Pryce said two men were more risky than one. But Scully didn't think so. John Scully was excited and proud to be chosen for the kind of mission I had never entrusted to him before.

Twenty

While it is easy to identify the unmitigated disasters that wreck a man's life, it is important not to overlook the inexplicable bits of coincidence that were absolutely essential to the catastrophe.

I ponder the fact that Pryce Lewis and John Scully only got to Richmond by a hair's breadth. Escorted by General Joe Hersey, they passed through the Union lines to the Potomac River crossing at Cobb's Point, but their canoe overturned in the river that night in an unexpected thunderstorm. They nearly drowned and were fired upon by Confederate pickets. There was a much greater likelihood of them dying en route instead of reaching Richmond to cause Timothy's death.

But they did reach Richmond, and they got Timothy killed, pretty much as Mrs. Warne had predicted, although even she could not have imagined the specifics. They arrived in early March with

letters from our agents introducing them as arms dealers and friends
of Timothy Webster, and they had no trouble finding his room at
the Montgomery Hotel, but when Hattie Lawton answered their
knock at the door, she was shocked by their arrival. From the door-
way they could see Timothy lying ill in bed. What they did not see
until they entered was that Hattie and Timothy had visitors. Captain Samuel McCubbin, chief of the Detective Force of General
Winder's Confederate Secret Service, was paying an innocent call to
the ailing Webster, whose poor health was of genuine concern to all
his Richmond friends. McCubbin was accompanied by another officer, Lieutenant Chase Morton.

Lieutenant Morton was the son of the renegade Senator from
Florida who left his wife and sons behind in their opulent Washington mansion when he fled at the outbreak of the War. Mrs. Morton remained active as a Rebel agent, until I searched her residence
and found numerous traitorous dispatches. She and her sons were
ordered to leave Washington with safe-conduct passes to Richmond. They were accompanied to the Baltimore train by my operative, John Scully.

What were the odds that John Scully and Chase Morton
would meet again in Timothy's hotel room? That Morton would
stare at him curiously, trying to place the face? There is no possible way the coincidence could have been imagined in advance.
What was totally predictable, however, was that John Scully
would panic.

In all the years he worked for me, he had performed his assign-
ments to my satisfaction precisely because I had never placed him
in a situation where his jittery nerves, in need of frequent fortification from alcohol, might betray him. Which is exactly what happened when he recognized Lieutenant Chase Morton in Timothy's

room. Instead of trying to bluff his way through it, Scully bolted out the door, fully arousing Morton's suspicions.

Pryce made his apologies and left, but they were both arrested before they even got out of the hotel. At the military prison Morton and his younger brother identified them. Their names were on a list that General Winder possessed of Pinkerton agents operating in Washington.

Timothy's name, however, was not on that list, so he was not yet in danger. Pryce held fast, refusing to reveal his mission or any connection to Timothy. It was Scully who broke when Winder got him drunk and described death by hanging. He offered Scully a pardon if he gave him information about Pinkerton's activities in Richmond. Useful information.

Scully revealed Timothy's identity.

I ONLY LEARNED of the arrests of Timothy Webster, John Scully, and Pryce Lewis and their subsequent death sentences when the news was published in a Richmond newspaper that was regularly delivered to our field camp. That was on April 6, four days after the main body of McClellan's Army of the Potomac had landed on the Yorktown peninsula for the assault on Richmond.

So began the worst weeks of my life, days that bore a strange resemblance to the nightmare of my aborted effort to save the life of John Brown.

McClellan argued that sending a white flag envoy to Richmond was an admission of guilt and would seal their fate.

The debate still rages about Little Mac's abilities as a general. I was one of his more steadfast supporters. Before launching his Peninsula Campaign, McClellan begged Lincoln and Stanton for reinforcements. They refused, citing the necessity of keeping *one hundred forty thousand troops* manning the perimeter of Washington, lest the Rebels charge across the Potomac and carry them off in the night.

Hadn't I told the morons to get the hell out of Washington when the War began?

On the eve of the Union advance, Stanton even *withdrew* General McDowell's forty thousand men from the peninsula to reinforce the defense of the Capital.

That was stupid, since Lee had wisely gathered his entire Army of Virginia and placed it between McClellan and Richmond. Despite that, McClellan got within five miles of the prize before his advance bogged down in the Chickahominy swamp in appalling weather. Rather than press on and risk losing the only Army the Union had, McClellan pulled back and Lee drove him all the way down the peninsula.

Lincoln's Menagerie immediately rose as one, pulling their thumbs out of their asses and waving their shitty fingers in every direction but their own to assign blame for the failure to capture Richmond.

At this horrendous juncture of events, McClellan was more concerned with his own survival than saving Timothy's life. In response to my pleas, the little fucker just shined me on.

Finally on April 21, ignoring McClellan, I met with Lincoln, Stanton, and the entire Cabinet. They were justifiably concerned about the situation, because we had a jail full of southern agents, including Rose Greenhow. The Cabinet authorized a flag-of-truce dispatch directly to Jefferson Davis, requesting that the lives of all three men be spared and a prisoner exchange take place.

After the Cabinet meeting, Lincoln and I had a brief moment alone. It was clear the Peninsula Campaign had failed miserably. His black moods had begun to descend upon him. As I left he gripped my hand and said to me, "It is a terrible thing, Mr. Pinkerton, what this war will force each of us to bear."

On April 23 I reached Fortress Monroe on the Virginia peninsula with the dispatch to Jefferson Davis. It was telegraphed to Norfolk and forwarded directly to Richmond. The dispatch with Lincoln's name at the bottom pointedly reminded Davis how many southern agents were currently held in Washington. Lincoln understood that some tense agreement was needed concerning the treatment of prisoners in a war between two factions of what had so recently been the same country. He would end up shipping all our captured spies to Richmond after they signed pledges to cease hostile activities toward the Union, pledges everyone knew would be broken.

Jefferson Davis, however, refused the offer to exchange prisoners. At the very last minute he commuted the death sentences of Scully and Pryce Lewis. Why then did he insist that Timothy die? I can only conclude that what flowed through Jefferson Davis's veins was tainted by some dark vision in his mind. He believed he was God's servant, creating a Promised Land for white men, where black people would forever be relegated to their proper role as animals. Since God does not measure the cost of His actions, neither did Jefferson Davis. People forget that he never surrendered, not even when the War was long lost and the remnants of the Confederate Army, his own countrymen, were being chewed to pieces by Grant's forces. Jefferson Davis did not surrender. Robert E. Lee finally did.

Who knows, maybe someone reminded him that Timothy Webster was the same fellow he had chatted with at the Spottiswoode Hotel, and it enraged him. Everything enraged him. Like Lincoln, he too disappeared for days on end to his room, descending into darkness.

He never surrendered. Instead, he torched Richmond and fled to Mississippi, where he spent eighteen cozy months confined to his home. They brought him back to Richmond in 1867 to stand trial for treason, but the trial never took place. No one said why, except that it was best for the nation.

ON APRIL 28, 1862, at 8 A.M., Timothy Webster was executed in Richmond, Virginia, in the least honorable manner, by hanging from his neck until he was dead. He was the first American executed as a spy since Nathan Hale in 1776, and he also gave his life for his country. It was Timothy's executioners who betrayed their country, and not one of them was ever punished for their treason.

General Winder even refused Timothy's request to be executed by a military firing squad.

For several years after the War, I kept track of General Winder's whereabouts. He took up a peaceful life in Richmond, along with so many other traitors of the Rebellion. I noted the occasion when his daughter had a second child. I intended to journey to Richmond, gather up Winder's extended family, and take them to the General's house, where they would form the party of official witnesses to a *proper* military execution. I intended to offer General Winder the blindfold he had refused Timothy, before I shot him. I would not have made him suffer while his family watched.

As he made Timothy suffer. Timothy was so weak from the damned feverish rheumatism that he had to be carried to the gallows, not in the yard of the military prison but in a park in the center of town, where Winder staged the event as a public spectacle.

Even with the noose around his neck, Timothy Webster managed to stand calmly at attention in the morning sunlight. When the trapdoor opened, he fell and hit the ground below with a sickening thud. They had botched it; the rope was too long. They dragged Timothy back up to the gallows and put the noose on him once more. His last words were, "And so I die a double death."

They pulled the noose so tight he gasped for breath while they took their sweet time measuring the rope before finally dropping him again and letting him swing, strangling, rather than snapping his neck cleanly, until he was finally relieved of his agony.

General Winder refused Hattie Lawton's plea to send Timothy's body back across the lines. Instead, Winder stuck him in a plain coffin and buried him in a common Richmond graveyard.

Perhaps it was my good fortune that certain events prevented me from visiting the retired General Winder, because I don't think I would have been able to execute him with the dignity of a single shot. I would have used my Navy Colt to shatter each of his kneecaps first. I would have stepped back and allowed his wife and children to rush to his side and soak in his blood and agony before I pushed them away at gunpoint. Then I would have approached General Winder and placed the barrel of my revolver in his mouth. As Winder was choking the way Timothy did, I would have told him that I would never have killed one of *his* captured operatives. Then I would have blown his brains all over his fine Richmond parlor.

As I noted, certain events prevented me from carrying out my intentions.

THE NEWS OF Timothy's execution arrived at Fortress Monroe via telegraph.

I went directly to George Bangs, who had been anxiously awaiting word, along with every other man in my unit. Until then, George had assured me there would be a last minute pardon, that the Rebels would not be so foolish as to invite retribution. When I told him Timothy was dead, his body went limp as if he'd taken a minié ball to the chest. He reached out and put his hand on my shoulder to hold himself up and comfort me at the same time. "Oh, dear God, Allan. Nothing will ever be the same."

Perhaps this is why, despite George's intermittent idiocy, perfidy, and disbelief in my ways, I have never fired him and never will. George has always stood on my side. At that terrible moment he did not question my judgment when I assembled my men and told them we were going to infiltrate Richmond and assassinate every Rebel leader involved in Timothy's murder.

I took my plan to Lincoln. A small group of operatives under my command would enter Virginia, don Confederate uniforms, swing around Richmond, and enter the city from the north. Lincoln looked at me as if I were a blasphemer. He had that expression of the pious whose religious sensibilities have been affronted.

What did the man think, that we were engaged in a game of whist? A lunatic had just cold-bloodedly executed Timothy Webster. There already had been a dozen attempts on Lincoln's life. We were at war!

Nevertheless, Mr. Lincoln had turned matters over to God. I was one of the first whom he informed of this. Soon he would announce it to the entire nation, rarely uttering another word in public without prefacing it with a disclaimer that the Author of his actions was not himself, but the Higher Power.

I told him that if it was in God's hands, he should know that God had told me to kill Jefferson Davis, on the condition that I inform the President first and obtain his signature on the field orders, or, if he wished, he could simply nod his head. God would correctly interpret the signal for me to execute His Will.

Lincoln insisted that God said to Abraham not to kill the son-of-a-bitch Davis. He actually wrote out orders to McClellan to that effect.

While I was desperately trying to save Timothy's life, there was no time to go to Mrs. Warne. When the news of Timothy's execution arrived, even as I wept with George, I knew that she, too, was weeping for Timothy and waiting for me to weep with her, but the urgency of organizing the mission to avenge his death kept me away. Or so I told myself. The truth was I simply could not face her.

"MR. PINKERTON, I cannot believe Timothy is gone."

She was dressed in black. Her eyes were red and she was quite pale. I had sent word ahead because I did not want to arrive unannounced. It was the middle of the day, and she was waiting for me in my office. There were others about, so when I walked in I closed the door behind me. I had carefully rehearsed my words, but I could not recall my lines and improvised them badly.

"Mrs. Warne, there is no way I can ever . . . there is nothing I can say or do, no apology I can make . . . to change the fact that my actions caused Timothy's death."

She looked at me as if she had no idea what I was talking about.

"Only *we* know the truth, Mrs. Warne," I said, more plainly now, remembering it as I intended. "Timothy would be alive today if I had followed your counsel."

She looked pained, as if she wished I had not mentioned this. I didn't understand. It had to be as clear to her as it was to me, yet she replied, "I have advised you on many things. Sometimes I have been right and sometimes not. No one could have anticipated what happened."

"But you did, Mrs. Warne." My voice rose. Why wouldn't she simply agree that I was to blame?

"Mr. Pinkerton, as always your actions were based on your firm convictions." Was she conning me? I stared at her in disbelief, until I realized that she was distressed for me. She forgave me!

How could she?

"Mrs. Warne, I was not acting from my convictions. I was not even thinking clearly. The truth is, I have not been thinking clearly for quite some time."

She comprehended in a heartbeat what I would not put into words. "Do you really believe that somehow we caused Timothy's death? Is that what you're saying?" I wanted to deny it, but I could not. That was exactly what I believed.

She took a step toward me and reached for my hand, her eyes filled with sorrow, a sorrow she wished me to share with her. "It's not true." Her voice had the urgency of a mother trying to convince a child his worst nightmare was only a dream.

I looked up and it was Kate who was staring into my eyes. She had broken her word never to appear in the light of day, to share our loss together.

But Kate was as guilty as I was. Besotted by the arrogant invincibility that only an illicit adventure such as ours can engender, we had willfully ignored the consequences. When I finally opened my eyes to the disaster looming before us, it was too late. And the casualty was Timothy Webster.

I drew my hand away. "Mrs. Warne, I have examined the decisions I made and the instincts that prompted them. I am not proud of either. But what about you?"

"What about me, Mr. Pinkerton?" Did she desperately hope I would once again lose my ability to obey my reason and fall back under her spell?

My jaw trembled; I could barely get the words out. But I had to. I had to kill Kate then and there. "I accept my guilt in sending Pryce and Scully. But if you had gone instead of them, you could have prevented Timothy's death."

"Or I could have died trying," she answered quietly.

I said nothing.

"Either way, Mr. Pinkerton, you would feel better right now, wouldn't you?"

As I looked at the woman I loved reeling from the blow I had delivered, a rigid paralysis gripped me. "There is nothing that would make me feel better right now, Mrs. Warne."

"Then the only thing I can do is leave you alone with your grief."

And that is what she did.

Twenty-one

In September of 1862, McClellan massed his army to face the Rebels at Antietam in Maryland. Lee had boldly taken the War into the United States of America for the first time. It was a sobering moment for the Union.

I hooked up with a company of regular cavalry and, bluffing my way with my major's rank, ordered a dozen cavalrymen to follow me. We found a Rebel artillery battery hidden on a hill awaiting McClellan's attack. Ordinarily, I would have returned to camp and pinpointed the battery on our field maps.

But there was nothing ordinary about my purpose.

What happens if you cannot confront the killer of someone you loved? If your comrade falls beside you, and there is no way you can peer across the field of battle and identify the man whose bullet brought your comrade down, your thirst for revenge becomes even greater, because it isn't one man's life you seek but the destruction of every man who wears his uniform. You may once have fought for a cause; now you fight for vengeance.

That night I ordered the men to camp without a fire. Before dawn we snuck up on the sleeping Rebel artillerymen. I plugged three in their bedrolls at close range with my pistol, and my thirst for revenge was briefly quenched.

Our attack raised an alarm across the ridge, and we were pursued by Rebel cavalry and fired upon by another artillery battery. As we crossed the creek back toward our lines, my favorite big black sorrel was shot from beneath me. I tumbled into the cold water and struck my head against a rock. I stood up beside my dead horse and drew my pistol. I was waiting for the first Rebel to come riding out of the stand of trees beside the stream, when I was suddenly wrenched by the shoulder up onto the back of a Union cavalryman's horse, and we charged out of there. I am not sure I thanked him for saving my life when we returned to our camp.

The next day at Antietam the bloodiest battle of the War to date was fought.

McClellan declared it a victory. It was not. He suffered twelve thousand casualties, and Lee briefly crossed the Potomac before making an orderly retreat, having made his point.

In November, Lincoln, with his usual lack of manners, sacked Little Mac and replaced him with General Burnside, who promptly disbanded the Secret Service of the Army of the Potomac. President Lincoln informed me that my services to the Union were no longer required, expressing his regrets for everything and, as usual, taking responsibility for nothing. Still, I felt that even if he only saw himself as a bearer of tidings, he considered me his friend, and despite how things had turned out, I felt the same way toward him.

There was nothing for me to do except return to Chicago with my operatives.

"WILLIE, PRAISE THE Lord, you're alive!" Joan exclaimed, as she hugged the young soldier, who looked damn smart in his corporal's uniform. "Oh, Allan," she murmured, gently touching the bandage on my forehead that covered the stitches holding together my skull, gashed at Antietam. I could not recall if I had written her of the event.

Joan repeated her gratitude to the Almighty for our safe return in the same tone of awe as men in the field camps spoke of just what the Lord, as they imagined Him, could taketh away in this war and what He could giveth.

While I'd been at the front, she had been there too, confronting not an enemy in uniform but a different bringer of death, the daily casualty lists in the newspapers, the ominous knock on the door, the mail itself. I had written her of Timothy's death, but I had never considered that she would read it thinking, *That could have been my son or my husband; thank God it was only poor Mr. Webster.*

"Allan," she murmured, "I'm truly sorry for Mr. Webster. He was a fine man."

I nodded, and she took Willie by the arm and led us down the platform. After an absence of over a year and a half, I was home.

I WAS AWAKENED in my bed the next morning by my daughters, Young Joan and Belle, who might as well have been Rebels who'd slipped past the sentries into camp in the middle of the night. I sat bolt upright, having no idea where I was. Little Joan was pointing something at me. I thought it was a pistol, but it was a piece of toasted bread. Joan, just seven, looked like she was about to burst into tears as I reached out for it.

Belle giggled, as if this were some fairy tale and the Monster in the Woods had to be tamed. She was barely five, and I might well have been some imaginary beast. Did she even remember me? I grinned widely and she squealed with glee, but her older sister frowned. She was always a serious little girl, and she has remained serious her whole life, not like her mother for whom she is named but like her father. She has grown up into a woman of unflinching principles, which has led her into incessant conflict with me, although I admire her guts. It is my hope that one day she will understand that my meddling in her life was only the result of deep affection and a protective urge to save her from making a costly mistake in the matter of matrimony.

"What's wrong, my dear?"

"The tea got cold." She pointed to the elaborate tray they had prepared for my breakfast in bed. "Mother said you'd be awake by now."

I was wounded by Little Joan's distress. "But, my dear, I prefer my tea cooled down. So it's perfect."

That delighted them both. "Puffect! Puffect!" Belle exclaimed, clapping her hands together while Little Joan fussed over the pouring of the tea, insisting that I remain in bed, propped up on my pillows to enjoy my morning meal. She stood by me as if I were an invalid in hospital, handing me my cup and saucer and more toast, until I let out a loud sigh of contentment. "That was quite delicious. Oh, yes, quite delicious. Thank you very much, ladies."

Belle was so excited that she jumped up on the bed and perched herself on my knees. I reached my hand out to Joan. "Come on, Little

Lady. Room enough in the ship for everyone." Belle waggled her stuffed bear in my face. "What's his name, Belle?" I inquired seriously.

Belle bit her lip trying not to give away the secret. She looked at Joan, who gave her an enthusiastic nod of permission, and Belle shouted out, "He's Major Da Da!" She held up the bear's paw and made it salute.

I smartly saluted back, and they howled with laughter as if I had told the funniest joke they'd ever heard. This inspired me to call upon my talent for accents to create an array of entertaining characters that put my little girls totally in their father's thrall.

They were already seven and five, and I barely knew them. But it was not too late! My heart nearly burst as I lifted Belle into the air, telling her this was what it was like to go up in a balloon, high in the sky, and look down at the world. Of course I did not mention that you were looking at the enemy below. She did not need to know of war and betrayal and grief.

Suddenly, the empty feeling I had endured on the long train ride home from Washington was replaced by the fullness of fatherhood. My little ladies needed me and loved me. I would do right by them.

JOAN INFORMED ME that the day after next, Christmas Day, we would be entertaining visitors. Christmas is abhorrent to me, a preposterous mythology wedded to hypocritical sentiments of goodwill toward mankind on the part of people who express no such thing on the other 364 days of the year. Nevertheless, I resisted the urge to return immediately to my office and instead engaged in holiday activities. I went out to purchase gifts, returning with them hidden on my person as the girls tried to sneak under my coat to find them. I enlisted Robbie's help in obtaining a fine tree, and we set it up on Christmas Eve. I felt genuine affection toward Robbie. He was older now than when I'd left him. He showed his brother Willie a bit of respect. This family harmony brought forth in me a feeling I had never experienced before toward Joan, the mother of my four children.

We even had sex that night. It was not the Sabbath, but it was Christmas Eve. As she drifted into her lightly snoring slumber, I remained awake, pondering Joan's role in my life in a new light. What if her brazen act of treachery in tricking me into fleeing my homeland really had saved me? I would probably have been dead a long time ago if I'd stayed in Scotland, having committed some utterly reckless act of rebellion.

I resisted the impulse to wake her and thank her. I was trembling with something approaching religious fervor, a sense that my life was not in my control and Joan might well be the mysterious agent of my salvation, if not in holy terms then in the equally important realm of earthly survival.

Every man has to have a home. At least this man must. I'm just not very good at making one. At that moment my chest swelled as I contemplated what my wife had done for me.

I was a lucky man.

As it turned out, this was a grossly distorted view of the situation. Joan soon set me straight by poisoning what might otherwise have been a decent Christmas.

THE HOUSE WAS full of people I'd never seen before. I had expected the usual crowd from church, with whom I'd long ago made a casual truce, allowing us to avoid discussions of religion and instead chat amiably about the virtues of Joan's choir singing. But only a couple of them showed up early and were gone by the time the refreshments were laid out and our real guests arrived, men dressed in expensive overcoats and beaver hats, accompanied by their wives in luxurious capes and bonnets.

Joan descended the stairs in a dark blue dress of silk brocade with a full bustle that I'd never seen before, as fashionable as any of the guests. She'd engaged an Irish girl to serve for the occasion, and I was confounded by the ease with which she assumed the role of hostess.

Each of the gentlemen arrived with an elaborately wrapped gift. I opened one out of curiosity and was amazed to find an expensive bottle of the finest Kentucky bourbon. I felt the other packages and realized they were all similar bottles.

Later I stood in my parlor, answering their questions about the sacking of McClellan and what, in my considered opinion, I thought was the most likely course of action Lincoln would now pursue. I was a military man and they were mere innocent civilians, and despite my personal doubts about Lincoln's ability to prosecute the War, it was my duty to bolster their morale. "Gentlemen," I assured them, "the Rebellion will be crushed by the spring of the New Year."

Rather than eliciting exclamations of relief, my pronouncement was met by skeptical looks and knowing winks whose meaning I could not at that moment quite fathom.

Then the front door flew open and George Bangs entered, covered with snow that had begun falling lightly outside. As he shook himself clean like a big dog, I was surprised by the chorus that arose—"Mr. Bangs, how good to see you again, sir!"—as if he were a long-lost relative.

George nodded sheepishly and glanced uncomfortably in my direction. I excused myself from the crowd hemming me in and ushered him into the kitchen. His eyes were bloodshot and his breath reeked of alcohol. "Allan, I can't bring myself to return to the office."

"What the hell are you talking about, George? Are you drunk?"

"Webster's gone!" He shook his head, as if he could not believe it. He stifled a sob. "And Pryce and Scully—"

I put my hand on his shoulder. I'd never done that before, but at that moment I wanted to touch him.

"I'm sorry, Allan."

"There's nothing to apologize for."

"Thank you." He took a deep breath and regained his composure.

"Who the hell are those men in my parlor?"

He took out his handkerchief and blew his nose. Then he spoke in a bitter tone I'd never heard from him. "They were formerly small-time commodities dealers, you know the type, buying lots here and there to sell to big men like Armour. But now that the Union Army must provide daily rations of tinned meat and salt pork for several hundred thousand soldiers, they don't need Armour. They can sell directly to Washington and make a steep profit."

"You seem to be on very familiar terms with them," I looked at him suspiciously.

"As soon as you left for the Capital, they started beseiging me with requests. Now that you've returned, they are even more eager to engage your services."

"What services?"

"Everyone in Chicago knows that Allan Pinkerton has connections at the highest level."

"Connections." I could not hide my disgust. I had heard the word bandied about too often in Washington. The Capital had always been a magnet for men seeking the lucrative political plums of federal jobs as postmasters or customs officials, but the War made those prizes mere pittances compared to a federal contract to supply the Union Army—if you had the right connections.

"Why the hell would I get mixed up in that sort of thing?"

The sheen of alcohol gave his eyes an unusually shrewd aspect. "For a fee, of course. For every contract you *procure*." He gave the word a spiteful twist. Once, any enterprise that produced a profit for the Agency would have elicited his enthusiasm, along with a condescending attitude if I interposed my principles in the way of revenue. But he had been changed by the death of Timothy Webster.

"They're brokers, Allan. They bet on futures, and right now they're betting on a long and *costly* war, because they will not bear the cost. Instead, it will go directly into their pockets."

I was ready to charge back into the parlor, show these pasty-faced carrion to the door, and toss their fancy coats and vile bribes out after them. But that would have greatly embarrassed Joan.

Over George's shoulder I watched my wife, surrounded by the ladies paying fealty to her, as they had been instructed by their wealthy husbands, to make a good impression on the wife of Allan Pinkerton, who could provide them with the lucrative connections they so eagerly sought.

LATER THAT NIGHT, after Joan put the girls to bed, we sat with each other beside the parlor stove. I puffed slowly on a cigar one of our guests had thoughtfully placed in my pocket, a fine Havana. Joan let out a long sigh, which I recognized as a prelude to her voicing some strong opinion.

"Allan, do you think you've got any chance of collecting what you're owed from the War Department? Out of sight and out of mind, you know." Although Joan frequently employs clichéd homilies, there is nothing harmlessly mundane in her syntax. My body stiffened in alarm.

I probably should have heeded George and more diligently pursued the overdue payments to my Agency from the War Department. But every time I went to them, they demanded not only the names of my undercover agents but the dates and specifics of their activities.

"Why not just send the invoices to General Winder in Richmond, you fucking moron?" I'd end up screaming, leaving unpaid. We were still owed thousands. I think. I didn't know the exact figure. I was sure Joan did.

"No sense crying over spilt milk," she replied with odd good cheer. "The gentlemen we entertained this afternoon do all their business with the government on a cash-on-delivery basis."

"Do they?"

"Yes, Allan. And they are eager to employ your services."

I wanted to say to my wife, *Services? You mean greasing assholes in Washington for these gentlemen to fuck?* Naturally I said nothing of the sort, maintaining a resolute silence. My refusal to rise to Joan's bait was often a more powerful weapon than unleashing my wrath.

Too bad this was not one of those occasions.

She began *singing*! An old Scots ballad proclaiming the birth of the Christ Child. She was smiling, quite pleased with herself. And why not? On this dark Christmas, Joan's messiah had reappeared at last, to guide her and her Righteous Army across the scorched battleground to pluck the coins right off the eyelids of the Union dead, the fools fallen for nothing! And then Allan Pinkerton himself would follow her meekly into battle for the only True Cause: profit.

Even if I wished to speak at that moment, I was struck dumb.

And she wasn't finished.

"Did I tell you, Allan, how Willie was going on this morning? What foolishness."

"*What* foolishness?"

"Oh, I'm sure he told you already."

"Told me what?"

Does the reader even understand? How can I make my predicament any clearer? I was *begging* her to bring her sledgehammer down on my own head!

"Some nonsense about reenlisting. Willie thinks he can get a commission. It's ridiculous. He's just a boy."

"He's a man and he proved it."

"He's sixteen."

"Seventeen in four months." I sounded like a six-year-old, defiantly sticking his tongue out at a street bully.

"They'll call Robbie next year too!"

"If they are called—"

"You can see that they aren't. With your connections."

Ah, the magic word. My skin crawled.

But how could I blame her? Hadn't my dear ma sacrificed so much for my escape from the mills?

I was exhausted. It was much more exhausting heading the Pinkerton household than the Secret Service of the Army of the Potomac.

If she had left it at that, though, she might have gotten her way. Instead, Joan could not resist gloating. "It's a terrible war, I know," she sang out, as I nodded, half asleep. "But at least something good has come of it." I opened one eye inquisitively. "Thank God, we'll never again have to risk everything, sheltering those runaway slaves."

It would be unfair of me simply to set down her words without including a possible interpretation other than the one I arrived at.

Was she genuinely praising the Lord for advising his servant Abraham to set them free in his recent Proclamation of Emancipation?

But I detected no feeling of goodwill toward anyone but herself. She rose and walked up the stairs with an unmistakable beckoning sashay of her bustle that positively horrified me. I leapt to my feet, threw on my overcoat, and fetched a gunnysack, filling it with my gifts from the war profiteers. I tossed the sack over my shoulder like a malignant Santa Claus and marched out into the snowy night.

Twenty-two

Fleeing my own home, my foul mood was made worse by the weather outside. The storm had turned into a howler off the lake. The temperature had plunged, and snow was blowing hard in my face as I made my way up Michigan Avenue, seeking the sanctuary of my office.

Knee-deep in the drifts, carrying the ridiculous sack of whiskey bottles over my shoulder, I struggled to climb onto the planked sidewalk. I'd left the house without a proper hat and gloves, and my fingers were numb as I fumbled with the frozen lock. As the bolt turned I was startled, sure that somewhere in my mind's eye a flickering light had just been extinguished.

I stepped back and looked up at the top floor of the building. All was dark. But had it been when I arrived? I couldn't recall. My head was down against the wind in my face. I looked around, but any intruder's footprints would have been obliterated by the drifting snow. I quietly opened the door and closed it behind me and stood in the downstairs vestibule, allowing my eyes to adjust to the darkness. I lowered the sack and removed one of my Christmas presents, slipping it out of its wrapping as a weapon.

I knew every squeaking board of the stairwell by heart, so I climbed to the landing at the top without making a sound. I stepped inside and stood motionless, bottle in hand, until I was sure no foolish Christmas Day intruder was about; then I took out my matches and started across the room to light the oil lamp. I was stopped by an ominous sound I knew well, the heavy click of a pistol's hammer cocked to fire.

"Don't move or I'll shoot you."

"Please don't do that, Mrs. Warne," I replied, as I lit the match and held it up to illuminate my face. We stared at each other in the pale light of the flickering flame, until it singed my fingers. I dropped the match to the floor, crushing it out with my boot. In the darkness I made my way to the lamp and lit it with another match.

"Is that a bottle of whiskey in your hand, Mr. Pinkerton?"

"It is. There's a whole sack of them at the bottom of the stairs. Christmas presents." She stared at me suspiciously, as if I myself had been drinking. "Mrs. Pinkerton was disappointed that you sent your regrets."

"I was not much feeling in the Christmas spirit."

"What are you doing here, Mrs. Warne?"

"I came in this morning to get started." She motioned to the mountain of file boxes that had accompanied us back from Washington.

"Why didn't you light a stove? It's freezing." She was dressed in her outer coat with her scarf wrapped around her neck.

"I didn't want everyone arriving in the morning to be greeted by an empty coal bin."

It made little sense to me. None of it did.

She seemed no more anxious than I to continue this awkward conversation. "I'll leave you to your work." Without waiting for a reply, she went into her office and closed the door behind her.

Our horrendous encounter in Washington after Timothy's death left us unable to exchange a single word more about him or us. Instead, we resumed our roles as Allan Pinkerton, head of the Pinkerton Detective Agency, and Mrs. Kate Warne, in charge of the Female Detective Bureau. Our task had been to bring our agents in from the field, pack up, and return home.

We had not spoken more than a few cursory pleasantries on the entire journey back. This was the first time I had seen her since I stepped down from the train.

As I got the fire going in the potbelly stove in my office, I wondered how long we could maintain these clumsy disguises? This time there were no misunderstood intentions separating us, only a chasm of recrimination.

Just then she knocked on my door and entered unbidden. "I did not ask what you intend to do about Mr. Stanton's request."

"What request?"

"Didn't George tell you?"

"He was drunk this afternoon."

"We received a telegram yesterday from the Secretary of War."

"What about, some invoice he won't pay?"

She held up a telegram several pages in length. I shook my head to indicate my complete disinterest in its contents. She continued, nonetheless, to press her case. "The Secretary of War wishes to retain the Agency's services once more."

"That is a pathetic joke, Mrs. Warne."

She ignored me and read aloud from the telegram. "He informs you that the activities of fraudulent northern contractors has reached *such epidemic proportions that the War Effort is being undermined and the Treasury bankrupted."*

I practically spat in disgust. "I told Stanton a year ago to hang the first ones we caught to set an example, but Lincoln wouldn't hear of it. When I continued collaring the President's campaign contributors, Stanton took the matter out of my hands."

"Apparently he now wishes to put it back in your hands."

"He's only asking me to clean up this mess so Lincoln can claim it's not his fault. Those two are quite a pair."

"Whatever they are, Mr. Pinkerton, for better or worse they are on our side."

Our side.

The way she said the words, and the look on her face, made my head spin. Despite everything that had happened, we were still on the same side. I suddenly realized that when she told me she would leave me alone to my grief, she had not quit me.

I reached for the telegram written in Stanton's usual high-blown gobbledygook. The gist of it described shipments to the Army that contained sawdust instead of Springfield rifles, cotton batting in place of wool blankets, and cartridge casings filled with gunpowder adulterated with sand.

"Mrs. Warne, Samuel Morse Felton of the Pennsylvania Railroad was kind enough to explain all this to me when he first sent us to Baltimore. He said that no one except a bunch of hotheads and radicals wanted this war, and he was right. Now that war has been forced upon them, men of commerce are literally making the best of the situation."

She grabbed the telegram out of my hand and waved it like a battle flag. "These men of commerce are no less traitors to their country than Rose Greenhow or Captain Ellison." It was a clarion call to a far different battle than I was being prodded into at gun-point by Joan.

"Let's just say for argument's sake, Mrs. Warne, that I took Stanton up on this. I wouldn't be anything more than a snooping private citizen, delivering reports to the War Department while the perpetrators go about their business." I couldn't help it. *Mrs. Warne, what should we do?*

She waved off my objections. "The Capital is now under martial law. You can demand the authority you need from Stanton. And this time he must pay us on a weekly basis, without those damned invoices." I must have smiled, because she was beaming.

"I would insist upon that."

"They can't win this war without you, Mr. Pinkerton, and it did not take them long to realize it!"

They didn't have a prayer without me! Hadn't I been indispensable to the Union from the day I saved Lincoln's life? I was the only man capable of defeating these new traitors. They were the most conscienceless foes the Union had yet faced: its own citizens, not content to reap huge profits *legitimately* but so infected by greed that they were sabotaging the Union Army beyond the wildest dreams of Rose Greenhow!

Timothy Webster had given his life for our Cause, and the War still had to be won, or he would have died in vain. Our course was clear. Mrs. Warne and I would return to Washington together.

The stove was glowing warm. She removed her coat and scarf, picked up a writing tablet, and sat down in the chair where she always sat when we had business to discuss. Her face was flushed with anticipation.

She was wearing a plain wool dress. Gray, without any bustle. Buttoned tight around her neck. Not a single piece of jewelry.

Her hair was done up close with a stack of pins. It was the way Joan usually dressed, except Joan was the one in fancy costume at the Christmas party, while Mrs. Warne was here in a plain wool dress.

A few stray locks fell across her forehead. I noticed for the first time tiny emerging crow's feet impressed upon the skin around her eyes. I had witnessed her transformation over the years to middle age, yet she looked as beautiful to me as ever.

She unself-consciously lifted the hem of her dress to cross her legs and rest her writing tablet on her knee, revealing a small patch of her black stockings, not the fine ones she wore in disguise but practical ones that disappeared into plain black boots above her ankles.

I wanted to drag her out of her chair and pull up that gray wool dress and press her down on my desk and cover her body with mine. I wanted to fuck her with a consuming desire that I had never felt for anything or anyone before.

My eyes burned her clothes to cinders, revealing Kate's naked body. I had not succeeded in killing her in Washington. Kate could not be killed. And now there would no longer be Kate and Mrs. Warne.

Only Kate Warne.

I had never been so frightened of anything in my life.

I could not look her directly in the eye as I spoke. "Your analysis of the situation is absolutely correct—I must return to Washington."

She nodded enthusiastically.

Then I mustered the strength to do what I had to do. "In the meantime it is essential to get the Agency running again at peak efficiency. There are numerous pending cases and a backlog of requests for our services." The sound of my voice was foreign to me.

It was a pathetic disguise. "Mrs. Warne, I have complete confidence leaving you and George in charge here during my absence."

She gave me time to come clean, but I just stood there as if what I had said was perfectly reasonable. And innocent. She lowered her gaze and murmured, "Is that what you really wish me to do, Mr. Pinkerton?"

"Yes, it is, Mrs. Warne."

But it wasn't! I wanted her to talk me out of it, as she always did when she knew better than I what I should do.

I did not hear what she said next.

"What?" I demanded, desperate for her contradiction.

"I said, *I understand, Mr. Pinkerton.*"

"Oh."

Of course she understood. So why the hell wouldn't she save me from this unholy mess?

She stood up and put her coat back on. I watched in disbelief as she carefully wrapped her scarf around her neck and buttoned the coat. When she walked out of my office without another word, I still did not believe what was happening until I heard her footsteps descending the stairway. I went to the window and stared down at her trudging through the snow in the street below until she disappeared into the darkness.

It was done.

When I had accused her of complicity in Timothy's death, that was only a slap across the face compared to the wound I just inflicted. This time I had succeeded in killing Kate.

EARLY IN THE new year of 1863, Willie and I shared a compartment on the long train ride to Washington. He wanted to squeeze every bit of instruction out of me on the techniques of criminal investigation, so I summoned the porter to retrieve our costume and makeup cases from the baggage car. For the next few hours I patiently taught him the same lessons that in the old days I imparted to every new operative.

Willie has always been an excellent student, unlike Robbie, who for some reason feels it is to his advantage to inform me, "I know that," whenever I reveal something he has never in his life heard before. That is why I do not trust my youngest son to find his own asshole to wipe after taking a shit, much less solve a case. William, on the other hand, became a credible detective at the age of seventeen. He came up with a remarkable inspiration. "When we get to Washington, I could pose as a supply officer. If you suspect a contractor is crooked let me approach him, and when he hands me a bribe, I'll cuff him and bring him to you!"

I frowned, as I often do when one of my operatives makes a good suggestion. Keeps them on their toes. I had already decided I would never make an exception for my own son. I waited for him to prove his case to me. He donned a Union officer's coat from the costume case and glued a beard and a scar on his face, so he looked old enough to pass for a lieutenant. I was delighted to see he had my gift for creating a fictitious persona. He imitated perfectly the voice of an arrogant young officer, giving me a rapacious look. "How much do y'think this contract for a hundred saddles might be worth to you, sir?"

I clapped him on the back. "William Pinkerton, you've got your first assignment as an operative of the Pinkerton Detective Agency." I felt as proud as my old master Larkin the cooper must have felt when his son completed his apprenticeship and joined the family business. Back in my ignorant youth I wanted to kill Larkin for dismissing me in favor of his own boy. Now I more than forgave him,

I embraced him. I *was* Larkin. And damn lucky my son wasn't a skilless fool like the old cooper's.

IN PHILADELPHIA WE had a four-hour layover. Willie was dying to see the city, so I gave him his leave, admonishing him to get back in time for the evening Pennsylvania Central to Baltimore. I made my way to the waiting room and found a table in the corner where I could be alone, where it had all started, when Timothy, Pryce, Scully, Hattie Lawton, and Mrs. Warne had gathered with me on this very same platform to embark on our journey to Baltimore.

I sat there defenseless against the onslaught of memory.

ALTHOUGH I HAD been gone for only a few months, the landscape of Washington had changed dramatically. Everyone and his uncle were now tripping over each other in pursuit of spies, and even good men like Seward were denouncing those suspected of southern sympathies, because it was an expedient way to jail your political opponents. Too bad it did little to diminish the Rebels' infiltration of the Union government.

Meanwhile, the new breed of traitors comported themselves with a brazenness that would have made Rose Greenhow blush. These jackals had something even more seductive than Mrs. Greenhow's sexual favors to offer government officials: wads of cash.

Washington was now awash with the profits of war, and business at the high-class bawdy houses Mrs. Warne had previously turned to our side had never been better. When I went to see Madam Tess Coburn, she was offended by my "insinuations against these patriotic Yankee gentlemen," as she referred to her new best customers.

I assured her that she would be well compensated for any evidence she could furnish to me regarding the activities of the few rotten apples among these patriots who might be engaged in defrauding the United States Government.

"Where is Mrs. Warne?" Tess Coburn demanded.

"She is in Chicago, supervising the Pinkerton Detective Agency, while I have urgently returned to Washington at Secretary Stanton's personal behest."

"Send Mrs. Warne my best," Tess Coburn replied, as she shut her door in my face.

IN OUR OLD headquarters, I pored over reports I obtained from Union field officers regarding fraudulent shipments they received. I tracked down every factory invoice, bill of lading, and transport receipt the contractors presented to the War Department. The papers were as bogus as their claims that the goods left the factories as ordered, but had been waylaid en route by thieves or crooked railway workers or mysterious bands of marauding Rebels. If the War Department questioned a claim, a helpful congressman from the contractor's home state was at the ready to vouch for it.

One of the most egregious offenders was a Mr. Jacob Bourne of Boston. Over a big steak dinner with Lieutenant Allan William, Mr. Bourne slipped the procurement officer for the Army of the Potomac's Third Regiment two hundred dollars in gold to make sure a consignment of ammunition was not too closely inspected.

Later that night, when Bourne staggered out of a nearby whorehouse, "Lieutenant William" was waiting. He delivered him to me, and I thanked him and sent him on his way. I did not want my son to witness what was about to take place.

I took Mr. Jacob Bourne upstairs to the old secret room, sat him down in front of a small desk, and placed before him a detailed confession of his illegal activities. Bourne laughed and asked if I knew who he was. I shrugged and replied I intended to find out. I asked him to sign the confession so I could deliver it to Stanton. He snorted derisively in the manner of men who think they are somehow protected from me by defenses I am too obtuse to perceive.

I yanked his hands behind his back, cuffed him, and put a gunnysack over his head. He tried to say something about what Lincoln would do, but I didn't catch his words as I backhanded him across the face so hard it snapped his head back.

"You're out of your mind!" he shouted.

By now I'm sure the reader knows this was not a very smart thing for Mr. Jacob Bourne to accuse me of.

"Mr. Bourne, by aiding and abetting the enemy in time of war, you have committed an act of treason against your country, whose privilege of citizenship you have abused, a privilege not shared by four million black slaves."

"Who the hell are you?"

That was a fair enough question. In America a man does indeed have the right to face his accusers, and here I had a sack over his head. But like His Excellency the President, I too had chosen in this desperate time to suspend certain rights.

I pulled him out of the chair and flung him on the floor. I took out my gun and poked it through the gunnysack into his ear. I held him still with a knee on his chest as he lay on his back, gasping for air. Since he couldn't see me, I took advantage of the element of surprise to discharge the pistol without asking him again to sign the confession. I held the gun away from his head as I fired, but the report probably reduced his hearing in one ear for life.

I was only mildly disgusted by the smell of shit in his pants.

I pulled him back up into the chair. He sat there, stock-still, perhaps deliriously hoping I was done with him. Instead, I cocked the hammer again.

He screamed and screamed and screamed, and I joined him. I felt better, screaming with him, until he broke into sobs. I knelt beside him, patted him like a good dog, and quietly asked if he would like to sign the confession. Then he could get cleaned up.

When I let him out the front door onto the city streets, I told him that if he left Washington by the end of the week I would bring no charges against him. If he stayed I would hunt him down and shoot him dead.

The next day Stanton summoned me before I could even request an interview.

Mr. Bourne had of course run straight to Lincoln, who immediately ranted to Stanton that my actions were intolerable.

At least we were all playing our roles.

Stanton smiled, a thin evil twisting of his lips, and whispered that Lincoln already had his secretary, Nicolay, drafting legislation that would make war profiteering a federal crime, obviating the necessity for the tactics I had been forced to employ on Mr. Bourne in the absence of legal redress.

Still, I didn't feel good about it. When I fired my weapon in the vicinity of Mr. Bourne's head, I wanted to kill him, not just scare him. John Brown never *wanted* to kill anyone, even though he killed more men in cold blood than I could imagine in my wildest dreams.

Once more I was painfully aware of how right Mrs. Warne had been—I would never be John Brown. I could only be Allan Pinkerton, a man who lived on this earth deaf to God's commands, serving only his lusts for blood, pussy, and what he believed was right.

It was getting harder to be that man.

That must have been why she would not speak to me in my nightmares when she visited me nearly every night. There was always some emergency, and we had to act quickly. I asked her what we should do?

But she was silent. Arms clasped across her chest, her face severe and disapproving, she refused to answer my question.

What should we do, Mrs. Warne?

Twenty-three

I n the spring of 1864, Stanton requested a confidential meeting with me to discuss *a politically important and highly sensitive situation confronting the War Department.*

The naval blockade the Union imposed on the South had succeeded in severely curtailing the overseas cotton trade, cutting off the Rebels' supply of cash and leaving them desperately short of raw materials and food for their soldiers. The blockade's unintended effect, however, was to put the northern cotton brokers and shippers, who had been making as much before the War as the southern planters, out of business.

As the price of the commodity rose sky high, the cotton brokers could not resist the lure of exorbitant profits. They circumvented the blockade by acquiring the "white gold" clandestinely, exchanging supplies for it that provisioned the Rebel forces slaughtering our soldiers. Finally, in early 1864, Lincoln made the unseemly situation palatable by decreeing that southern cotton would henceforth be confiscated as contraband in areas controlled by the Union Army. The government would sell the rights to that cotton to legitimate brokers who could then legally resell it on the overseas markets.

In our meeting, Stanton revealed to me that there was nothing legitimate about most of these brokers. They claimed rights to futures they did not control but only hoped to, through bribery or clandestine deals with southern planters. The port of New Orleans, captured early in the War by the daring naval officer Farragut, was the center of the cotton futures market. Stanton wanted me to go down there and clean out the swindlers.

Now, why the hell would I want to traipse off a thousand miles from Washington just to chase another despicable class of crooks? I wouldn't—and Stanton knew it.

At this late juncture in my narrative it is still possible that a small number of readers do not yet comprehend what I am talking about when I refer to "my Enemies." They may even be sympathetic to that most absurd charge that I *imagine* the machinations and plotting that goes on behind my back.

For you skeptical simpletons, I will spell it out: Edwin McMasters Stanton, Secretary of War of the United States.

When I told Stanton there was no way in hell I was going to drag my ass down to that malarial hole at the bottom of the Mississippi, the Secretary of War sighed, his heavy lids dropping over those beady eyes. He stroked his long thin beard like he was rubbing his crotch. Then he leaned across his desk and whispered that what he was about to divulge had to remain an absolute secret and could he trust me?

What did he expect me to say? He looked around as if we might be overheard and told me that this was an extremely delicate matter that could cause immense political embarrassment to a man we both admired greatly, but whom we both knew was often a victim of his own innocence. President Lincoln.

Following this dramatic prelude, Stanton revealed that the most flagrant cotton frauds were being perpetrated by some of Lincoln's closest cronies, including none other than my old friend Colonel Ward Hill Lamon.

Surely you now see how my Enemies will stop at nothing to bring me down! Or do I have to spell this out too?

All right, then. Since I had accomplished most of Stanton's dirty work in Washington by rounding up the most egregious crooked contractors and putting the fear of God into the rest, he now wanted me out of town. And New Orleans was as far away as he could send me.

But he knew I wouldn't go for it, so he cleverly masked his true intentions by raising the possibility that I might put the Fat Fuck and a few others on my list in jail. It was like waving a red flag in front of a bull.

I should have realized what Stanton was up to, but I missed it. I marched out of Stanton's office and told Willie to pack his bags for New Orleans.

It was the biggest mistake of my life. Stanton had set me up.

WILLIE AND I found suitable accommodations in a guesthouse in the French Quarter on a narrow street off Jackson Square, run by an Italian named Grosso. This was Willie's chance to fight his own war, and he marched in and out of the Military Governor's Head-quarters with a swagger. When we made a collar, I let him bring the man in to face charges. He took to wearing striped silk shirts you could find for a song in the shops of the Italian tailors, a wide-brimmed hat, and a drooping mustache like one of those old-time fire-eating Secessionists. The disguise enabled him to slip easily into the seamy underworld of cotton dealers and fixers.

He liked to carry a hidden derringer along with the Navy Colt I issued him. He was no fool, I made damn sure of that, and no braggart. I wasn't going to let him get suckered into something he couldn't manage. He listened respectfully when I taught him how to size up a situation and not take any risk he didn't have to.

Meanwhile, the War raged on. Gettysburg had been no turning of the tide but a close escape from disaster. In May of 1864, Grant got near enough to see the church towers of Richmond, and he attacked, pulling back after three thousand Union soldiers died in twenty minutes. But who was counting? He had lost ten times that many in what is now called the Battle of the Wilderness.

Early in 1865, Mr. Grosso delivered a telegram from George Bangs containing his sincere condolences on the death of my beloved daughter Belle, only seven years old.

She had been sickly her whole life and couldn't shake the fever and cough that beset her during the past harsh winter. Once we were in New Orleans, I had been unable to make the long arduous journey home, as I had done at regular intervals when Willie and I were still stationed in Washington.

Now we boarded a river steamer and set forth on an odyssey of grief. I never felt so adrift in my entire life. I had been in the proximity of the sudden violent deaths of thousands, yet this one death struck my heart as if the world had ended. Joan had never mentioned in her letters any turn for the worse in Belle's condition. My little lady was dead, and it was George who informed me. Why hadn't Joan told me?

AT THE CEMETERY, Joan's grief exploded in a wailing keening song that pierced the chill May morning like a crow's cry. I looked helplessly to my sons. Robbie stood at his mother's side and fixed me with a look from across the open hole in the ground as if he did not trust me. William seemed as helpless as I. Little Joan clung to my hand, telling me through her tears that she was frightened I would leave again, and she would die next. Where'd she get that idea?

Back at the house, Joan retreated to her room and would not receive any of the visitors who'd come to pay their respects. I went to comfort her and asked her, not at all accusingly but only trying to relieve her sorrow, why she had borne the burden of Belle's illness alone. Why hadn't she told me?

She attacked me like one of those ferocious storms down in New Orleans that comes roaring in off the gulf to pound the city. She pelted me with the gruesome details of Belle's feverish hallucinations in her final weeks, crying out helplessly for her da who wasn't there, who she was convinced was dead; Da Da was dead, he had to be or he would be here, Ma; and Joan telling her, It's all right, my darling, your da is in Heaven with the angels.

She told Belle I was dead? My daughter passed from this earth thinking her da was dead!

"How could you do that, Joan?"

Her voice crackled with malice. "Would it have been better if I'd told the poor girl you had more important matters to attend to than your daughter?" There was a black purity to her grief that gave her accusations a peculiar, unassailable force.

You see, Joan blamed me for Belle's death.

She had made me promise years before, for the sake of her unborn child, our little girl Belle, that I would never let John Brown in our house again. And I had broken the promise on which Belle's life depended.

I had killed her baby girl.

She said those very words and more, which I am too weary to even recall, much less record here. I said anything I could think of to shake her out of her madness, but it did no good. Joan's grief infected our family forever.

THE NEXT DAY I went to my office. George wished to discuss our current cases with me before Willie and I returned to New Orleans. I did my best to pay attention, to offer suggestions, but my heart wasn't in it.

My heart was broken.

At the end of the day, when George and all the others had left, I sat at my desk, unable to gather the strength to return home. *Home.* It sounded like the names of those once-innocent places that overnight became synonymous with horror: *Chancellorsville, Vicksburg, Shiloh.* I stared out the window, wondering how it had come to this.

There was nothing for me to do but grab Willie and get the hell out of there. We headed back to New Orleans the next day.

WHEN LINCOLN WAS finally assassinated on April 14, 1865, five days after Lee's surrender at Appomattox, I took the blow hard. It was inconceivable to me that he was gone, that there would never be another occasion for him to exasperate me. Despite my beliefs, which he never shared, I felt an affection for him I've known for no other man. Yet his passing could not squeeze a tear from me, because I had none left to shed. Willie cried for both of us, unashamed, like a million other young men who had been drenched in death wept across the land for Lincoln. But they had never met him, as Willie had. In our stifling hotel room in New Orleans, Willie insisted that I tell him every story about Lincoln I could recount. Lincoln was Willie's Captain, the way John Brown had been mine.

WE SHUT DOWN our operation in New Orleans and got back to Chicago a few days before the funeral cortege arrived on its last stop in its cross-country journey. There Lincoln's casket would be transferred to an Illinois Central car that would take him to his final resting place in Springfield, Illinois.

William Herndon, Lincoln's old law partner, who had been his most trusted adviser right up until the end, was decent enough to invite me to ride on the train. I planned to take George with me and, of course, Willie. The day before we were to leave I called them into my office to discuss our itinerary. It was a comfort to me to have these two at my side, the closest men left in my life.

Willie looked at me strangely. "Da, shouldn't Mrs. Warne be coming with us to Mr. Lincoln's funeral?"

I shrugged dismissively. Willie fixed me with a dark stare.

I flat out did not know what to do. "George, please see to it that Mrs. Warne is informed."

"Allan," George replied gently, "wouldn't it be more appropriate if the invitation came directly from you? She's in her office as we speak."

"I had no idea."

George just nodded and left me to the task.

WE HAD NOT spent a moment alone together in more than two years, since I left for Washington without her. Each time I returned to Chicago, George informed me almost apologetically that Mrs. Warne had been called away on "urgent Agency business." Sometimes to Detroit or Cincinnati or just Springfield, but far enough to avoid me. On the few occasions she was not out of town, she left files on my desk for my perusal and avoided a face-to-face meeting.

At Belle's funeral she had stood beside George with her jaw set hard, and I could not intuit what she was thinking. The next day when I was sitting at my desk she had knocked on my door. "Come in," I practically cried out.

She had opened the door but did not enter, instead calling to me as if from the far shore of a lake, "I wish to offer you my sincerest condolences on your terrible loss." When I had asked her again to come in, she just shook her head sadly and left.

Now it was my turn to knock on her door.

"Yes?"

"Mrs. Warne?"

She opened the door but did not bid me to enter. "Mrs. Warne, there's a matter of business I wish to discuss with you."

"I don't think this is the appropriate time. I can think of little else right now except the death of Mr. Lincoln."

"I understand. That is what I wish to discuss with you."

Reluctantly she stepped away from the door and I entered. I hadn't been in her office since that Christmas night when she pointed a gun at me, and now I wished she had shot me then. As I looked around at the details of her life, I recognized the painting on the wall, a New England landscape I'd hung for her the day I gave her this office. I always liked the masculine character of the brass lamp that sat on her desk. The carpet was new, though. My heart sank. It was the same one that had lain on the floor of her bedroom in Washington.

"What is it you wish to discuss, Mr. Pinkerton?"

"I would like you to accompany George, Willie, and myself to Mr. Lincoln's funeral."

She could not hide her surprise.

"I can't imagine our going without you, Mrs. Warne."

AS SHE MADE her way down the platform to meet us at the train, I was standing in conversation with Mr. Norman Judd, who had played such a crucial role in our thwarting the Baltimore Plot. When he saw her, his grief seemed to evaporate. He grasped Mrs. Warne's hand warmly, telling her with genuine emotion that it had been too long since he'd had the pleasure of her company.

After the funeral in Springfield, William Herndon, and John Nicolay and, yes, even Ward Fucking Lamon approached Mrs. Warne, to give her their warmest regards. We soon found ourselves in the hotel saloon, doing what old soldiers inevitably do, exchanging war stories.

The men wanted to hear hers, having heard their own too many times. She was, as always, a magical storyteller. "Of course, the one I will never forget is the night I spent in his train compartment, with him dressed in that outlandish disguise, sneaking to his own inauguration as President of the United States. But of course, the situation did not dampen his sense of humor or his fondness for an appreciative audience for his jokes."

"And you were always that," I added. I was sitting beside her at the round table in the corner. Mrs. Warne was in her element, surrounded by seven men in a saloon. They urged her to go on, and she recounted the entire scene from four years earlier. It seemed like an eternity. We had all heard Lincoln's stories many times, but never in her voice, a remarkable imitation of Lincoln, punctuated by her imitation of her own younger self, full of the dizzying energy and purpose that once filled us both.

She finished with a succinct coda recounting his safe delivery to Washington and my return to Baltimore.

Our eyes flickered across each other's gaze. We both knew what had happened next. I was positive we were sharing the memory of our first encounter in her hotel room in Baltimore. My heart was racing as my eyes darted to the others, but they were just smiling, warmed by this recollection of their fallen leader and friend.

They suspected nothing.

They had no idea I was really two men. One of them was sitting at the table with them, engaged in this world of human events and time passing and grief shared. The other, however, lived in a world unknown to anyone else except the one sitting right beside him, the one who had created this secret world with him, the one who shared it with him still.

I LEFT A note at the hotel desk, asking her to meet me early in the morning for breakfast before the departure of our train back to Chicago. I was drumming my fingers impatiently on the table in the hotel salon, nearly deserted at that hour, when she entered the room through the doors at the far end. I asked her to sit down so we could speak privately before the others arrived.

While it had been weighing on my mind for weeks, I had only just discovered new evidence concerning the most important case I had ever confronted. She was the only one whose opinion I could rely on. At least, that is what I told myself.

"Mrs. Warne, there are disturbing circumstances surrounding the death of Mr. Lincoln that bear closer examination."

She remained silent, waiting to hear what I had to say.

"I could have saved Lincoln's life if I had been with him in Washington."

"Of that I have no doubt, Mr. Pinkerton." I knew she could not possibly imagine what I was about to reveal to her.

"The precautions taken to guard Lincoln, not merely that night but for weeks before, were woefully inadequate."

"Yes, I learned as much from a brief conversation with Nicolay after the funeral." Her tone was professional, as if, So what?

I then related to her all the evidence I had accumulated since Willie and I first received the news in New Orleans. "To begin with, Stanton didn't see fit to inform me of the assassination until five days after it occurred. Even then, the news was telegraphed to the Military Governor's office. Every foot soldier in the Union Army knew Lincoln had been killed before I did."

I was heartened by the penetrating look I knew so well. I went on urgently. "Naturally I telegraphed Stanton, offering to return to Washington to assist in apprehending the perpetrators and uncovering the identities of everyone connected to the vile plot."

"And what was Stanton's response?"

I reached into my coat pocket and took out the telegram I had shown William Herndon the day before. I scanned the room to make sure we were still alone before I slid it across the table to her.

ACCEPT MY THANKS FOR YOUR TELEGRAM OF THE 19TH RECEIVED THIS EVENING. BOOTH AND TWO OF HIS ACCOMPLICES ARE STILL AT LARGE. SOME OF THE OTHERS HAVE BEEN SECURED. BOOTH MAY HAVE MADE HIS WAY TO THE WEST WITH A VIEW OF GETTING TO TEXAS OR MEXICO. YOU WILL PLEASE TAKE MEASURES TO WATCH THE WESTERN

RIVERS AND YOU MAY GET HIM. THE REWARD OFFERED FOR
HIM NOW AMOUNTS TO ONE HUNDRED THOUSAND DOL-
LARS OR OVER. ASK GENERAL CANBY TO GIVE ORDERS IN
HIS COMMAND FOR HIS ARREST.

"I didn't get this telegram until the end of the month. By then
Booth was dead and in the ground, along with all the others they
claim were part of the plot, and the trail was cold."

I paused to see if she had put it together the way I had, but her
expression was impassive.

I waved the telegram in my hand. "This is utter shit! Stanton knew
perfectly well that Booth wasn't heading for Mexico. He wanted to
send me on a wild goose chase so I wouldn't get anywhere near Washington. Don't you see? That's why he sent me down to New Orleans
in the first place, while assassination plots were being hatched all over
the Capital!

"Stanton claims he gave orders for Booth to be taken alive for
questioning, but somehow his captors couldn't restrain themselves.
What a coincidence, don't you think, Mrs. Warne?"

"What does Mr. Herndon make of all this?"

"He thinks it is *not* a coincidence that Secretary of State Seward,
who stands ahead of Stanton in line for the presidency, was vi-
ciously attacked by still unknown assailants the same night as Lincoln
was murdered and only survived by luck. Now Seward is incapaci-
tated, Vice President Johnson is ignored, and Stanton rules Washington as if he'd been crowned King."

Mrs. Warne looked at me narrowly. "What do you believe can be
done?"

She still did not understand! "Neither Mr. Herndon nor myself accepts the implausibility that Booth acted without aid from

others whose identities have not merely gone undiscovered but may well be protected by the same men who have now seized power."

"But Mr. Pinkerton, was Lincoln killed because he was the enemy of the South? Or the enemy of Radicals like Stanton, who wish to impose upon the defeated Rebels the very punishment you yourself prescribe but Lincoln would never have meted out?"

"That is what must be determined, Mrs. Warne!" I was growing impatient with her refusal to see to the heart of the matter. "Mr. Herndon is willing to aid me in any way he can if I take on this case as a private detective."

She was silent.

"I intend to return to Washington in strictest secrecy. I will need assistance in this operation."

"Is that what you are asking me to do, Mr. Pinkerton?"

Of course it was!

"Mrs. Warne, Lincoln is—"

"Dead. He is dead, Mr. Pinkerton."

As I started to speak she held up her hand to stop me. I felt myself retreating from the edge of my seat until my body was braced against the back of the chair.

"We have served this cause as best we could. But there is no battlefield left for us to fight upon." I knew she was saying it the only way she could. "The War is over, Mr. Pinkerton, and we have no choice but to accept it."

I admired her bravery, I will admit that, the way she faced me without dissimulation. At last it was perfectly clear between us.

"Allan!"

My head snapped around at the sound of George's voice. As if in a dream I stood up as my old friend and my son approached, smiling.

The sight of me and Mrs. Warne, engaged in serious conversation once more seemed to lift their spirits.

Mrs. Warne greeted them with her firm handshake. We bade them sit down and join us for breakfast. We had donned our new disguises.

Twenty-four

T he end of the War inaugurated a brand-new age that continues to this day. Lee's signature on his surrender at Appomattox was barely dry when the first spikes were driven into the rails of the Transcontinental Railroad, the spine of a vast new empire of commerce. Slavery was no longer an impediment to westward expansion, and the factories of the North that had only recently manufactured rifles, cannon, and ammunition now churned out plows, reapers, and railroad rolling stock to settle the frontier.

It is a law of nature as immutable as gravity that where commerce goes, crime follows. In 1866 the Pinkerton Detective Agency was still the only reliable national police force, and the demand for our services had never been greater.

We opened offices in New York, Atlanta, and Philadelphia, and while I naturally retained absolute control over every detail of my far-flung organization, I made my sons William and Robert assistant superintendents. I sent Robbie to New York City, while Willie took nominal charge of the day-to-day operations of our home office under my close supervision.

Mrs. Warne expanded the Female Detective Bureau in Chicago as well as in our branch offices.

While we never spoke of the past, of Timothy Webster, or, for that matter, of what had happened to us, I detected no undercurrent of anger or recrimination from her. We went over cases together much as we did in the old days, and she often left my office with the words, "Thank you very much, Mr. Pinkerton."

I valued her thanks. After all, I was making an extraordinary effort. This new play in which we were cast in the roles of near strangers, who were in fact nothing of the sort, was unbearable to me.

EARLY IN 1867, George informed me that Timothy Webster's unmarked grave had finally been located in Richmond. I sent George to bring Timothy home.

On a chilly wet March morning, Timothy was buried in Graceland Cemetery in a large plot I had purchased as the permanent resting place for myself and my family members. I felt it fitting that Timothy should lie there too.

I spared no expense for the ceremony honoring him, including a military band. His grave was marked by a magnificent tombstone on which I had inscribed an epitaph of my own creation that briefly recounted the life and exploits of the greatest operative the Pinkerton Detective Agency has ever known.

I read the inscription aloud to the assembled mourners, and after the blowing of taps, the crowd dispersed. Willie and Robbie accompanied their mother home. Joan had bravely attended. I held my breath during the ceremony because I was not sure if the event would ignite another explosion of tears, which occurred often ever since Belle's death.

George had recently taken it upon himself to speak to me of Joan's condition. "Allan"—he tried to reassure me—"just give her time. She will get over it."

I thanked him for his concern but did not tell him that there are some things you never get over.

After the others departed, George and I waited for Mrs. Warne, who was seated on a bench across the path from Timothy's freshly dug grave. The cold rain had petered down to a mist. I finally told George to go; I would wait and see her home.

After a while I approached her. "Mr. Pinkerton, I wish you had consulted me before including my name on Timothy's memorial."

"Mrs. Warne—"

"It doesn't matter, I suppose." Then she was seized by a dry hacking cough I had noticed during the prior week at the office.

"Shouldn't we get out of this chilling dampness? I have a carriage."

"Yes, in a moment." Since she was not yet ready to leave, I wiped the rain from the wooden slats on the bench and seated myself beside her. She reached under her cape and produced a flask. She unscrewed the cap, filled it and held it out to me. "To Timothy?" I took it from her, and she raised her flask, and we drank to the memory of Timothy Webster.

Only then did I recognize it as the very same silver flask she had shared with me on our train ride north from Baltimore to save Lincoln. "Timothy gave me this flask," she murmured. I never knew that. It seemed incomprehensible that we could be drinking from it, while sitting beside his body lying in the ground. I desperately needed to make sense of things. Everything.

"Mrs. Warne?"

"Yes?"

"Did Timothy know about us?"

She seemed pained by my question.

"Please, I finally need to know."

She peered off in the only direction visible to us at that moment, the past. Her words came reluctantly. "He made me swear never to tell you. Yes, he knew."

"You told him?"

"Of course not!" She was outraged at my assumption. "I denied it vehemently when he confronted me, but he waved off my denial. He was too good a detective, after all."

It ached deep inside to imagine Timothy finding out the truth. "It was that night, the three of us, before he set out again to Richmond, wasn't it?"

"Yes."

"How did he take it?"

I was not sure if she had heard my question, and I started to ask it again.

She cut me off sharply. "He laughed and wished us luck."

"That's ridiculous!" Why was she defiantly blackening his memory?

She pursed her lips, refusing to say another word.

"Mrs. Warne, tell me the truth!"

She looked at me like a sawbones doctor in a field hospital contemplating whether to attempt the amputation of a patient's limb that is beyond salvation, the gangrenous retention of which endangers his life. She finally made her decision. "Mr. Pinkerton, Timothy and I were never engaged to be married."

"Of course you were!"

"Did Timothy ever tell you he was going to marry me?"

I tried to recollect but could not. "Why would you make it up?" I asked helplessly.

"Would you have risked what we risked, unless you believed there was a boundary between us that you would never cross? You would never take your best friend's fiancée from him, would you, Mr. Pinkerton?"

"No," I muttered, not sure if it was true.

"That's why I convinced you that I was engaged to Timothy. The limitation eased your mind. Or at least as much as your mind can ever be eased."

"But"—I grasped for the words—"even if you weren't engaged, you were—"

She held up her hand, shaking her head, as if we had gone far enough, too far, and nothing good could come of going any farther.

"I have to know!" I was desperate.

Did some feeling of pity arise in her, even as a feeling of loathing arose in me for asking for her pity?

"We were quite fond of each other. That's all. I was not in love with Timothy."

The last ten years were rewritten with a single pen stroke.

"You did not cause his death, Mr. Pinkerton."

"We don't have to rake over those old coals, Mrs. Warne."

She suddenly became irate. "You squeezed what you wanted out of me! Now, I'll be damned if you aren't going to hear all of it!"

My heart stopped. I was waiting for the next beat in my chest, but there was nothing.

"When you ordered me to go to Richmond, I knew I might be able to save him. At least there was a small chance of it."

"But you would not take the chance because you weren't really in love with him."

She looked at me sadly, shaking her head. "The great detective still can't solve the case."

"Then why didn't you go?" I was slumped forward, elbows on my knees, my head bowed.

"I would not go to Richmond just to assuage your guilt that somehow we had put Timothy in danger. He put himself there. That was his fate. His life." She stopped and waited until I looked her straight in the eye. "I would not risk dying for him because I wanted to live for you, Mr. Pinkerton." Then she turned away, as if she could not say this next thing to my face. "I fell in love with you the day I walked into your office. It was not my intention. Love has no intention."

Will the truth set you free? To this day I do not know. I held out my little cup, like a beggar. I wanted more from her. But she only gave me whiskey.

"Kate," I whispered gently, "don't you know I've always loved you?" She looked at me with great suspicion. I realized, only then, that she had never expected to hear those words from me. Or if she had, she long ago told herself that her expectations would go unfulfilled. I reached for her hand. "My life has been almost more than I can bear without you." Still she said nothing. "Do you understand me?"

She finally answered, almost regretfully. "Yes." Her eyes made the practiced, almost unnoticeable sweep an operative makes to be certain he is not being observed. Then she leaned toward me and kissed me on the lips.

Time stood still. We sat there side by side staring into space, trying to understand how we had gotten to this place.

"It is time for me to go, Mr. Pinkerton."

I misapprehended her words. "I suppose we should return to the office."

"No, it is time for *me* to go." I still did not understand her. "Don't you remember, a long time ago I told you if we were ever discovered, I would disappear?" Of course I remembered. "We have finally been discovered. By ourselves." She stood up. I could not believe she meant it until I saw the look on her face. I could never mistake that look of determination.

"You can't go! What about *us,* Kate?" I stood up in front of her, as if I could keep her from going.

She started to say something, but then she stopped and shook her head. I did not urge her to say anything more; I was too desperate for her to hear me out.

"Listen to me." I tried to control the urgency in my voice to make what I was saying sound rational. "When you told me you would disappear, you also told me I could come with you."

"I don't recall."

"Goddammit, you know you did!"

She sighed. "Is that what you really want, Mr. Pinkerton?"

"It's the only thing I want."

I don't know what response I expected, but the calm expression on her face was the same as the night she agreed to run guns to John Brown for me. We had never ceased to be comrades. Or conspirators.

IT SEEMED SO familiar, the matter-of-fact way we always discussed a plan, dispassionately assessing the stratagems and the risks.

"You must first resign from the Agency in a way that seems natural, even logical."

"I will say that I am returning home. That my father is ill."

"Perfect."

My disappearance would be more problematic. We had to make it look like foul play. I certainly had enough enemies. Mrs. Warne was amusingly enthusiastic in her suggestions for the way I could meet my end, and how we would stage it so that while the body would not be found, the fact of my death would be accepted by all.

I estimated it would take me a month to put all my affairs in order. She agreed that William and Robert were ready to assume control of the Agency with George's help.

I honestly believed I would be doing the best for everyone, including Joan. This was not a rationalization but an accurate assessment of the situation. Although I am exhausted from the labor of producing this complete account, I will not flag at the finish but instead take the time to explain, in a manner even my most unsympathetic audience can comprehend, exactly why abandoning my wife and family, in a manner some might choose to characterize as deceptively cruel, was in fact the greatest act of benevolence I could bestow upon them.

I have never interfered in the lives of those closest to me out of an appetite for domination, but only to instruct them in regard to what is right and what is wrong. Nevertheless, by that point in my life, I had come to the painful realization that my selfless motivation would be misunderstood until my dying day. Hastening this event would be doing them a great kindness. Once I was dead, or at least believed so, my daughter could marry whomever the hell she wanted, and Willie and Robbie could buy the largest desks made in America to put their feet up on and run the Agency that bore their name. As for Joan, my wife would be well provided for and no scandal would attach to her if my feigned death was accepted as real. She would take great comfort knowing that my soul was roasting in Hell while she acted the grieving widow for her beloved congregation. It was the role Joan was born to play.

WE LINGERED AT the cemetery, repeating the details of the plan to each other as if affirming our vows.

The next day Mrs. Warne appeared before the entire staff and, with tears in her eyes, announced her resignation from the Agency she had helped build. George could not hold back his own tears as he hugged her and wished her well. I informed everyone that Hattie Lawton would assume the post of head of the Female Bureau of the Pinkerton National Detective Agency.

MRS. WARNE AND I stayed in contact via coded letters. According to our plan she would remain in Chicago for the month, on the pretense of wrapping up her personal affairs before returning to her family back east. In reality, she would be busy organizing the circumstances for my demise.

Then, upon my disappearance, she would postpone her departure from Chicago ostensibly to help George and my sons in the investigation. In reality, she would make sure no clues turned up to point to what had really happened to me and deflect any connection that might arise between my disappearance and herself. When the inevitable conclusion had been reached by all that I had suffered an untimely demise, she would grieve with them before proceeding with her previously stated intention to leave the city.

That is when we would meet up and embark on our lives together.

What I could not possibly have foreseen was how difficult it would prove to turn over to my sons the responsibility they had been clamoring for to run the Agency. In my initial enthusiasm I had grossly overestimated their capabilities. When put to the test, Robbie made a complete mess of the first important assignment I gave him, and I had to travel to New York to sort it out personally. Since time was short, perhaps I was a tad rough in my correction of Robbie's unacceptably sloppy methods. That in no way justified the little snot in taking umbrage at my tutelage and resigning.

I had to waste two full days enduring his whining litany of complaint before he agreed to resume his post, after extorting from me a raise in salary! When I returned to Chicago, I was shocked to discover how much Willie still had to learn about the intricacies of running the head office. And why did George choose that moment to inform me of what he called a "cash flow crisis?" My only interest was that he solve it and stop pestering me with financial obscurities like a bank panic he claimed was throwing the entire country into a depression.

Then Joan came down with an awful flu. I had to race back and forth from the office to the house to help young Joan nurse her mother.

The weeks went by so quickly, I was not close to being ready to leave before I realized that the month was almost over. I composed a letter to Mrs. Warne, explaining that in no way had my intentions changed, but I felt it was best for our future together that we allow sufficient time for me to set my affairs in order.

I suggested that she adhere to her announced schedule of departing Chicago the next week so as not to arouse suspicion. I advised her to choose an intermediate destination not far away and wait for me to join her there in no longer than six months' time. I told her to reply as soon as possible, informing me of her exact destination.

THE NEXT DAY I received no reply. Nor the next, nor the day after.

What was wrong? I strode down Michigan Avenue and turned onto the side street where her boardinghouse was located. Her landlady greeted me familiarly. Over the years we had met several times. She seemed confused and then a bit suspicious that I had no idea Mrs. Warne was gone. A wagon and drayman had come the day before and removed all her possessions. No, the landlady replied slowly, looking at me strangely, she had not left a forwarding address.

"Mr. Pinkerton, surely she informed you of her destination."

I tried to hide my panic. "Yes, of course." I had to get back to the office as quickly as possible. I tipped my hat to go.

"It's a terrible thing." The landlady's words chilled me

I nodded in agreement, unwilling to let her know what I did not know.

"Mrs. Warne's illness." She sighed. "A terrible thing."

Twenty-five

T he greatest detective in the world could not locate the whereabouts of Mrs. Kate Warne.

Seizing upon her landlady's revelation that she was ill, I methodically visited every physician in the city, inquiring whether they had recently treated her. None of them had. I felt better, although it seemed like she'd deliberately left a false clue. Then I checked the recent departing passenger lists on every train leaving Chicago as well as lesser modes of transportation. Her name was on none of them. It was becoming depressingly clear that her intention was to disappear.

SEVERAL WEEKS LATER, George and I were going over the books in his office as we did at the beginning of each month when he closed the ledger on the previous one.

This time George proudly announced that we were making money. He slid the summary sheet across his desk. I picked it up, making no attempt to hide my indifference. He removed the spectacles he had lately taken to wearing and carefully cleaned them with his silk handkerchief.

"It's not the same around here without her, is it, Allan?"

My throat was too thick to answer. I shrugged and pretended to look at his balance sheet, but the numbers appeared squiggly through my watery eyes.

He put his glasses back on and peered at me intently. "I don't suppose you've received any word from her, or you would have shared it with me?"

"No. Yes . . . of course." Goddammit, he was prying! But I didn't mind. Pry harder, George.

I looked up helplessly, and when our eyes met I was certain George knew the truth about myself and Mrs. Warne.

George, I was going to tell you. I knew I could trust you.

Of course you can, Allan.

I was going with her. I just had to make sure I put everything in place first. Why didn't she believe me?

You don't have any idea, Allan?

I am not sure I ever knew what was in her mind.

But I said no such thing. Nor did I ask George if he knew about us. I just sat there, helpless, until he helped me, whether he intended to or not.

"Allan, I'm sure she's fully occupied getting settled with her family. We'll hear from her in time."

Sometimes the solution is so simple you can jump right past it. She had told me exactly what she was going to do. She was going home.

I WENT OVER every word I could recall from her initial interview some ten years before and the few references she had made since then to her past.

I went to Boston, not letting anyone know the purpose of my mission. While she had never identified the exact town, she said it was west of the city. I methodically visited the town halls of each community, examining the records of births and deaths, until I found what I was looking for.

Alfred Warne, b. April 22, 1828
Alfred Warne, dec. August 5, 1853

I could barely control my anticipation as I pulled the ledger from the shelf that contained the records of marriages. There it was, recorded in a lighter hand.

On November 10, 1852, Alfred Warne had married Kate Shipley.

SITTING ON A bench on one side of the three-cornered town common lined with stately elms, I tried to imagine Kate Shipley emerging from the white clapboard Congregational Church on her wedding day nearly fifteen years before. I watched young women of the age she had been then, strolling with their mothers across the green expanse. They stopped and paid their brief respects at the newly constructed bronze memorial to the town's Union Soldiers who had died in the War of the Rebellion. Then they strolled on as before, chattering animatedly about things Kate Shipley would have had little interest in. I couldn't imagine she had much interest at all in this orderly, confined New England community.

That's why she left. It wasn't Alfred's idea. It was hers. She had to leave this place.

And she had not returned.

When I went into the church and asked to speak to the Reverend Shipley, I was met with suspicious looks. I explained—lied, actually—about my connection to his daughter Kate, and I was finally ushered into the church vestry and introduced to a man in his forties, the Reverend William Tremont.

He told me that Kate's father, Henry Shipley, had died three years before, a widower for several years and a lonely man. It was a source of grief to the Reverend that his daughter had disappeared from his life, Tremont said—almost accusingly, because I had some connection that he did not quite understand to Henry Shipley's daughter.

I couldn't help it. "But hadn't they quarreled?"

The Reverend Tremont's face softened. There was, after all, some religion in the man. "They did. And Henry Shipley was a proud and unforgiving man. Kate took after him." He sighed. "He never should have let her go that way."

No, he should not have let her go that way.

I WAS SURE that she had finally done what she had long ago set out to do. She had made her way to California. A place for disappearing.

After several months I discovered this was yet another incorrect assumption.

Mrs. Warne never left Chicago. All this time she had been living under an assumed name, not a mile from our office, in a boardinghouse run by Abbie Grunewald. Naturally, I had questioned Abbie, along with many other old informants in the Chicago underworld, at the beginning of my investigation, but I failed to appreciate how these women with whom Mrs. Warne had formed her closest associations over the years would protect her at all costs. I could imagine the story she concocted for them, probably something about that dreadful man, the Eye That Never Sleeps, pursuing her for something of which she was totally innocent.

Abbie's place was a favorite haunt for the best class of con artists and whores passing through the city. I had to smile at Mrs. Warne's ironic choice of a new residence.

But why had Abbie Grunewald betrayed her now and sought me out, without Mrs. Warne's knowledge, to ask me to come in person?

WHEN I ARRIVED, Abbie was alternately defensive and hostile, as if intuiting without knowing the particulars that I was somehow to blame for the entire situation. Before letting me enter, she made me promise to go along with her story that I had somehow managed to track down Mrs. Warne on my own.

I was exasperated by the woman's petty concerns. "I will cooperate with you in the charade."

She was insulted. "She's not well, Mr. Pinkerton." There was no mistaking the tone of accusation. "She is dying. That's why I summoned you."

"I don't believe it." The woman wanted money from me. That was what this was about! I didn't give a damn, I just wanted to see Mrs. Warne. "I will bring a doctor after I see Mrs. Warne, and you'll be well paid for your help."

"I don't want your money, and Mrs. Warne doesn't need a doctor. She's been under the care of Dr. Lowry since the beginning." Her hard look turned to sorrow. "It's the cancer."

How could that be? Lowry was the best physician in Chicago and the first one I'd gone to looking for her. He denied to my face that he'd ever treated Mrs. Warne. Had she managed to get him to protect her as well?

Abbie had me sit in the kitchen and wait while she went to tell Mrs. Warne I was there. "If she won't see you, Mr. Pinkerton, you must leave quietly and not return."

I nodded my agreement, and for the next half hour I waited in agony, until Abbie's footsteps on the stairs brought me to my feet. She motioned for me to go up. "Top floor. It's the only room."

When I reached the landing I stood outside the door uncertainly before knocking.

"Yes," came the weary, familiar voice. I entered and closed the door behind me. She was propped up in her bed with a blanket pulled up to her waist. She wore no makeup and her hair hung loose. She was obviously terribly ill, but she still looked achingly beautiful to me.

"Why didn't you tell me?"

"Tell you what, Mr. Pinkerton?"

"The truth."

"I told you the truth. Every word of it."

"But you knew how ill you were. Why didn't you tell me that?"

She pursed her lips and stared down at her hands clasped together on top of the blanket. "That is all I intended to tell you. I waited until the others had left the cemetery. After our toast to Timothy, I was going to tell you. . . . But before I could say anything, you insisted on hearing things I never wished to tell you. And then you proposed to me." She looked up at me. "I had to find out if you really meant it. I did not trust any declaration you'd make if you knew my true condition, so I said nothing about it. For that deception, I do apologize."

"Of course I meant it!"

She lay back exhausted, as if this was taking more energy than she had left in her body.

"I didn't lie to you!" What could I say to convince her?

"You told me what you believed." Her voice was almost inaudible. "That's more than most of us is capable of."

I felt my knees buckle. "Whatever you need . . ."

She looked out her window. "Mr. Pinkerton, I apologize again, but there is nothing more I can do for you."

I RETURNED THE next day and brought a nurse. When she left, I told Mrs. Warne the nurse would come by each day to assist her in any way.

"Thank you. Now if you would be so kind as to hand me what is in the top drawer of my bedside table."

I was shocked to find what I recognized from many years trolling among the worst elements of the city.

"Oh, please." She snorted at my unconcealed disapproval. "Laudanum ceased to be of use months ago. Abbie acquired this opium through reliable channels."

I handed her the pipe and a packet and watched as she carefully unwrapped it. The opium had an iridescent black sheen like a panther. She took a hat pin and speared it. "It requires an open flame. Lift the chimney from the lamp," she instructed. Then she twirled the black ball over the flame until it gave off a sweet, pungent smell. She popped it into the small opening of the pipe bowl. With effort she shifted over onto her side and propped her head on the pillow. She held the pipe so that the bowl was directly over the flame as she put her lips to the end of the long stem and drew in slowly. Her steady inhalation consumed the opium in a glowing ball. She closed her eyes and held out the pipe. I took it from her hand.

"Is there anything else you need?"

Her eyes opened halfway. "Could you please sit down so I don't have to look up to talk to you? It gives me a crick in the neck."

I smiled, recalling that was what she said to me the first time she sat in my office, and quickly pulled up a chair beside her bed.

"Tell me how Hattie Lawton is managing the Female Detective Bureau."

We discussed the Agency's current cases. That became the pretense for me to visit her each day in the late afternoon. It was a pretense, but not a cover. We no longer needed a cover.

"IT WAS ALL for nothing, wasn't it?"

I was startled. She was not well that day. Shortly after my arrival she had held up her hand and closed her eyes. As I watched her fall into an opiated sleep, I must have closed my own eyes and dozed off, because her voice now awakened me.

"What was all for nothing, Mrs. Warne?"

"Everything we fought for. Do you remember Detective Scobill?"

"Of course."

"He now mops floors in the sheriff's office here in Chicago."

I frowned and sighed. "Yes, I know. I got him the job. How did you find out?"

She gave me a heavy-lidded wink. "I keep up with matters that still interest me. Such as Detective Scobill."

"It is an unfortunate situation. I'm sorry."

"I know you tried to keep him on as an operative. But you could hire an entire female detective force before you could employ one black detective. Even Scobill."

She was right, of course. General McClellan himself could not force me to remove John Scobill from the United States Secret Service, but after the War was won, the most powerful lawman in the country could not employ a black man as a detective, for Scobill's own safety. Lynchings of free blacks were as common in Cicero, Illinois, and Cincinnati, Ohio, as they were in Mississippi. I couldn't risk his life to make a point. Instead, he mopped floors after a million men had been killed and maimed to win his so-called freedom.

Her voice had a mournful quality to it. "It is not something I will miss, Mr. Pinkerton, the endless war over the fate of those for whom we fought so long."

"You never really believed it could be won, did you?"

"I suppose not. There never seemed to be an appropriate time to tell you." She gave me the same ironic, intimate smile I had seen before when we lay naked beside each other and talked. Beautiful, fantastic talk with my beloved in my arms.

"How could you have fought the way you did, if you didn't believe in our cause?"

"I believed in something else. It did not matter whether we won or died fighting. It was our life, the only one we had together."

I pondered that. "It wasn't so bad, was it, Kate?"

"No, Mr. Pinkerton, it was rather grand."

I STOPPED BY earlier than usual on the afternoon of December 31, 1867. There were several galas that night celebrating the eve of the New Year that I was obliged to attend. As soon as I entered her room, though, I knew this was the end. I could not let her die alone. I lit her pipe and she took it, practically forcing herself to inhale.

"Please. Another."

This time she smoked avidly, as if life had returned to her emaciated frame, but it wasn't life, only the relief of pain.

"Mr. Pinkerton, please prepare another pipe."

"Surely you've had enough."

"I have. This one is for you."

"It's not necessary."

"I insist. Remember that time on the train from Baltimore to New York? I had to insist you share my bourbon. What if I hadn't? So I insist now. You can't refuse me."

No, I could not. I pulled the chair over and fixed the pipe, but the thing is not designed for sitting in a chair. She watched me intently, her glistening eyes almost the color of the opium itself, waiting for me to realize the predicament. Then she spoke in a whisper that caused me to lean close to hear her words.

"You must lie on your side." With great effort she slid over in her bed and motioned for me to lie down beside her.

I removed my coat and laid it on the chair. I sat on the edge of the bed and hesitated. I had to remove my boots. I wasn't going to soil her sheets. Then I lay down on my side facing away from her. In the small bed she pressed against my back, and I was startled by how light she felt against me. She reached over my body to steady the pipe as I held it over the flame of the lamp on the bedside table. I had seen her do it enough times, and I drew in, steadily, watching the glowing ball of opium consumed by the flame before my eyes, feeling the smoke reach my brain even before it was fully consumed by the fire.

She deftly took the pipe and placed it on the bedside table, leaving her hand resting on my shoulder. "This is nice. After all this time, here we are once more in bed together, even if it is my deathbed."

"It's not a joke, for God's sake!" I sat bolt upright.

Luckily she grabbed me, as my head spun and my stomach rose up to my mouth. She gently lowered me onto my back, laughing. "Why do you think those Chinamen lie on their sides with their heads propped up on their little porcelain stands?"

Then she pulled me over so I was facing her, placing a pillow under my cheek. She curled up on her side, so close I was staring at her lips moving as I heard the words. "You can't let the blood leave your head suddenly." We held each other's hands, like two opium fiends. Except it was each other we were addicted to.

"I was surprised just then when you invoked the Lord's name. After all, He has never liked us much."

I shuddered. "Dammit, Kate, why didn't we run off together a long time ago?"

"What does it matter? I would be dying in some boardinghouse in San Francisco instead of here in Chicago. It is God's Will that I spend my last night in this world in this bed, in this room, in your arms."

"There is no God," I murmured like an incantation to ward off an evil spirit.

"You are entitled to whatever belief best eases your pain. Mine is nearly over."

"Kate?"

"Yes, Mr. Pinkerton?"

"Will you call me by my name? Allan?"

"I'm sorry, Mr. Pinkerton. I could never call you that."

"Why?"

"Even if we had married and had three children, I would have called you Mr. Pinkerton."

Of course—the opium made it clear—what she had always wanted. My eyes squeezed shut, and I could see Kate and Mr. Pinkerton and our three children. One of them named Timothy.

"Yes, that is what I wanted." Was her voice coming from her lips or my mind? "I managed, somehow, to rarely allow myself ever to consider the possibility, because it was not possible. Hence all our disguises and our lies to the world, but most of all to each other. Because of the complications." I shuddered, and she held me tightly. "In your last letter to me you revealed the truth, intentionally or not. You could not leave and start a life with me because you already had a life, Mr. Pinkerton, and a family of your own that you could not abandon." Then she spoke the words that echo in my mind right to this moment. "We loved each other. Nevertheless."

I held her until her last breath left her body.

I could not move because from the pit of my being the full flower of grief emerged, unlike anything I had ever known before or since. A hand reached deep into me and pulled me inside out, so that I was no longer covered by my own skin; I had no covering at all, no protection against the howling fire of this world. It hurt so much that a soundless wail came out of me, a silent scream that practically ripped my jaw from my face to let this cry emerge, like a baby from the womb, but I was not giving birth to life, only my own death. My life's end had begun.

I walked out of the boardinghouse in the early morning light as the church bells of Chicago rang in the New Year. I had lost her.

Twenty-six

I whipped my tired horse in the darkness. It was the fall of 1868, the worst fucking year of my life, and the only thing that felt right was tracking killers in the dead of night. Willie and Robbie and three operatives could barely keep up with me as we raced across the plains of Indiana.

The sons of bitches I was after hadn't just robbed a train, John Reno and his gang had killed the engineer and paymaster in cold blood. It was the first time it had ever happened on a train under the protection of the Pinkerton National Detective Agency, and it would be the last.

A decade before, the Renos had ridden with the murderous slaver Quantrill in Bleeding Kansas against John Brown. When the War broke out, the Renos and scores of other bloody vigilantes like them had a license for mayhem—bushwhacking Federal troops, rounding up Rebel deserters and runaway slaves, and executing them on the spot. They didn't surrender with Lee at Appomattox.

I was the only man in America who understood that the War of the Rebellion was not over!

John Reno, his brother Frank, and their henchmen had taken over the town of Seymour, Indiana, and turned it into a Rebel stronghold. My operatives infiltrated the town, smuggled out maps and information, and gained the confidence of the locals who harbored and abetted the Reno gang. When they returned from another train robbery, we rode down on them hard. I put John Reno and most of the gang into custody, but Frank escaped and made it all the way to Windsor, Ontario.

The British were extending their famous hospitality to American outlaws, offering them diplomatic immunity in that filthy Canadian town on top of the lake. I followed Frank across the border and cornered him in a bar. He was surrounded by his pals, laughing. He was laughing at the Eye who'd never catch him. But no one escapes Allan Pinkerton.

Willie and Robbie were right behind me. I wanted Willie at my back, because he was cool under fire. I wanted Robbie there because it was about time he learned what the hell our business was about.

So I walk right up to Frank Reno, my gun in my holster, and stare him in the face until he recognizes me. He jumps up and draws his Navy Colt and points it at my chest. Then he tells me how he's going to send my soul to hell, but his hand is trembling like he's looking at a ghost.

The jackass. Why's he giving me a sermon when he should have shot me? I lunge for his pistol and stick my finger between the trigger and the steel of the ring so he can't fire, then I rip it from his grip so hard I hear his shoulder pop out of its socket.

He goes down howling in pain, and before he even hits the saloon floor I'm kicking the murderer to death. See, if you get the hard toe of your boot into a man's ribs, they keep cracking till they puncture his lungs and he drowns in his own blood. It's a useful technique, and I wanted to show Robbie the particulars, but Willie grabs me and then the others do too. It takes five of them to pull me away. My own fucking operative asks me if I'd gone crazy! I spit in his face.

Next day the British Consul himself comes marching down to the dock with his troops to stop me from loading Frank on a boat to take him across the lake to Detroit. The fat ponce starts shouting about extradition treaties and how I'm creating a major diplomatic incident.

What did I care? The only thing my Scots eyes saw was blood when I laid eyes on those Redcoats. I don't know who fired first, but next thing I know we're in the icy water and Reno is drowning in his chains. I wasn't going to let him escape the noose! I kept going under till I finally hauled him back up in the boat.

After I stuck Reno in a cell in Indiana, I rode trains all night, my clothes still soaking wet, but I couldn't take time to stop and change. I had to get back to my Agency. I'd left my flanks unprotected, and my Enemies had seized this opportunity to try to destroy me at last!

I ran down Michigan Avenue and bounded up the stairs of the Pinkerton National Detective Agency. I entered with my gun drawn and a finger raised to my lips to silence my astounded clerks. My crooked grin assured them that all would soon be made right. Then I approached his office to confront the traitor lurking behind that door, the mastermind of the whole conspiracy: *George Bangs*!

Of course it was George!

Who else could penetrate my defenses with his pretensions of loyalty? I would snuff out his treachery without mercy.

I burst into the office and grabbed the ledger book out of his hand. He tried to distract me with pathetic expressions of concern for my well-being, trying to get me out of the room so he could cover up his dirty work, telling me I was risking pneumonia in my damp clothes. "Allan, for God's sake, what is a fifty-year-old man doing chasing killers across the country?" Though I had not slept in five days, I ignored his insinuation that I was delirious with fever.

Instead, I found the evidence I was looking for!

I slammed the ledger book down on the desk, stabbing at the incriminating entry with my trembling finger.

He just stared at me with that innocent look of denial so many criminals have tried unsuccessfully to put over on me. "Allan!" He feigned astonishment. "Why would I steal twenty dollars in expenses? I sign all the checks!"

How the fuck should I know *why*?

Then he tried to tell me I wasn't in my right mind!

Oh, *that* was the clincher! Isn't that *exactly* what my Enemies have always claimed? Except, at that moment, staring into George's eyes, I realized this time it might be true.

I had been out of my mind since she died.

As I considered that, an explosion went off in my skull. It felt like when I went flying off that horse at Antietam. I toppled over and my head hit the floor. Then there was blackness.

FOLLOWING A BRIEF announcement that Allan Pinkerton had been in the hospital for several weeks recovering from a fever contracted during his apprehension of the Reno gang, the appearance of normalcy was restored. The usual stream of correspondence, reports, and contracts flowed from Chicago to our branch offices. Business was so good that Allan Pinkerton was regrettably too busy to meet with his clients in person, sending in his stead his sons,

Assistant Superintendents William and Robert Pinkerton of the Pinkerton National Detective Agency. No one knew my true condition.

MOST PEOPLE THINK being paralyzed doesn't hurt since they can stick pins in you and you don't feel anything. Then again, as I have made abundantly clear in this memoir, most people are morons. My paralysis was not the kind suffered by the thousands wounded in the War who took a minié ball to the spine, but my symptoms were similar. I'd had a stroke. Even though it rendered most of my body insensate and flaccid, just being hoisted out of my wheelchair to take a shit or wrestling with my one good arm to grasp a pen to make chicken scrawls on a piece of paper set off frantic alarms to the few remaining working muscles in my chest, neck, and legs, causing them to pull and twist and rack my body.

I wasn't about to give anyone the satisfaction of knowing what the pain was like. I couldn't, anyway. It took me thirty seconds to spit out three damned syllables. I could only move my tongue with monumental effort. Curiously, my lips still moved, but only up, so I appeared to be smiling more than I ever did before my incapacitation.

My condition was proof to Joan that God runs an orderly universe. As she fed me with a spoon, her blue eyes up close had a frightening sheen of fanaticism. She was quite pleased with this new arrangement. After all, I was wholly reliant on her for my most basic needs, and, even better, I was mute and unable to challenge her endless recitation of dogma and homilies.

For the next two years I secretly visited America's finest hospitals, even as I maintained the public deception that nothing at all was wrong, but the doctors could do nothing for me. Then I heard about a man named Kreutzman who had some kind of sanitarium way the hell up in Michigan. I read earnest testimonials from men he had healed, survivors of the War who had staggered home wrecked in body and soul.

I decided to go see him. George took me.

THE APPROACH OF dawn illuminated my rustic cabin, whose spare details I had come to know intimately. The previous night I slept like the dead, as I had nearly every night since my arrival a year before. The quality of my rest was the only noticeable improvement in my condition. Kreutzman's daily regimen of immersing me in alternating tubs of crushed ice and water hot enough to scald the hide off a pig had so far failed to restore any lost function to my body.

But I didn't mind.

Even if I regained the use of my limbs, or just my tongue, I didn't particularly have any destination I wanted to reach or orders to give—or, for that matter, one word I wanted to say to anyone again. I had lately begun to entertain the not altogether unpleasant thought that my life was truly over.

You see, I had done all that I could do, and whatever I had not accomplished, those things had simply not been possible. Even a man like me who possesses an indomitable will cannot extend his grasp beyond his reach.

I had done it all in a way I could never have imagined, but who can? Much less imagine that it can end, suddenly, with such stunning finality?

It is as if you're galloping across a field on a moonless night, full of passion and purpose and certainty, and you suddenly ride into some depression in the earth, an almost imperceptible gully, filled with a pocket of low-lying fog that hugs the ground. Without thinking you draw hard on the reins of your horse. You're blind and dare not race on, lest your horse stumble or you ride smack into a tree. Having come to a complete halt, all momentum is lost. Then you slowly realize that this interruption has no end, this fog will not lift, its edges are beyond your ken, and you will never emerge from it to take up your life's journey again.

You've arrived at a lonely, hopeless place. While you are not dead, you might as well be, but it is not entirely a bad thing. Your mind need not race about for a course of action, because there is nothing left to do. You have done all you can, lived the life that was parceled out to you, and what remains is memory.

For the first time in my life I felt some kind of acceptance.

There was a knock on my cabin door. I was looking forward to Kreutzman's next treatment. Someone else had finally taken charge of things. But when the door opened, it was Joan who unexpectedly entered.

I motioned with my chin toward the one rough little chair in the spartan cabin. She ignored my gesture and instead came closer, looming over me. She sighed. I had forgotten how much disapproval of my person Joan could convey with a single exhalation of breath.

"Allan, I've come to fetch you. You must return home."

I wanted to tell her that I was unable to accommodate her request, since I was still engaged in my rehabilitation, which would probably occupy the rest of my days. I could not talk, though, so I just shook my head like a recalcitrant child.

"You cannot stay here," she stated emphatically.

I tried to size up the situation. Was this some plot to lure me back into her captivity?

"Why?" It was the only syllable I could utter. Unfortunately, that's the last thing a man ever wants to ask his wife.

She had tricked me into asking, and now she was going to tell me, having positioned herself to deliver the crushing blow to my chest. "Allan, Willie knew all about your activities with Mrs. Warne."

Unable to speak, I could not tell Joan that I did not wish to hear any more about it, so she continued with what she had come so far to tell me.

"It wasn't long after he joined you in Washington. He was delivering some secret dispatch from the field. He arrived at your headquarters late at night and you weren't there, so he hid to wait for you. When he heard sounds from upstairs, he snuck up, and when you came out of her room, he saw you . . . kissing her. So he snuck out."

"Why?"

"Why didn't he tell you, Allan?" I nodded helplessly. Now I really wanted to know. Joan smiled. "Because Mrs. Warne told him not to."

My mind was disintegrating.

"He came in the next morning with the dispatch, and he went to her. He wanted her to explain that it wasn't like it looked. But she said, *Willie, it is so.* Willie was so fond of Mrs. Warne, called her Auntie, remember? So she says, *Willie, you are a man, and you can understand this. It is so, but there is no harm. Your ma is your ma and your da is your da.* That's what she told him. And he believed it, because he loved you, Allan."

It was true. Maybe her story had a happy ending?

"But something happened to you when Mrs. Warne died." Joan stopped and frowned. "That's when Willie came and told me about it. He wanted me to tell him it was all right. Imagine that?"

I could imagine anything.

"I told him it was all right. What else was I going to say?"

Was she asking me to answer that question?

"But after you had your stroke, Willie brooded on it. Then you left to come to this place, and it seemed like you were never coming home again, so he told Robbie. And Robbie said, *Well, Da got what he deserved,* so it was up to them now to look after the family. That's why they're going to court now to let everyone know the state you're in and have you declared incompetent so they will be put in charge of your Agency."

I felt relieved. What would be wrong with that?

Obviously a lot or Joan wouldn't be here. She was an even more unsentimental judge of her sons' abilities than I was. She had ascertained that Willie and Robbie, left unchecked, would put the Agency out of business and impoverish her. *That* she could not abide.

"You must come back, Allan. I'm afraid of what your sons will do."

Still, she had not said a word in regard to her own position concerning Willie's revelation. She had known about me and Mrs. Warne for at least three years. She probably assumed I'd been fucking Mrs. Warne from the day I hired her, that it was the very reason I hired her. She was wrong, but that was a small detail in the big picture that was finally coming clear to me. Too late.

My mind silently screamed, *Duck!* But I could do no such thing. As Joan leaned closer, all I could do was press my head back against my scrap of pillow until I felt the pressure of the bed slats beneath the mattress, as she spoke into my face.

"Do you ever think, Allan, about what your life would have been like if we'd never left Dundee? That beautiful place in the country. You built a fine house for our family. Built your own cooperage. You could have been sheriff too. It was Paradise. Was it worth it, Allan, what you sold your soul for? Do you ever think of that?"

Without waiting for my answer, she turned and walked out of the cabin.

Joan is undoubtedly the most formidable adversary I ever confronted. That was an act of pure genius. To ask a paralyzed man whether he ever thinks how his life might have turned out. If only . . . if only . . .

A little thing to consider, no weightier than a pine needle coming loose and floating through the air until its tip lands against the engorged boil of your being, so full of pus and horror that this tiny prick is all it takes for it to explode.

Twenty-seven

After Joan revealed to me the terrible burden Willie had been carrying for so long, I resolved to make it right between us. Kreutzman outfitted me with a harness of wood and leather that made my legs rigid, so I could actually walk with stout crutches strapped to my shoulders. It required effort beyond comprehension, but several hours a day of staggering up and down the path from my cabin through the woods brought results. Muscles that I forgot existed came back to life. He doubled my immersions in the fire and ice, and after six months I sent for George to bring me home.

I could barely stand the anticipation, until at last I was sitting once more behind my desk as Willie and Robbie walked into my office to greet me. I stood up, leaning on my stout blackthorn cane. I could even speak, almost, calling them over so I could hug them with my one good arm. I couldn't hold back my tears. They were such fine-looking young men in their smart new suits. They were both married, and Willie was a father! I had done the right thing by coming back.

Robbie, naturally, was nervous. He knew I was aware of his shenanigans to wrest control of the Agency from me, but I reassured him that I understood why he felt he was doing the best thing for the family, and that it didn't matter. All that was behind us. There were more important things to discuss.

I told them to sit down. I wanted to collect my thoughts, even though I had been rehearsing the speech I intended to deliver since Joan walked out of the cabin at Kreutzman's sanitarium. I had no apologies to offer my sons, only the facts of my life: what I believed in, what I stood for, and what I'd fought my whole life for. These are the only measures of a man that count for anything, and it was high time they understood that.

But before I could even begin, Robbie started going on the way he always does to justify his misdeeds, accusingly, as if I *made* him do it, by announcing that they had closed down the Female Detective Bureau without consulting me!

"How the fuck could you let him do that, Willie?"

Maybe I shouldn't have put it on Willie quite that way, but goddammit, Willie knew better!

Then Robbie gave his brother a knowing look that made my stomach churn, and I realized Willie had finally caved in to the little cretin. He didn't say a word when Robbie started lecturing me about how times had changed and clients wouldn't accept women coppers these days. That we couldn't hire quality operatives because a gentleman today would not work alongside a female.

When he finished his sermon, he looked me straight in the eye. Robbie was daring me to contradict him the only way I could.

By bringing up Mrs. Warne.

I shot Willie a look, but he just stared at me grimly, waiting to see what I would do. Did he really doubt me? There was no way I would back down from my own sons!

"Robert," I began, trying to control my desire to strangle him, "you were too young to take part in this Agency when Mrs. Kate Warne founded the Female Detective Bureau. Her contribution was essential to our success, not just in solving cases but in saving the life of President Lincoln and securing for the Pinkerton National Detective Agency its place in history for the service we rendered to the Union in the War of the Rebellion."

Why was I talking to my son like some lardass politician making a Fourth of July speech? That wasn't why I had come back from the dead!

"Willie, for chrissakes, tell him!"

Willie just hung his head. He couldn't even look at me.

Robbie's smile grew wide. Triumphant.

"Willie, what the hell is wrong with you? What do you have to say?"

"Nothing. Da."

Willie had nothing to say. And I could say no more. I couldn't make my speech about my principles, or why I had done what I had done.

ROBBIE KEPT UP his relentless attacks. He was itching to get involved with "industrial protection," but each time he brought up the idea I refused. Last year they both marched into my office, and Robbie put Andrew Carnegie's offer on my desk, an offer he had negotiated behind my back. I told him I'd known Carnegie since he was barely out of short pants, and the son of a bitch didn't have a single bone of principle in his scrawny little Scots body. I'd be damned if I'd *protect* his steel mills! I reminded my sons that, good business or not, it was an abomination to hire ourselves out to a bunch of very rich men in their insane quest to get even richer off the backs of their workers. It was a wholesale betrayal of the General Principles upon which I founded this Agency!

Robbie looked at Willie with a smirk. Then Willie stared at me with a look in his eyes I never dreamed I'd ever see. He was disgusted. Or worse.

I had to do something. I finally decided to ask George to talk to Willie.

But I waited too long.

Only a month ago, Willie handed me a telegram from New York containing the news that George had died. I should have seized that moment for us to finally talk, but I couldn't say anything. I was choking, and I couldn't stop the tears from rolling down my cheeks.

George was gone.

Willie looked embarrassed and walked out before I could say a word.

NOW, WILLIE, YOU and your brother are just waiting for me to die so you can proceed with your intentions. Maybe reading these pages will give you pause. After all, Willie, you're the one I wrote this for. I don't give a shit what anyone else thinks of me. I would gladly burn the whole damn thing, instead of hiding it away for you until after I am dead, if I thought we could sit down just one more time and set things straight between us while I am still alive.

But I don't trust myself to find the right words.

If only she were here to help me. She would know what to say, Willie, to bring you to your senses the way she did for me so many times.

On my own, I am at a loss.

Mrs. Warne would have known what to do.

Acknowledgments

Without whom . . .

Alan Ziegler, Leonard Cohen, Eleanor Jackson,

Jack Macrae, and Jennifer K